P9-AOA-492

Dear Reader,

During my career as an air force officer, I became
an avid student of military history. As a transplanted
Oklahoman, I've become just as intrigued by this
state's fascinating history.

Countless warriors have marched across the mountains
and prairies of Oklahoma. Their ranks included Native
Americans; the Vikings rumored to have rowed up the
Arkansas River and carved runes in the rocks; Spanish
conquistadores; and French dragoons.

In 1803 the United States Army assumed responsibility
for exploring and mapping the vast territory acquired in
the Louisiana Purchase. In *A Savage Beauty*, I detailed
the adventures of the first U.S. military expedition into
the area that eventually became Oklahoma.

This novel opens some twenty years later and is set at
the first military outpost in Indian Country. It's a tale
of extraordinary courage, convoluted politics, fierce
passions and betrayal.

Hope you enjoy it!

All my best,

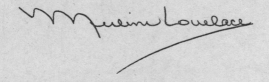

Merline Lovelace

Untamed

MIRA®

ISBN 0-7783-2075-8

UNTAMED

Copyright © 2004 by Merline Lovelace.

www.MIRABooks.com

Printed in U.S.A.

To my own handsome Oklahoman.
Thanks for bringing me to the land of blue skies
and endless horizons, my darling.

UNITED STATES TERRITORIES, 1830

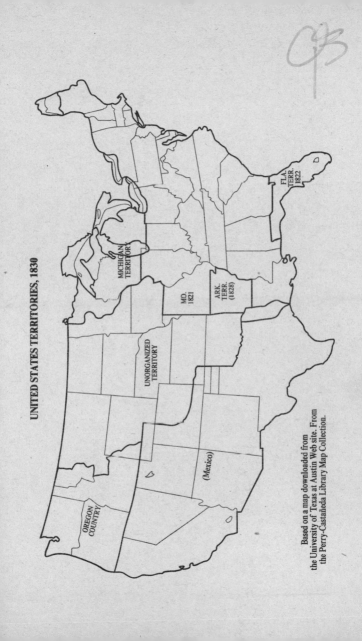

OREGON COUNTRY

(Mexico)

UNORGANIZED TERRITORY

MICHIGAN TERRITORY

MO. 1821

ARK. TERR. (1828)

FLA. TERR. 1822

Based on a map downloaded from the University of Texas at Austin Web site. From the Perry-Castañeda Library Map Collection.

Legend of the
Blue-Eyed Maiden

She was born to a woman of the People and one of the pale-skinned warriors who rowed up the river and wintered in the land where eagles flew. Violent storms struck after these warriors departed in their canoe with its great, carved prow. Long droughts followed. The People suffered. Blaming the child with the strange blue eyes, they cast out both her and her mother.

Ever after, it seemed, the birth of a babe with light-colored eyes presaged disaster. Crops failed. Spaniards in iron hats raped and pillaged. Frenchmen bartered for furs and sold the vast land that wasn't their own to men who called themselves Americans.

These men, too, brought disaster. They pushed farther and farther into the land of the People, dug up the earth with their plows, drove away the game. Then they built a fort where the three great rivers flowed together....

1

Indian Country
October, 1832

"Git off my land!"

The farmer planted his feet wide at the door of his cabin. His face twisted with rage, he glared down the long barrel of his rifle at the squad of soldiers who'd come to evict him.

Lieutenant Zachariah Morgan kept his horse steady and his finger easy on the trigger of his pistol. His small troop of mounted rangers were spread out on either side of him as he tried yet again to reason with the moose-headed squatter.

"I repeat, Billingsly, this is not your land."

"The hell you say! I got me a piece of paper with my name on it that gives me legal claim to this patch of dirt."

Zach smothered an oath. He'd heard this same song sung many times by whites duped into believing they'd bought title to land in Indian Country. Each time, he'd been forced to remove the angry squatters at gunpoint. This time looked to be no different.

"Your quit-claim deed is fraudulent. This land belongs to the Cherokee."

Or the Osage, he thought wryly, depending on which treaty a man chose to consult.

President Thomas Jefferson had first proposed moving all tribes living east of the Mississippi to the vast, uncharted Louisiana Territory at the time of its purchase in 1803. Successive presidents had heeded the clamor of their land-hungry white constituents and negotiated treaties with the various eastern tribes to cede their holdings in exchange for lands in the West.

Some tribes had begun voluntary migration decades ago. Others, like the Cherokee, still resisted, although bands of that tribe had already relocated to the vast area officially designated as Unassigned Territory but already becoming known as Indian Country.

Then, two years ago, President Jackson pushed the Indian Removal Act through Congress over the violent objections of such outraged legislators as Tennessee congressman David Crockett and Virginia senator Henry Clay. Cherokee chief John Ross had taken to the courts to challenge the act, but most tribes had given in to the inevitable and ceded their remaining lands in the East. Unfortunately, so many different officials had scribbled so many hurried cessation treaties that no one was quite sure which tribes were supposed to settle where.

The resulting confusion had only increased the age-old hostility between the Osage and the tribes migrating into the territory they'd long considered their own. Years of bloody confrontations had led to the establishment of Fort Gibson, smack in the middle of Indian Country, and the futile hope that one regiment of infantry and a company of mounted rangers could keep peace between the tribes. In the process, they were also supposed to keep out the white settlers already attempting to claim a piece of Indian Country.

Like this one.

Zach tried again to reason with him. He'd spent two years practicing law before accepting an appointment to West Point. He knew the intricacies— and the absurdities—involved in claims such as this man's.

"Listen to me, Billingsly. You can get your investment back from the company that sold you that false quit-claim. If the company won't give it to you, the state that certified the deed must pay you back. You can take your case to the courts and—"

"I ain't taking my case nowheres," the burly squatter snarled. "This is my land, I tell you."

Zach was fast running out of patience. He and his

men were tired, dirty and hungry. They'd been out on patrol for close on to a week now. In that time, they'd escorted a Pawnee raiding party back north of Kansaw, returned three Osage captives to their tribes and forcibly evicted two other stubborn squatters like this one.

"You have a choice," he snapped. "You can pack your wagon, round up your livestock and come with me voluntarily, or travel to Fort Gibson in chains."

"I'll send you to hell afore I let you take me any-wheres."

"They're soldiers, Thomas!"

The nervous cry came from the woman cowering just inside the cabin.

"Maybe you should listen to the lieutenant."

She edged out into the harsh sunlight and added her voice to Zach's. She was small and birdlike, almost lost in her homespun skirt and short-blouse. Her brown hair fell in untidy strands. When she brushed them back with a nervous hand, Zach's breath left on a hiss.

Her face looked as if the farmer had taken a barrel stave to it. Or both of his hamlike fists. One of her eyes was completely closed. Ugly purple bruises rimmed the other. A red scar cut across her temple, and livid finger marks ringed her throat.

"Your pa tried to tell you that deed wasn't any good." Her voice was little more than a hoarse whisper. "We could—"

"Close your mouse-hole, woman!"

She put a timorous hand on the man's arm. "We could go back to Georgia. Your pa would help you with this court business. You know he would."

"I told you to shut your hole!"

The squatter released his grip on his rifle long enough to fling out his arm and send the woman crashing back against the cabin wall. She hit with a mewling cry.

The buckskin-clad sergeant mounted next to Zach spit out a curse. "You cow-handed bastard. Why don't you try your fists on someone nearer to your own weight?"

"I'll show you who's cow-handed." The farmer slammed his rifle butt against his shoulder.

Zach didn't hesitate. A boyhood spent in Indian Country and years of military training had taught him a simple formula for survival. When confronted by a snarling beast of the four-legged variety, back away. When facing one of the two-legged variety, try reason. If either approach looked as if it would fail, fire.

Zach saw murder in Billingsly's contorted features and squeezed off a shot a mere heartbeat before the farmer's rifle belched fire.

The man's wife chose the same instant to throw herself at her husband in a desperate attempt to deflect his aim. Billingsly's shot went wild. The ball

Zach had intended for the man's right shoulder took him square between the eyes.

He went down like a felled ox.

Zach's sergeant spit a wad of chewing tobacco into the red dirt. "Good shooting, lootenant."

Accepting with a nod what amounted to a high compliment in the ranger company, Zach swung out of the saddle and strode to the woman. She stood rooted to the dirt, staring down at the blood spurting from the neat hole in her husband's forehead.

"I'm sorry. I shot to wound, not kill. My aim was off."

The last was a lie, but Zach didn't want the woman thinking she'd helped precipitate her husband's death.

He needn't have been so concerned. When she raised her head, the eye that wasn't swollen shut blazed with joy.

"I'll thank the Lord every night for your poor marksmanship!"

Grabbing Zach's hand, she brought it to her lips and covered it with fervent kisses.

"Here now!" he protested. "There's no need for that, Mistress Billingsly."

"My name's Hattie. Hattie Goodson. I wasn't married to that…that pig. His pa bought my indentures, then passed them to Thomas."

"Yes, well, you're free of the pig now. Bundle up

your things and we'll take you to Fort Gibson. You can stay there until you arrange passage back to Georgia."

"I can't go back there with Thomas dead. His pa will come after me and make me serve out my time!"

Her bruised face, which had showed such fierce exultation mere moments ago, now folded into tight seams of desperation.

"He has a meaner fist than his son. He'll kill me for sure."

"No, he won't."

Zach knew full well indenture constituted a time-tested means for individuals to pay off debts, learn a trade or find homes for large broods of children who might otherwise starve. The law required those who'd sold themselves, or been sold, into service to fulfill their obligation. He also knew the law protected those in service from the kind of mistreatment this woman had endured.

"I'll write a paper for you to take to the magistrate," he promised. "In it I'll describe the beatings you've taken. I guarantee you won't have to serve out the rest of your time."

She looked doubtful but had little choice in the matter. An hour later, Zach helped her scramble onto the back of a mule. The meager possessions his men had scavenged from the cabin were piled behind her. A milk goat baaed and balked at the end of a rope lead.

Zach swept Billingsly's mounded dirt grave with another glance and swung into his saddle.

"Fire the cabin," he instructed his sergeant.

"Yes, sir."

The late-afternoon sun slanted at a sharp angle by the time Zach's small troop topped a hill and spotted Fort Gibson below.

The outpost sat on the banks of the Grand River, some three miles up from its juncture with the Arkansas and the Verdigris. A natural rock shelf on the east bank extended into the river and provided a landing spot for the steamboats that chugged up the river with ever-increasing frequency.

One of which, the rangers saw with whoops of delight, was tied up at the stone quay this very moment. The lanky woodsman who wore sergeant's stripes shot Zach a brown-toothed grin.

"Now there's a welcome sight! She'll mean an extra ration of whiskey tonight for sure."

"That she will."

It also meant newspapers, letters, visitors, and, of late, another boatload of Creek, Cherokee or Choctaw en route to new homes in the West. Resigned to the escort duty he and his fellow officers would be asked to perform in the coming days, Zach urged his weary mount down the sloping track to the fort.

* * *

The return of a patrol would normally excite attention at the post. The return of a ranger patrol provided even more than the usual entertainment.

Unlike the infantry, the rangers were not regular army. The men were volunteers, and colorful ones at that. Colonel Matthew Arbuckle, Fort Gibson's commander, had recognized early the impossibility of patrolling the vast Indian Country on foot, much less keeping up with mounted Indian warriors, and lobbied hard for a troop of dragoons. Ever parsimonious, the War Department had granted him authority to mount a company, but no funds to recruit, train, horse or equip it. The result was a unit of rugged frontiersmen with no uniforms, no training and precious little discipline.

Some of the rangers who cantered down the hill wore moleskin trousers, coats cut from green blankets and floppy brimmed hats decorated with turkey feathers. Most chose fringed buckskins topped off by a variety of headgear ranging from wolfskin caps to shiny black beaver top hats. They were a ragtag bunch at best, but the poorest shot in Zach's squad could take down a deer at a hundred yards.

The regulars in their canvas pants and blue wool shirts paused at their work details to call out greetings to the arrivals. Several pressed around the troop, eager for news. One of those wore the shoulder pips of a lieutenant. A tall northerner with sandy hair and luxuriant mustaches he combed three or four times a day, Nathaniel Prescott had graduated from the Point a year behind Zach.

"You've timed your return perfectly, Morgan. The steamboat delivered another band of Cherokee for resettlement. We'll no doubt— Good Lord!"

His startled gaze locked on the battered face of the woman sitting astride her mount.

"Who's that?"

"Her name's Hattie Goodson. She was indentured to a squatter."

Prescott's glance swept the dismounting squad. When he saw no evidence of the squatter, he drew the inevitable conclusion. "I assume this squatter was so unwise as to tangle with you rangers?"

"You assume correctly."

He tipped a nod toward the woman. "What are you going to do with her?"

"I'm hoping Sallie Nicks will take her in," Zach replied, referring to the gracious and much-courted widow of the fort's original sutler. "At least until I can make arrangements for her to return to her home."

"I'm sure Sallie will oblige you if she has room. The steamboat discharged a full load of passengers." A note of excitement charged his friend's voice. "I must tell you, the *Bonne Chance* has delivered the most ravishing Englishwoman ever to set foot in Fort

Gibson. I've exchanged a mere half-dozen words with her and already I'm hopelessly in love!"

Zach snorted. "You fall hopelessly in love with *every* passable female under the age of fifty who so much as smiles at you, Prescott."

"That's true," Nate admitted cheerfully. "But when you see Lady Barbara, you'll agree she's a diamond of the finest cut. And you will stare, I'm sure, when I tell you she's come in search of your mother."

He had the right of it. Zach gaped at his friend in utter astonishment. "An English lady has come in search of my mother? Why?"

"She was somewhat vague as to her reasons, but evinced considerable interest when she learned Louise Morgan's son is an officer. Of sorts," Prescott added in a good-natured jibe.

Regular Army right down to his leathers, the New Englander still shook his head over Zach's decision to serve with the rangers.

"Colonel Arbuckle assured her he'd release you from your duties long enough to escort her to your parents' plantation. You lucky dog!"

The homestead Zach's parents had carved out of the wilderness hardly qualified as a plantation, but he didn't bother to correct his friend. He was still puzzling over the fact an Englishwoman had business with his mother.

"What was this woman's name again?"

"Lady Barbara Chamberlain. From the little intelligence I've been able to gather about her, she's the daughter of Sir Harold Chamberlain, now deceased, and sister to Sir Harry Chamberlain. She's also unmarried."

"She's putting up with Sallie Nicks, you say?"

"She is. But don't try to steal a march on me," Nate warned with a growl. "I saw her first."

"Only because I was out on patrol. Will you look out for Mistress Goodson for a few moments? I'd better make my report to Colonel Arbuckle."

Nate eyed the young woman's bruised face and shapeless garments with some apprehension, but consented readily enough. Zach lifted Hattie out of the saddle, explained that he was leaving her in the lieutenant's care for a bit, and strode across the trampled grass toward the post headquarters. He was just passing the coal house when a flutter of lace on the path that led to the river snared his attention.

Zach's step slowed, then halted completely. Unless the steamboat had delivered two ravishing creatures, he'd just spotted the Lady Barbara Chamberlain. She stood staring out over a bend in the river, a frilly parasol held aloft to shield her face from the fierce rays of the late-afternoon sun.

Damned if Prescott didn't have the right of it, Zach thought on a swift, indrawn breath. She *was* a diamond of the finest cut.

Her lavender gown fell in soft folds over seductively rounded breasts and hips. A paisley shawl dripping yards of fringe dangled from her elbows. The profile shaded by the parasol was one of porcelain perfection.

And her hair...

Zach had never laid eyes on such a mass of glorious, shimmering gold. Altering his course, he started down the path to the river.

2

She would have to change her plans. Considerably.

Her forehead creased in deep concentration, Barbara stared unseeingly at the marshy cane lining the banks of the river.

She'd traveled thousands of miles in search of the half-breed mistress of a long-dead trapper. She'd sailed through a vicious Atlantic storm. She'd endured weeks aboard a packet from New York to New Orleans. More weeks aboard a steamboat paddling up the Mississippi and Arkansas Rivers to this dismal little outpost.

She'd arrived at her destination only this morning and learned the woman wasn't the ignorant savage she'd been led to expect, but the wife of a prosperous landowner. Even more disturbing, her son was an officer assigned to this very fort. All accounts indicated he was an educated man, one who'd studied law before donning a military uniform, no less!

Barbara's frown deepened as she turned that unwelcome bit of information over in her mind. The scowl was an uncharacteristic expression. She'd learned at an early age she could achieve far more with honeyed smiles than pettish pouts. The lesson had stood her in good stead for most of her twenty-two years, a good number of which she and her brother had spent fleecing well-heeled gentlemen on several continents.

But Harry's usually razor-sharp instincts had failed dismally in his last scheme to line their pockets. He'd picked the wrong prey, a seemingly vacuous English lordling touring the Italian coast. Unfortunately, the young lord's uncle turned out to be a chancellor of the courts. He'd been waiting with a long list of charges when the Chamberlains returned to London. After a farce of a trial, the judge had sentenced Harry to transportation. Barbara's brother was now in leg irons and confined to a prison hulk anchored off Bermuda.

With a clutch of pain just under her breastbone, she recalled how thin and ravaged Harry had looked during the one visit she'd been allowed with him. Five months in the hulks had taken their toll. He wouldn't survive his ten-year sentence. Barbara had needed only one glance at his gaunt face and gray pallor to recognize that fact.

Her hand tightened on the carved ivory handle of her parasol. Harry would not serve those ten years. He *could* not! Barbara would take whatever measures necessary to secure his release. If those measures included relieving a French trapper's relic of every farthing she possessed, so be it!

First, though, it appeared Barbara must deal with the woman's son.

Her lips pursed again, this time in a moue of distaste. Lieutenant Zachariah Morgan. How Puritan. She could only hope the lieutenant wasn't as sanctimonious as his name implied.

Ah, well. It mattered not. She'd beguiled more than one seemingly staunch and upright gentleman with her seductive smiles and murmured half promises. She'd beguile this one, too, if necessary.

The sound of footfalls on the path behind broke in to her thoughts. Startled, she spun around and snagged her gown on one of the thorny pea vines lining the path.

"Hell and botheration!"

Muttering Harry's favorite oath, she tugged on the soft kerseymere. She had few enough decent frocks left in her trunk. The maid who'd tended to her hair and her wardrobe had declined to accompany her from Bermuda to the wilds of America. The fact that Barbara was several months in arrears with the woman's wages no doubt contributed to her stubborn refusal to set foot aboard another ship.

The possibility of being forced to cope with a torn hem didn't disturb Barbara nearly as much as the figure striding down the path in her direction, however. He wore his jet-black hair clubbed at his nape, not shaved in a scalp lock like the aboriginals she'd observed since entering Indian Country. In all other respects, though, he mirrored the native tribesmen. Quills and beads adorned his fringed buckskin trousers and shirt, which stretched taut across frighteningly wide shoulders. He carried a rifle in the crook of one arm, and his skin was so weathered by wind and sun, Barbara couldn't tell if it was white or red or something in between.

She took a nervous step back at his approach. The thorny vine brought her up short. Reminding herself that an entire garrison of troops was just a scream away, Barbara straightened her shoulders and fixed a cool smile on her face.

"Good day, sir."

"Good day."

The fact he spoke English relieved her, although the deep, rough timbre of his speech wasn't particularly reassuring. He was really quite intimidating. And rather dirty, she now saw. Grease stained his buckskin trousers in several places and a rusty splotch that looked suspiciously like blood darkened one sleeve.

Her smile slipping a bit, she slid her hand behind her and gave her skirt another tug. The prickly vine refused to yield.

Observing the surreptitious movement, the man lifted an ink-black eyebrow. "Caught, are you?"

"It appears so."

"I'll help you get free of that—"

"No!"

She flung up a hand to halt him. His size and his pungent aroma of leather, sweat and horse chased away her smile. She wrinkled her nose delicately.

"I do not require your assistance, sir."

Something gleamed in his dark eyes, quickly come and as quickly gone. Cocking his head, he seemed to be considering his response.

"Looks to me you're snared tighter than a rabbit."

"If I am, I'll free myself."

The tart reply earned her a long look. "Well, now, missus, I'm guessing you'll stay snared 'less I cut you free."

His accent seemed to grow thicker and coarser with every word. The slow drawl and uncouth garb confirmed Barbara's suspicions. She had his measure now. He was a frontiersman.

She'd heard many a tale of this rough-and-tumble sort during the steamboat voyage. Most were outcasts, misfits who penetrated deep into Indian Country despite every attempt to keep them out, illegally peddling whiskey or trade goods. Like the white settlers who, she'd been told, persisted in staking claims to lands west of the Mississippi, these men had no respect for boundaries or for laws.

Having danced around the law more than a few times herself, Barbara nevertheless viewed such low-bred ruffians with the contempt characteristic of her class. It was best to take a firm hand with men of this ilk.

"I must ask you not to refer to me with such familiarity.'"

"How am I to call you, then?"

"If you must address me, you may refer to me as Lady Barbara."

The honorific was purely fictitious. As the heir of a baron, Harry was entitled to hang a "sir" in front of his name, but Barbara had no claim to the title of "lady." With his characteristic disregard for convention, Harry had bestowed the title on her years ago to boost her status in the eyes of their gullible marks. She was confident this colonial wouldn't question her rank, though, and so he didn't.

"I reckon I ain't niver met a real lady before."

"No, I shouldn't think you had."

"You sure you don't need help?"

"Quite sure."

Instead of accepting the cool dismissal, he stood there, big and broad shouldered as an ox. The standoff looked to continue indefinitely. Finally, Barbara released a small huff of disgust, turned to one side and gave her gown a determined yank. The dratted kerseymere proved tougher than canvas. Forced to admit defeat, she faced him once more.

"It appears I shall require some assistance after all."

There it was again. That indecipherable glint. For an incredulous moment, Barbara thought he might actually be laughing at her. Her back stiffened, but his response held only affable agreement.

"'Pears you do to me, too, missus."

Her eyes narrowed. Was he deliberately trying to rile her? If so, he had a good start on it. She was considering her response, when he propped his rifle against an oak and drew a knife from the beaded scabbard at his waist. Its monstrous blade knocked the breath back down Barbara's throat.

Along with the other lessons her harum-scarum life had taught her, she'd learned never to show fear. Yet that wicked blade sent a shiver rippling down her spine. She would have stopped the man from approaching once again, but his long legs quickly covered the few yards still separating them.

She managed to hide her nervousness as he hunkered down beside her. His shoulders were really most ridiculously broad and his buckskin shirt so very thin. Quite unlike the padded frock coats and starched linens worn by gentlemen. She could see the play of his muscles as he sawed through the tough weed.

Unaccountably, she found the rippling movement as disturbing as his scent. It was sharp, to be sure, but not overpoweringly so, she was now forced to concede. Nor was it as cloying as the effusive perfumes and pomades the men of her class used so lavishly.

When he finished his task and rose, she exhaled a silent breath of relief. Relief gave way quickly to outrage when she realized he'd brought the hem of her skirt up with him.

"Sir!"

Seemingly unaware that he'd exposed her petticoats and the silk drawers that had become so popular among well-bred ladies, he plucked at a bit of thorny vine still embedded in her hem.

"Don't be a-fidgeting or you'll tear this pretty dress."

Barbara had no choice but to stand rigidly still until he worked the thorn free and tossed it aside.

"Thank you. Now if you'll loosen my skirt, I'll return to the fort."

Various admirers had described her as slender and willowy. Her brother, Harry, put it somewhat less charitably by claiming she stood as high as a gatepost. Yet as tall as she was, Barbara had to crane her neck to look into the woodsman's face. What she saw there gave her instant pause.

He wasn't done with her yet. She knew enough of men to grasp that instantly. He confirmed her suspicion with his next words.

"Surely you'll be payin' me a reward before you go on your way."

"You expect payment for this paltry service?"

Disdain tightened her lips. "I have no coin with me at the moment. Give me your name and I'll have one delivered to you."

"Oh, you needn't be payin' me in coin. A kiss will do."

"A kiss will most definitely *not* do! Release my dress at once!"

"Just a peck, sweeting. One little peck."

There was no mistaking it now. That was most definitely laughter dancing in his eyes. Her lips thinning, Barbara came to the humiliating conclusion her earlier supposition was correct. The man was toying with her.

He was also maintaining a firm grip on her skirt. She had two choices, she supposed. She could deliver a resounding slap and risk further unpleasantness or pay the toll he demanded.

"Present your cheek."

A rakish grin sketched across his face, altering it quite astonishingly. Barbara barely had time to appreciate the transformation before he turned and offered a bristly patch of skin.

Rising up on tiptoe, she delivered a quick buss. Or attempted to. He turned his head at the last second and caught her lips with his. The contact startled her, but the skill he brought to the kiss astonished her. Before she quite knew how it had happened, he'd covered her mouth with his.

Barbara had been kissed before. A goodly number of times, if the truth be told. She'd even surrendered her virtue during one escapade gone sadly awry. But none of the titled gentlemen she and Harry had enticed into their snares had heated her blood as hot—or as swiftly!—as this rough frontiersman.

As confounded by the heat that surged through her as she was infuriated by the man's impertinence, she jerked back, balled her fist as Harry had taught her and put every ounce of strength she possessed into a punishing blow to the woodsman's midsection.

Her fist slammed into a wall of solid muscle, so hard her knuckles cracked and pain shot straight up her arm. His startled grunt more than made up for the pain.

"That, sir, is only a taste of the payment you'll receive if you dare to touch me again."

Yanking her skirt free, Barbara stalked past him.

Zach rubbed his aching middle and grinned as the golden-haired beauty flounced up the path to the fort. Despite her haughty airs and aristocratic accents, Lady Barbara Chamberlain delivered a wallop that would do a mule skinner proud.

Zach deserved the punch. He'd be the first to admit it. Although a body couldn't tell it by looking at him right now, he was an officer and a gentleman. True, he'd traded his gold braid and tasseled sword for buckskins, but he shouldn't have allowed his amusement at the lady's assumption she was dealing with a rustic oaf to goad him into acting like one.

Oh, well, he'd had his fun and received a solid punch to the middle as a reward. Time to mend a few fences and discover what this English beauty wanted with his mother.

He retraced his steps and found her standing next to Nate Prescott, staring in sympathetic dismay at the female Zach had left in the lieutenant's charge.

She wasn't the only one who stared. Word had spread like summer lightning that the rangers had brought a squatter's woman back with them. White females were a rare enough occurrence in this remote wilderness. Two showing up at the fort on the same day would provide fodder for late-night chawings for weeks to come.

A small crowd had gathered. In their eagerness, the men pressed too close. Their avid curiosity drew a whimper from Hattie and a curt command from Zach.

"Stand away, men!"

At the sound of his voice, Hattie's head lifted. She spotted him shouldering his way through the crowd, gave a little keening cry and slumped to the red dirt.

"I say!"

Nate Prescott tried to catch her and missed. Smothering a curse, Zach went down on a knee beside the fallen woman.

His fellow officer hovered at his shoulder. "Is she ill?"

"I don't know."

"For pity's sake!" Lady Chamberlain protested. "Stand back and give the poor woman some air."

Shoving her parasol into Nate's hands, she dropped down on the woman's other side and laid the back of her hand against her neck.

"She's not feverish. She must have fainted. Fetch some water. *Now,*" she bit out when no one responded quickly enough to suit her.

A quick nod from Zach sent one of the soldiers scurrying. The man returned mere moments later sloshing water from a tin ladle and passed it to Zach.

The Englishwoman pulled a lawn handkerchief from its tucked position in the bosom of her gown. When she dipped the handkerchief in water and bent to bathe the unconscious Hattie's face, Zack feasted on the glimpse she gave him of lush, creamy breasts.

Some moments later, the unconscious woman stirred. Her one good eye opened and fixed on Zach. Another small whimper escaped her. At the pathetic sound, Barbara regarded him with seething contempt.

"You brute! Did you cause these bruises?"

Stealing a kiss from a high-arched female was one matter. Letting her think he'd take his fists to any woman, much less this bit of a thing, was another kettle of stew.

"No, ma'am, I did not."

"Oh, so?" She arched a disbelieving eyebrow.

"Then why did this poor woman faint dead away at the sight of you?"

Zach supposed he couldn't blame her for her skepticism. Hadn't he just taken a kiss from her against her will?

"Could be because I put a bullet between her master's eyes only this morning," he admitted.

The lady's mouth opened. Before she could respond to his outrageous statement, however, Hattie reached up with a trembling hand and grasped Zach's wrist.

"I'm sorry to make such a fuss, Lieutenant Morgan."

The moment Hattie said his name, Zach knew he was in for it. The English beauty stiffened and flashed him an incredulous look.

"*You* are Lieutenant Morgan?"

"At your service, ma'am." He gave her a rueful smile. "I intended to introduce myself but became, ah, somewhat distracted."

The fury that leaped into her turquoise eyes came close to distracting him yet again. A now thoroughly embarrassed Hattie reclaimed his attention.

"I expect I'm just hungry. I haven't had anything to eat since yesterday morning," she added apologetically.

Zach cursed under his breath. He and his men had been in such a lather to return to the post after a week in the saddle, he hadn't thought to offer the woman so much as a bit of hardtack during the long ride.

"We'll right that situation immediately."

Scooping her into his arms, he pushed to his feet. Nate scrambled to offer the blonde a hand. She rose with a grace that belied the anger still staining her cheeks.

"I should like to continue our unfortunately abbreviated conversation," Zach said to her. "May I call on you at Mrs. Nicks's after I've found Mistress Goodson a bite to eat and reported to my colonel?"

"You may." Ice coated the words. "But I must warn you, Lieutenant Morgan, I very much dislike being made a fool of."

A lesser man might have withered under the icy blast, but Zach knew there was fire under the frost. Despite her haughty airs, this was no bloodless aristocrat. Zach had sensed her heat during those brief moments his mouth had covered hers. He'd felt it most forcefully when her fist plowed into his middle. Thoroughly intrigued by the woman, he stood aside as she snapped open her parasol and turned to his friend.

"Lieutenant Prescott, will you be so kind as to escort me to Mrs. Nicks's quarters?"

"With pleasure, ma'am!"

Grinning under his mustaches, Nate marched off with his prize while Zach cradled Hattie to his chest and headed for the officers' mess.

3

The officers' mess was situated in a cluster of buildings on the grassy flats outside the pallisade enclosing the blockhouses, armory and enlisted men's barracks. The one-story log structure served as a communal dining area, gaming room and social gathering spot for the officers assigned to Fort Gibson.

Whitewash brightened the interior walls, and a somewhat frayed carpet covered the plank floor. The furnishings included a well-scrubbed oak table set astride two barrels and two rows of cane-back chairs. An open-shelf cupboard displayed a stack of pewter plates, eating utensils, an assortment of dust-covered brandy bottles and each officer's silver drinking mug. Since graduates from every West Point class after 1825 had seen service at Fort Gibson, a good number of the mugs were engraved with that institution's insignia as well as the officer's name and regimental arms.

When Zach entered with Hattie, the mess was empty of everyone except the hulking private who served as its steward. The Polish recruit could speak barely five words of English but his incredible way with a ragout had earned him the coveted post of mess steward over others with more fluency and time in service.

Sure enough, Walenowski had just brought a pot of venison stew in from the kitchens behind the mess. The tantalizing aroma set Zach's mouth to watering and the woman in his arms to gulping convulsively. Carefully, he lowered her into one of the chairs.

"Rest easy a moment, Hattie, and Private Walenowski here will fetch you some fresh-baked bread to have with that stew."

The private quickly supplied her with the requested items, along with a flagon of ale. She fell on the food like a starving wolf, her spoon clattering against the tin plate. Sympathy for the wretched woman tugged at Zach as he watched her down every morsel before sopping up the broth with a bread crust.

"Would you like another serving?"

"Yes, please!"

She started to swipe her mouth with the back of her hand, but stopped with her arm halfway to her mouth. Coloring under her mask of bruises, she reached for the linen square Walenowski had placed beside her plate.

"I'm forgetting my manners. My mam taught me better, but living these past years with Thomas... Well..."

With a daintiness that surprised Zach, she patted away the drop of broth at the corner of her lip.

"Will you be comfortable with Private Walenowski if I leave you for a while?" he asked, reluctant to abandon her yet again. "I must make my report to my colonel, then call on Mrs. Nicks to see if she'll take you in."

"You'll come back for me, won't you? All these strangers..." Her voice trailed off helplessly.

"I'll come back."

The promise reassured her. Zach left her with a second plate of stew. Rasping his palm against his chin, he decided he'd best rid himself of some of his trail dirt before attending to his errands.

Since the rangers bedded down in tents some miles distant from the overcrowded fort, Zach made a quick detour to Nate's quarters. Along with his abundant mustaches and side-whiskers, Prescott possessed the most extensive collection of personal linens west of the Mississippi. He wouldn't mind if Zach borrowed some shaving soap, a clean shirt and a fresh stock. Not a great deal, anyway.

Scrubbed, shaved, pomaded and smelling considerably more aromatic, Zach once again made his way toward the post headquarters. The officer of the guard had already advised Colonel Arbuckle of the rangers' return. He now awaited Zach's formal report.

At the colonel's gruff command, Zach marched into his office and offered a smart salute.

"Lieutenant Morgan reporting back from patrol, sir."

Arbuckle returned it and leaned back in his chair. "Let's have your report, Lieutenant."

Matthew Arbuckle was a good man and a fine officer, one of the best Zach had served under. He'd commanded the Seventh Infantry Regiment for more than a decade and Fort Gibson since its construction eight years ago. Assigned the almost impossible task of resettling the eastern tribes and keeping peace among the warlike Plains people, he took great pride in the fact that not one of his soldiers had killed an Indian during his tenure as commander. Zach knew he wouldn't be best pleased to learn one of his officers put a bullet into a white squatter.

The bewhiskered colonel took careful note of Zach's account of the Pawnee raiding party, nodded when he reported the return of the three Osage captives to their tribe and scowled as Zach described the incident with Billingsly.

"This selling of false deeds to land in Indian Country must stop," Arbuckle muttered. "Where did you say this Billingsly had settled?"

"Only fifteen miles northwest of here, sir, on the land reserved for the Cherokee."

Zach pointed out the spot on the hand-drawn map nailed to the wall. Frowning, Arbuckle tapped a stack of opened letters Zach guessed had arrived by steamboat only this morning.

"Although that stretch of Indian Country is sparsely populated as yet, I've just received a dispatch from the War Department. We may expect additional emigrants for that area any day now."

The information surprised Zach. "I thought Chief John Ross swore no more Cherokee would leave their homes now that the Supreme Court has ruled that Georgia law doesn't hold over them."

The ruling had been a controversial one, to be sure. Ever since gold had been discovered on Cherokee land in northern Georgia, that state had been among the most vociferous in attempting to force the provisions of the Indian Removal Act on its native populations.

Just last year, the U.S. Supreme Court recognized the Cherokee Nation as sovereign, thus rendering them immune from Georgia laws. The ruling had infuriated Andrew Jackson. The president was committed to moving all eastern tribes to land west of the Mississippi. Angrily, Jackson had declared that if Chief Justice Marshall insisted on making the law, he could damn well enforce it.

Various states had interpreted his denouncement

of the ruling as a signal to increase the pressure on their native populations. Lootings, beatings, even killings went unpunished. Yet the Cherokee had vowed to continue to fight the Removal Act through the courts. Or so Zach had thought.

"It appears there is increasing division among the Cherokee Nation," Colonel Arbuckle now informed him. "Some of their leaders believe they must bow to the inevitable and move west. Others have vowed to fight removal." Sighing, he tugged on his side-whiskers. "I don't have to tell you, Morgan, this is a bad business."

"No, sir, you don't."

"All these damn treaties only make it worse," Arbuckle grumbled. "No one can say with absolute certainty what land belongs to which tribe. Those unscrupulous land speculators back East have taken great advantage of the situation. They're selling false deeds as fast as they can print them. Ah, well, perhaps the commission President Jackson has appointed will sort through the mess."

"Perhaps."

Privately, Zach held little hope that the three-man commission expected to arrive at Fort Gibson any day now could untangle decades of conflicting negotiations.

"In the meantime, we must continue resettling the eastern tribes as best we can. I'll expect you to make yourself and your company ready for escort duty after you deliver Lady Barbara to Morgan's Falls."

The lines of worry faded from the colonel's face. A fatuous smile replaced them. A longtime bachelor, Arbuckle nevertheless had an eye for the ladies.

"You'll be most grateful to me for assigning you this task when you encounter the lady, Morgan."

"I've already encountered her, sir."

"Indeed? Is she not utterly captivating?"

"Utterly."

"She was most surprised and interested to learn the woman she's traveled so far to find had a son under my command."

"Did the lady indicate *why* she's come in search of my mother?"

"I didn't wish to pry, but I formed the impression it has something to do with one of your mother's business interests."

Zach supposed he shouldn't be surprised. His mother was a shrewd trader and financier who'd invested in a number of enterprises over the years. Her varied interests included a steamship line operating out of New Orleans, timber sales to several sawmills and a tannery that cured the beaver, mink and muskrat pelts she'd once trapped with her French-born first husband. Yet somehow Zach couldn't envision Barbara Chamberlain being concerned with the fluctuating price of beaver pelts.

"I'm sure she'll explain all when you speak with her," Arbuckle said.

"Yes, sir."

After promising to deliver a written copy of his report before departing for Morgan's Falls, Zach crossed the grassy flats and made for the establishment of Mrs. Sallie Nicks. He didn't doubt the generous-hearted widow would take Hattie in, but he didn't want to just show up on her stoop with the woman in tow if her house was as full to overflowing as Prescott had indicated.

The gregarious Mrs. Nicks was the widow of General John Nicks, who'd secured the lucrative license to sell provisions to the garrison at Fort Gibson. Upon her husband's death, Sallie had taken over duties as supplier to the garrison. She was a merry-eyed, shrewdly competent woman much courted by the officers and visitors to the post. The rumor that she'd inherited an estate valued at more than twenty thousand dollars from the general along with the right to continue operation of their store only added to her charms.

She occupied a two-story plank house close by the river and the warehouses where she stored her goods. As Nate had warned, the residence was full to over-flowing with visitors who'd arrived via the steamboat. And with every officer in the garrison not currently on duty, Zach soon discovered.

They crowded shoulder to shoulder in the parlor where Mrs. Nicks presided over a silver tea tray. Zach presented himself first to the widow, then to her guest. Sallie acknowledged him with a warm smile, Lady Barbara with an infinitesimal dip of her chin.

"I've come to beg a favor," he said to the widow. "I hate to ask it when you're entertaining so many guests, but I wonder if I might impose upon you to take in one more. I brought a woman back to the post with me."

Sallie's eyes twinkled. "A woman? Your mother will be pleased to hear it, if every unmarried female in Indian Country will not. Who is this woman?"

"Her name is Hattie Goodson. She's the indentured servant of a squatter we were forced to evict. I should tell you, ma'am, she had a rough time of it at the man's hands. Could you find a corner for her until I can make arrangements to send her home?"

"Of course! Bring her here at once."

"Thank you, I will. But first…" His glance went to the blonde surrounded by scarlet and blue uniforms. "Lady Barbara, may I beg a few words of private speech with you?"

His fellow officers responded to his request with a round of protests. Nate Prescott led the chorus.

"I say, Morgan! You'll have the lady to yourself when you escort her to your parents' place tomorrow. Surely you wouldn't be such a dog as to snatch her from us tonight!"

"It's about the journey that I must speak to her," Zach replied. "If she can tear herself away from your company, that is."

"I shall contrive to do so," she returned coolly before turning a brilliant smile on Nate. "You will remember you're taking me in to dinner this evening, will you not?"

"How could I forget!" He threw a smug glance Zach's way. "Too bad you won't be able to join us, old fellow. I know you don't have a decent frock coat here in camp. Although..." His eyes narrowed. "I must say, that shirt looks as though my tailor might have sewn it."

"He did."

Ignoring his friend's sputter of indignation, Zach escorted the lady to the small back parlor Sallie indicated they might use. It was crammed with the bedrolls and backpacks of the visitors she could not squeeze into the rooms upstairs, but otherwise unoccupied.

With a show of bored disinterest, the Englishwoman twitched the fringe of her shawl into place. Zach realized he'd have to grovel like a mud-bellied carp before he was restored to her good graces. If then!

"I must offer an apology for my earlier behavior," he began.

"Save your breath, sir. I consider your conduct inexcusable."

"All I can do is plead a misplaced sense of the ridiculous and beg you to forgive me for funning the way I did."

"Let me be sure I understand you. You beg pardon for allowing me to think you the oafish boor, but not for kissing me in that detestable way?"

One corner of his mouth kicked up. "I'll be sorry indeed if you found that kiss detestable. I, for one, found it most enjoyable."

Barbara didn't doubt it for a moment. He'd molded his mouth to hers with an expertise that bespoke long practice. Seeing him now with his prickly whiskers gone, most of the dirt scrubbed from his person, and that roguish smile in his eyes, she suspected more than one local miss had allowed him to steal a kiss.

Well, Barbara was no local miss. Necessity had taught her to select with great care the men she allowed close to her. She didn't base her choice on their rakish smiles or, as in this case, admittedly splendid physique, but rather on their bank accounts and family holdings. And this man's family holdings must of necessity be the sole focus of her interest.

"May I have your assurances you'll refrain from such *funning* during our journey to your parents' home?"

"You may." In direct counterpoint to her coolness, the smile in his eyes deepened. "But I give them reluctantly."

"Very well. If it is convenient for you, perhaps we could depart after breakfast tomorrow."

"It's quite convenient, but curiosity compels me to ask why you want to go to Morgan's Falls."

Curiosity and a son's desire to protect his dam, Barbara guessed.

"My business is with your mother," she said with a shrug. "I will discuss it with her."

The smile left his eyes. Without moving so much as a muscle, he went from affable to hard and still and somewhat dangerous. She guessed this must be the face he showed his men.

Or his enemies.

"I'll escort you to Morgan's Falls," he said slowly. "But only if *you* give me assurances you mean no harm to me or mine."

"I resent both your tone and your inference, but if it will ease your mind, I will assure you I mean no harm to you or yours."

The lie came easily, like the many others Barbara had uttered over the years. And so naturally, the lieutenant stared at her for only a moment or two longer before accepting it.

"Very well. I'll take you to see my mother."

She hid her relief behind a polite smile. She would have made the journey with or without his assistance, but much preferred to travel in the company of a man who knew his way about this wilderness.

"The trip will be faster if we go by water," he told

her. "I'll arrange matters and come for you in the morning, just after mess call."

"I'll be ready."

Barbara would make every attempt at it, anyway. She had yet to master the art of packing her trunks and valises with the same efficiency her maid had. Perhaps she could beg the assistance of the servant who took care of Mrs. Nicks's personal needs. With luck the attendant might have some skill with arranging hair, as well. Barbara had grown quite tired of drawing it up herself in this unsophisticated cluster of curls.

With a nod to the lieutenant, she allowed him to escort her back to the crowded parlor. His dashing friend with the silky mustaches jumped up at their return. While Prescott and his fellow officers jostled for position, Morgan took temporary leave of his hostess and promised to return shortly with Mistress Goodson.

True to his word, he reappeared a short time later with the bruised woman. Mrs. Nicks's manservant admitted them just as Barbara and her hostess were preparing to mount the stairs and dress for dinner.

With a gentle hand, the lieutenant nudged his charge inside. The timorous woman had found time to brush the red soil from her skirt, Barbara noted. And to knot her hair in a thick, smooth coil of some intricacy. Her interest piqued, she took a keener inventory while the lieutenant introduced the woman to Sallie.

"This is Mistress Hattie Goodson, ma'am. As I said, she's had a rough time of it."

The widow clucked in sympathy. "So I see. You may leave her with me, Zach. I'll see she's made comfortable."

"Thank you."

Hattie clutched at her rescuer's arm. "You won't forget the paper you promised to write for me?"

"I'll draft it tonight and deliver it to you in the morning."

With that, he sketched a bow in the direction of the other two women and departed. Mrs. Nicks bustled back down the stairs.

"Come with me, Hattie. I'll have the servants make up a pallet for you in the pantry room. It's cool and dry and will afford you a measure of privacy."

"I...I can't pay for my keep, ma'am."

"I'm not expecting payment, my dear."

Overhearing the exchange, Barbara made an impulsive offer.

"I'm in need of a maid. Mine chose not to journey to America with me. Do you think you could attend to me?"

Hattie threw her a surprised look. "Attend to you?"

"Help me with my hair and wash out my linens. I'll pay you for your services."

"How much?"

"We'll determine that when I see how handy you are with a brush or curling tongs. Should I be pleased with your efforts and you choose to accompany me when I leave Fort Gibson with Lieutenant Morgan tomorrow, the arrangement could prove beneficial to both of us."

"You're leaving with Lieutenant Morgan?"

"He's escorting me to the home of his parents. Do you wish to try your hand with my comb or not?"

The question ended on a somewhat tart note. Barbara wasn't used to conducting such protracted negotiations with an underling.

Looking properly abashed, the woman bobbed her head. "Yes, ma'am. I do wish it. I promise, I'll do my best by you."

"Very well. You may accompany me upstairs now and show me what your best consists of."

Hattie hastened up the stairs after the lady. Her thoughts all atumble, she could scarcely credit her amazing fortune.

Only last night she'd made the near-fatal mistake of attempting to keep that pig, Thomas, from bending her over the table and ramming into her yet again by telling him she had her monthlies. He'd near killed her when he'd yanked up her skirts and found it to be a lie. In the dark, desperate hours of the night, she'd decided to plunge a carving knife into the bastard's back the very next time he turned it to her. Lieutenant Morgan and his men had ridden up before she'd had the chance.

The lieutenant was her savior. Her hero. He could never know that Hattie had seen how he'd aimed to wound, not kill. Could never suspect she'd shoved Thomas directly into his line of fire. That secret would stay buried forever in the grave that held Thomas's rotting carcass.

Now Hattie would travel with the lieutenant to the home of his parents. Her fortunes had indeed taken a turn!

4

Zach arrived at Sallie Nicks's house just as the bugler sounded morning mess call. The crisp October air echoed to the tramp of the infantrymen's boots as they marched to their breakfast.

Zach soon discovered Barbara Chamberlain wasn't as accustomed to living by the bugle as the residents of a military community. Nor was she a creature of punctuality, apparently. He cooled his heels in Sallie Nicks's front parlor for close on to thirty minutes before the lady descended the stairs.

To his consternation, Hattie descended with her, as did two of Sallie's menservants carrying an assortment of bandboxes and valises.

"I've asked Mistress Goodson to accompany me," the lady informed him. "She was in need of employment, and I of a maid."

She said it casually, with barely a nod in Hattie's direction, but Zach remembered how she'd dropped to her knees in the dirt to aid the fainting woman. He began to suspect a warm heart beat under the lady's cool, porcelain exterior.

"That was well done of you."

She looked surprised that he would presume to comment on her actions and shrugged aside his words of praise.

"If you will direct these men to your boat, they can load the luggage while I make my farewells to Mrs. Nicks."

"I should have described our mode of transportation in more detail last night," Zach said ruefully. "We travel by canoe, not keelboat. It will accommodate you and Hattie, but not all those bags."

"Then you must procure an additional canoe."

Zach hid a smile. He'd already accepted that inevitability. Not one of his sisters could travel so far as the next settlement without carting along what seemed like every ribbon and shawl she owned. The lawyer in him, however, was reluctant to cede the issue without at least a token debate.

"A second canoe will be easy enough to procure. The men to paddle it are another matter."

"Surely you can hire someone?"

"I suppose I could."

"If it is a matter of payment," she said stiffly, "I shall be happy to recompense you."

Zach's eyes glinted. "I might collect on that, if you allow me to decide the manner of payment. In the meantime, you'll want to change your frock."

"I beg your pardon?"

He skimmed a glance over her coffee-colored taffeta day dress and matching silk-lined cape. One careless splash from a paddle would ruin it.

"Perhaps you have something more serviceable in one of those bags," he suggested. "Something water won't ruin."

"Do we canoe to your parents' home, or swim?"

The tart retort drew a laugh from Zach. "I spent my boyhood paddling these rivers, ma'am. I've learned it's always best to be prepared for the worst. I'll return for you shortly."

It took him only a brief time to arrange for another canoe, somewhat longer to hire the men to paddle it. He finally reached an agreement with two Choctaw.

Zach knew them both. He'd spent some weeks in their winter camp a few years back. They'd come to Fort Gibson to inquire about the arrival of the provisions promised by the government to their tribe and were only too happy to travel back downriver with him.

He returned to the Widow Nicks's home to find the delectable Lady Barbara changed into a gown of hunter-green gabardine. A fringed shawl was draped over her shoulders and a straw bonnet trimmed with white netting and green ribbons shielded her face.

"I hope this frock meets with your approval?"

"Most decidedly."

"You cannot imagine how that relieves my mind."

Grinning, Zach waited patiently while she went in search of Sallie Nicks. Hattie waited with him. She also wore different attire, he noted. Her homespun skirt and much-darned short blouse had disappeared. She was now attired in a dress of sensible striped cotton. Its ruffled collar hid the livid finger marks that ringed her throat, and the cherry-colored ribbons added a touch of whimsy to the otherwise sturdy fabric.

"Do you like it?" she asked shyly when she saw she'd caught his attention.

"Very much."

"Lady Barbara purchased it for me from Mrs. Nicks's store. She said she couldn't have her maid going about looking as though the ragman had clothed her."

Her fingers plucked at the cherry ribbons.

"She was going to give me one of her castoffs, but she's so big, her dress fell right off me."

Zach bit back a smile at the artless disclosure. He'd hardly describe the slender, graceful blonde as big, but he supposed anyone would seem overlarge to the sparrow-size Hattie.

"Well, you look very fetching, Mistress Goodson."

She colored under her bruises and preened a bit. Her cheeks were still red when her new mistress swept back down the hall with Sallie in tow.

"Thank you again for this lovely gift," the widow said, raising her left wrist to display the fan dangling from a tasseled cord.

"It's little enough recompense for your generous hospitality."

"You must promise to stay with me again when you return to Fort Gibson. Which will be soon, I hope. You can't miss the Cotton Balers' Ball."

"Your field hands hold a ball?"

"No," Sallie laughed, "our soldiers do. That's their nickname, the Cotton Balers."

"How very odd."

Zach stepped in with an explanation. "The Seventh Infantry Regiment stood with General Jackson, our current president, at the Battle of New Orleans. The artillerymen used cotton bales coated with mud as gun platforms and embrasures."

The Americans under Old Hickory had soundly trounced the British in that particular battle, but Zach decided not to mention the redcoats' humiliating defeat.

"The ball won't be what you're used to," Sallie warned, "but it's quite lively and very colorful. Zach's parents always attend, as do many of the local chiefs."

The Englishwoman sidestepped gracefully. "My plans are as yet indefinite. I'll make note of the occasion and attend if possible."

Now *that* would be a sight to see, Zach thought

with a grin. The exquisite Barbara Chamberlain dripping silk and lace while she trod the boards with a Creek or Cherokee chief. Resolving to make sure he also claimed her for a dance, Zach stood aside to allow her and Hattie to precede him out the door. The two servants followed with their burden of bandboxes and valises.

The small procession caused no end of a stir as it wound its way past the fort's outbuildings. The soldiers harvesting what looked like a bumper crop of pumpkins from the gardens paused in their labors to stare. So did the blacksmith and his minions. Even the whack of the laundress's paddles stilled as the small cavalcade approached the river.

With each step closer to the red mud banks crowded by birch and oak ablaze with fall colors, Zach felt the burdens of his military duties ease. He loved serving with the rangers, felt right at home among their rough-and-tumble company. Yet the prospect of leaving the fort and his men behind for a few days and paddling through the distant reaches of the land that had bred him started his blood singing.

Eager to shake free of the trappings of civilization, he introduced his charges to the men he'd hired to paddle the second canoe.

"This is Chula Humma. Red Fox in our language. And this is Ok-Shakla. His name translates loosely to Deep Water. They're of the Chata, or Choctaw, people."

Like so many who'd migrated from the East, the Choctaw braves displayed the mix of cultures that had shaped them. Their fringed deerskin trousers were quilled and beaded in the style of their people. Their wool shirts, suspenders and flat-crowned hats could only have come from a trader's stock.

Barbara offered the two men a small nod. Hattie hung back nervously until Zach assured her he knew them personally. Even then she had to be persuaded to climb into the second canoe. Zach arranged the valises around her and made sure she was comfortable before stowing the rest of the bandboxes in the first canoe and holding out a hand to his passenger.

"Lady Barbara."

She eyed the thin bark strips with a frown, gave an almost infinitesimal shrug, and put her hand in his.

Her fingers felt warm through her gloves, her grip surprisingly firm. Zach handed her into the canoe and saw her securely seated before he shoved away from the bank.

The bark boat tipped when he swung into it. At the motion his passenger grabbed for the sides. She sat stiff as a rail post while Zach's paddle cut into the water and steered the craft toward the current.

A quick look over his shoulder assured him the second canoe had launched without mishap. Like her mistress, Hattie gripped the sides. Neither woman relaxed until the current took the boats and the paddlers found their rhythm.

A few moments later they rounded a bend of the river. Fort Gibson disappeared from view, and with it all signs and sounds of settlement. As swiftly as that, the wilderness claimed them.

Zach could only wonder what his passenger thought of the tangled brush lining the riverbank and still, silent forests beyond. Her bonnet hid her face from his view until she felt secure enough to relax her grip on the canoe's sides and twist around.

"How far do we travel this river?"

"Until it joins with the Arkansas. We'll follow that to where the Canadian empties into it. Morgan's Falls lies fifteen miles up the Canadian."

"How long do you anticipate our journey will take?"

"If we hit no snags or unexpected delays, we should arrive in time for supper."

Nodding, she faced forward again.

The Grand carried them swiftly down the three miles to its juncture with the Arkansas. Muscles straining, Zach used his paddle to negotiate the swirling currents. With sure, clean strokes, he took his craft into the main channel. The second canoe cut through the rippling waters right behind him.

Much wider and swifter than the Grand, the Arkansas constituted the main waterway through Indian Country. Keelboats and paddle wheelers now coursed it regularly, hauling supplies, recruits and, of late, more and more of the migrating eastern tribes. At the moment, though, the occupants of the two canoes had the long, winding river to themselves.

The muscles in Zach's arms bunched and stretched in easy rhythm. Long years of experience had him keeping a constant vigilance for sunken logs and hidden sandbars.

In between, his glance lingered on the green ribbons trailing from Barbara's bonnet. He couldn't imagine what a woman of her background and breeding must make of Indian Country.

He got some sense of her thoughts when they broke their journey at noon. They'd covered a longer stretch of the Arkansas than Zach had hoped for and were able to bank their canoes at John Jolly's plantation. A shrewd merchant who'd obtained a license to act as government provisioner to the Chickasaw Nation, he operated a store and sawmill some miles above the point where the Canadian River fed into the Arkansas.

He and his Chickasaw wife welcomed the travelers and treated them to a hearty meal of fried corn, buffalo steak and pumpkin bread. Zach shared the news from Fort Gibson with Jolly, who in turn related the unwelcome information that a Creek hunting party had surprised two Chickasaw braves and relieved them of their weapons and horses. In retaliation, the Chickasaw had raided the Creeks' village.

"They took two captives," the agent muttered, shaking his head. "I'll have a devil of a time getting either side to cry peace."

The meal done, Zach lit up a fat cigar and waited by the canoes with the other men while the ladies made visits to the necessary. Barbara emerged first and joined Zach at the river.

The October afternoon had warmed enough for her to slip off her shawl and fold it over her arm. She stood silent, watching the rippling water. After a moment, her gaze lifted to the bluffs standing sentinel above the river. Tall pines dotted their granite ledges and speared into a cloudless blue sky. Hawks circled above the pines, wings spread, talons back, ever vigilant and ready to dive on their prey.

"This land is quite awe inspiring," she murmured. "So wild and untamed."

"River country has its own beauty," Zach agreed, "but you'll see no more remarkable sight than a storm rolling across the prairies. Or a more frightening one than a buffalo herd thundering over the hills in your direction," he added dryly.

She turned a curious glance on him. "You speak as though you love this land."

"I do. I'm sure you couldn't tell it from my refined manners," he added on a teasing note, "but I was born and bred here."

"Yet I understand you've only just returned to Indian Country after a good number of years away."

"I studied at a university in the East and practiced the law for a few years before going into the army. After that, it was anyone's guess which post I'd be assigned to until headquarters formed a company of mounted rangers. I promptly applied to serve with them and came home to Indian Country."

"I know little about the army, but I've heard service in a regular unit holds more honors and prestige than your irregulars."

Zach's mouth curved. "Been talking to Nate, have you?"

"It's the same in the British army, I would guess."

"You'd guess right," he admitted with a shrug, "but the rangers suit me."

She made no reply to that. She didn't have to. Zach was sure she considered him eminently suited for the rough-and-tumble irregulars.

"Will you tell me about your parents?" she said after a moment. "I don't like arriving on their doorstep knowing little more than their names."

Was that all she really knew of them? Zach wondered as he blew a cloud fragrant with the perfume of sweet Virginia tobacco.

"My father spent a good number of years as a rifle sergeant in the 2d Regiment of Foot."

"Ah, another military man. It's a tradition with your family, I see."

"More or less."

His father's military career had taken as many

twists and turns as his own. Daniel Morgan had enlisted in a rifle regiment and eventually rose to the exalted position of sergeant major, only to be stripped of his rank and cashiered from the service.

He'd then served as guide, surveyor and consultant to the army's elite corps of topographical engineers until the War of 1812 precipitated his return to uniform. His service during the Battle of New Orleans had won him special recognition from his commander, General Andrew Jackson, and reinstatement of his former rank. In recognition, Old Hickory had recommended the sergeant major's son for admission to West Point years later.

"My father was a member of the first official United States expedition to explore this territory," Zach said with more than a touch of pride. "He paddled down this very river twenty-six years ago. That's when he met my mother."

He dropped the bait deliberately, curious to see if she would take it. She did.

"I understand she's half-French."

"That's right."

"She was married to another Frenchman, was she not, before she wed your father?"

Well, that answered Zach's question. The lady knew a good deal more about his parents than their names.

"She was married to a fur trapper by the name of Henri Chartier. He died the same day my father stumbled on their camp. A mountain cat ripped out his throat. It happened not far from here."

Barbara suppressed a gasp. He'd intended to shock her, she guessed at once, and he'd succeeded. Suddenly the pine-shrouded bluffs lost their air of stillness and took on one of menace.

As unease rippled down her spine, she debated whether to continue her inquiries about Henri Chartier. She wasn't ready to tip her hand yet, but her brother's desperate circumstances weighed heavily on her mind.

Eyes cool, she surveyed the man next to her. For all his size and self-proclaimed tendency to give in to a sense of the ridiculous, he was no fool. Once Barbara's anger at being made the butt of his joke had burnt out, she'd been forced to acknowledge just how skillfully he'd played her.

Almost as skillfully as he'd kissed her.

She had yet to erase the memory of his mouth covering hers. What's more, she had only to see the ripple of his muscles as he pitched his cigar into the river to experience a surprising and rather annoying quiver low in her belly.

She'd have to decide how best to make use of the heat that kiss had stirred.

5

By midafternoon, the small party of travelers had left the Arkansas River and turned up the Canadian. Gradually the high, rocky bluffs fell behind them and the land flattened to rolling hills, although the mountains remained always in sight.

The going was slower now. The men paddled against the current, passing only the occasional Indian village. As the sun sank toward the hills, the October air lost some of its warmth. Barbara had just begun to believe her long-anticipated meeting with Louise Chartier Morgan might be delayed yet another day, when her ears picked up the faint sound of splashing water.

Moments later, a bend of the river revealed the source of the sound. A stream emerged from the undergrowth covering a steep hill. From there it tumbled in a silvery cascade over glistening black rocks before dropping a good twenty feet into the Canadian.

Atop the hill sat a two-story house with a commanding view of the river in both directions. Unlike so many of the rough-hewn log dwellings Barbara had seen since her arrival in Indian Country, this one was of smooth-planked wood painted a gleaming white. Low wings flanked the central structure on either side, while windows of thick, wavy glass reflected the gold of the slowly setting sun. Behind the main house sat a cluster of outbuildings that included barns, stables and what looked like quarters for servants or slaves. A windbreak of tall trees separated the outbuildings from the cleared fields beyond. Unless Barbara missed her guess, she'd finally arrived at her destination. Swallowing, she fought to still the sudden flutter in her chest.

"Is this Morgan's Falls?"

"It is," the lieutenant replied with a touch of pride.

Her glance swept the cluster of buildings and acres of cleared fields. "The plantation is larger than I expected."

"My father was granted the original two hundred acres in recognition for his services as scout and surveyor, and my mother claimed title to the rest through her Indian blood. Like Sallie Nicks and John Jolly, she also holds a trade commission from the government."

Barbara's nervous sense of anticipation increased

as the lieutenant took his canoe past the falls to a point where the hill sloped down to the river. The prow hadn't so much as nosed the red mud bank before a boy in canvas work pants and a loose-sleeved work shirt dashed down the hill.

"I spotted you a mile and more away!" he shouted.

"Did you? Good eye, Theo."

Skittering the last few feet on the seat of his pants, the boy goggled at Barbara. He was as brown as a chestnut and sported a good-size lump over one eye. Like a gangly pup, he hadn't yet grown into his hands and feet but their size and his easy familiarity with the lieutenant suggested they must be brothers.

Splashing into the river, Morgan pushed the canoe toward the bank. "Lend a hand here, Theo."

The boy scrambled to help drag the craft onto the grassy slope. Once there, the lieutenant gave him an affectionate cuff on the shoulder.

"Been fighting again, I see."

"It's that cussed Urice. She whacked me with a—"

"Mind your tongue, Theo, and say hello to our guest, Lady Barbara."

Aggrieved, the youngster rubbed his shoulder and turned his attention to the woman his brother handed out of the canoe. "How do you do, ma'am?"

"Quite well, thank you."

"This scamp is my youngest brother, Theophilus.

Here, Theo, take the lady's bandboxes while I help the others."

As the second canoe neared the shore, the boy's gaze darted to Hattie and lingered for a startled moment on her bruises before dropping to the bandboxes piled in the canoe.

"Urice is going to fall into raptures when she sees all these," he predicted somewhat glumly. "There'll be no talk of anything but ribbons and laces for days to come."

"Urice is my sister," the lieutenant explained as he beached the second canoe. "She spends more time poring over dress patterns than she does her lessons. Unlike Vera, another sister, who is just the opposite."

With a shy smile, Hattie put her hand in his. "Urice? What an unusual name."

"Yes, it is."

Barbara watched the byplay with a raised eyebrow. She would have to teach Mistress Goodson the proper etiquette for a woman in service, which did *not* include gazing up at her betters with such obvious adoration.

"My mother lost a fierce battle with the priest who baptized us," Zach explained, tucking one of the bandboxes under his arm. "The priest held fast for biblical names instead of the native names she'd chosen, so she started at the end of the alphabet and worked forward. We range from Zachariah, Youris and Xavier to Vera, Urice, Theo here and the youngest, Sarah. Only Washington was spared."

Barbara allowed him to take her elbow and escort her up the steep path to the house. Hattie, the boy and the two warriors followed.

"Washington, one must assume, was named for your country's first president?"

"No, for an old friend of my parents, Washington Irving."

Barbara tripped over her feet and would have fallen flat on her face if not for the lieutenant's firm grip. Her heart thumping against her stays, she struggled to keep her voice steady.

"Do you refer to Washington Irving, who penned *The Sketchbook of Geoffrey Crayon, Gentleman?*

"I do." He smiled down at her. "How gratifying to know one of our American authors has won the attention of European readers."

"Attention and acclaim."

"He's been living abroad for some years. Have you met him?"

"Once, very briefly."

She and Harry had been seated across the dinner table from the author during a dinner hosted by a Bohemian baron. The meal became quite lively when their host let slip that he'd presented the charming Lady Barbara with the diamond bracelet she was wearing. His baroness had expressed severe and rather vocal displeasure.

"You say Mr. Irving is a family friend?"

"More of an acquaintance, really. My parents met him when they went East some years ago. They've maintained a somewhat erratic correspondence with him ever since. He's always promising to come West for a visit, but has yet to… Here, watch this patch of pea vines." He slanted her a quick grin. "You won't want to snag your gown again."

With the lieutenant's strong hand under her arm and the ever-ready gleam of laughter in his dark eyes, Barbara allowed herself to relax. From the sound of it, his family claimed only a passing association with the author. Certainly nothing that might interfere with her plans. She let out a relieved breath, only to swiftly draw it in again as the woman she'd traveled so far to confront burst from the house.

"Zachariah!"

Aside from her lustrous black hair, Louise Chartier Morgan held little resemblance to her son. Nor did she in any way resemble the ignorant, half-breed savage Harry had told Barbara to expect.

Slender and petite, she wore a sensible, if surprisingly modish, gown of dove-gray wool. Its three-tiered embroidered collar flattered her heart-shaped face and made her look more sister than mother to the tall, broad-shouldered woodsman who swept her into a fierce hug. Her face was alight with joy when he released her.

"Me, I could not believe my ears when the servants tell me you are come! Have you taken leave from your duties at Fort Gibson?"

"Only for a few days. I've brought you guests."

"So I see."

Eyes a deep, startling blue looked over Barbara before flitting to Hattie and the two warriors who'd accompanied them. The woman was really quite beautiful, Barbara thought. And so very exotic. With those remarkable eyes, glossy hair and high, copper-tinted cheekbones, she might have posed for a portrait by Sir Thomas Lawrence of an American princess.

She had time for only that one thought before the woman's gaze fixed on her once again. Louise Morgan cocked her head, and for the strangest moment Barbara felt as though she was seeing more than just a rumpled, travel-worn visitor. The odd sensation passed as her son made the necessary introductions.

"Mother, this is Lady Barbara Chamberlain. She's traveled all the way from London to meet with you."

Astonishment filled the woman's eyes. "To meet with me?"

"It's true," Barbara confirmed with a smile. "Although had I known how long and arduous a journey it would be, I might have thought twice before undertaking it."

"And me, I make you stand here while we talk about it! Zachariah, tell me the names of these other guests you bring and let us take them inside so they may freshen themselves."

The lieutenant introduced Hattie, then lapsed into a native tongue unintelligible to Barbara but comprehended by his mother. She replied in kind and elicited animated comments from the two Choctaw. Clucking, Louise Morgan shook her head.

"It is so absurd, this tangle of treaties."

"Yes," her son agreed, "it is. President Jackson has named a commission to sort matters out. I'll tell you and Father about it over dinner."

"Pah!" Still shaking her head, she led the way inside. "That Jackson, he is beyond anything a rogue."

Barbara paid scant attention to the conversation. She had little interest in the politics of this provincial backwater, but the obvious signs of wealth that greeted her when she stepped inside Louise Morgan's home snared her instant attention.

The house was filled with the scent of waxed oak floors, a feast of rich colors and the echo of laughter. Two rooms gave off the central hall, one a parlor, the other a dining room. Both contained furnishings that might have graced a country home in Sussex or Kent. The dining room boasted chairs covered in striped silks, a table that looked as though it could seat a dozen comfortably and a three-tiered silver epergne filled with fall fruits and nuts.

Family possessions were scattered about the parlor. Leather-bound books. An embroidery basket spilling skeins of bright silk. Pipes stacked in a rack beside a leather tobacco pouch. A bow and quiver of arrows propped in a corner of the dining room.

This was a home well lived in, Barbara thought. The kind of home she dimly remembered from the years before her father had lost his estates to an unlucky turn of the cards and his life to a pistol shot on the field of honor. Barbara had just celebrated her fifth birthday when she and her brother went to live with a distant and sternly disapproving cousin.

The subsequent years were turbulent to say the least, as their relative attempted to crush Harry's reckless spirits. Their fierce arguments had finally led to an exchange of blows. Harry and the then-twelve-year-old Barbara had slipped out of the house in the dead of night and embarked straightaway on their adventurous, if somewhat up-and-down, life.

She loved the freedom such a life allowed her. She truly did. Harry had taught her to throw off so many of the conventions that narrowed life to a dull routine and live every moment to the very fullest. It was only at odd moments, when Barbara caught a glimpse of a comfortable, well-appointed house like this one, that the treacherous desire for a home and family of her own crept into her heart.

Sternly, she quashed the insidious longing. What was she thinking? Harry was her family. Her *only* family. He was depending on his sister to free him from the foul prison where he breathed in the stink of unwashed bodies every day. Her back stiffening, Barbara turned to the woman she and Harry had selected as their next prey.

"May I beg a private word with you after I remove my travel dirt?"

"But of course. Come, I take you and Hattie upstairs to refresh yourselves. Zach will bring your valises. Theo, take Chula Humma and Ok-Shakla to the kitchens so they may eat before they go back to their village. And ask Lula to fetch hot water for our guests."

The bedchamber Louise Morgan showed Barbara to obviously belonged to her daughters. Cloaks and colorful shawls hung from pegs, and the open doors of a tall wardrobe showed a profusion of sturdy calico, dainty checked gingham and lustrous silks. Sweeping up a sunbonnet that had been tossed carelessly on the bed, her hostess tucked it into the wardrobe while her son deposited one load of bandboxes and went downstairs for the rest.

"This is a lovely room," Barbara said, struck by the view its dormer window gave of the river and the green mountains beyond, "but I shouldn't like to dispossess your daughters."

"They won't mind. Urice is happy to give up her bed if you'll speak to her of the latest fashions in feather bonnets. Vera, too, if you'll share your views on radical feminine philosophers."

"I would, and gladly, if I knew any."

Laughing, the slender matron headed for the door.

"Vera will no doubt inform you. She teaches in our mission school and loves the chance to discuss these so-modern ideas. I'll send someone up with clean bed linens. If you wish to speak with me before dinner, I wait for you in the parlor."

Barbara was trying to decide which boxes to have Hattie unpack when the lieutenant carried in the rest of her things.

"Do you have all you need?"

"Yes, quite. Tell me, is dinner a formal affair?"

"Only when my parents entertain nobility," he replied, a smile in his eyes. "Two months ago they hosted Iesh, a Caddo chieftain. His presence, of course, caused a flurry of baking and silver polishing. I'd guess yours might merit the same."

Barbara suspected it would. Deciding she would need all her armor and then some when she confronted Louise Morgan, she directed Hattie to the appropriate valise.

"You'll find a blue silk gown and a Norwich shawl in there."

The gown was sadly crushed. While Hattie went to find a pressing iron, Barbara used the interval to shed her traveling dress, scrub her face and hands, and change her underlinens. Clad in a chemise of fine lawn, a lace-edged corset and silk stockings trimmed with delicate embroidery designed to draw the eye to a neatly turned ankle, she dug through the opened valise for her jewelry case.

Her hand closed around the embroidered case, then stilled. Chewing on her lower lip, Barbara released the case and felt for the slit in the valise's lining. Slowly, she withdrew a piece of oilskin folded to a small, flat square. Inside the protective covering was the document Harry had lifted from the dead body chained next to him.

Blindly, Barbara stared down at the folded oilskin. She didn't need to extract the document inside or read the French phrases. She'd burned them into her brain the very first time she'd read them in the dank, squalid visitors' cell.

They'd been written by the bishop of Reims. In bold, flowing script, the cleric certified that a Jesuit priest by the name of Père Jean Sebastian had indulged in a series of debaucheries with a young female more than thirty years ago. Père Sebastian had fled to French-held Louisiana to escape censure and had been defrocked in absentia. All rites performed by the priest in the New World, the bishop declared, were null and void.

Those rites, the possessor of this document had gasped to Harry with his last, rattling breaths, included the marriage of one Henri Chartier to a half-breed squaw. The woman wasn't his wife. Had *never* been his wife. The fortune she'd inherited from Chartier should have gone to his descendants in France. To him, through his great-grandmother!

Ever one to seize an opportunity, Harry had lifted

the tiny square of oilskin off the dying man. Months later, he'd passed it to Barbara.

Carefully, she slid the folded square back into its hiding place. She'd have to choose the best moment to produce the document. Not tonight, certainly. As Harry had taught her, one must always bait the trap before springing it.

Fishing out her jewel case, she crossed to the gilt-edged stand the Morgan girls used as a dressing table. She'd just seated herself on the padded bench, when Hattie returned and held the blue gown up for Barbara's inspection.

"Well done! You have a light hand with a pressing iron."

A blush rose under the woman's bruises. "My mam always said so."

"I don't have time to brush out my hair. Will you tuck in the loose strands?"

Laying the dress across the bed, Hattie took up the silver-backed brush and put her nimble fingers to good use. Not only did she tame the flyaway strands, she teased the side tendrils into feathery curls.

Her hair attended to, Barbara's impatience to be downstairs mounted. She stepped into her gown and tried not to fidget while Hattie fastened its buttons on the shimmering silk.

"I've never seen the like of this gown," the maid murmured.

"It's Italian in fashion." A little tug lowered the rounded neckline and bared her shoulders. The full sleeves puffed up to Barbara's satisfaction, she sorted through the contents of her jewel case.

The case that had once held a sparkling collection was now almost empty. She'd sold her ruby earrings to pay the barrister who'd defended Harry at trial— *most* ineffectually, it turned out. Her rope of pearls and magnificent, square-cut Russian emerald had gone for bribes to ensure her brother received what comfort he could in the prison hulks. Barbara's diamonds had paid for her own voyage, first to Bermuda and then to America.

The sapphires and a few inexpensive trinkets were all that remained. They, too, would go unless she succeeded in the mission Harry had sent her on. Setting her jaw, she clasped the filigree strands studded with sapphires around her neck.

"You may straighten up in here, Hattie, then go to your supper."

"Yes, ma'am."

On her way to the door, Barbara stopped and swung back. "I have a lotion of distilled pears in that valise. You may put some on your face and neck, if you wish. It will help ease the discoloration."

As she smoothed the lotion over her cheeks, Hattie marveled once again at her astounding change in fortune.

Not three days ago Thomas was slobbering all

over her and near suffocating her with his stink. Now here she was, daubing the essence of distilled pears on her skin. She'd smell as fine as any lady—including the one who pranced about with her nose so high in the air it was a wonder she didn't trip over her own feet.

Awash in a cloud of fragrance, Hattie threw a glance over her shoulder. The door was firmly shut. Giving in to avid curiosity, she poked through the jewel case sitting on the dressing table.

A choker of glittering jet made her gasp in delight. She held it to her throat, imagining how it would look when the finger marks faded. Returning it to the case, she continued her explorations. A small brooch lay buried under a string of Venetian-glass beads. The pin was just a trinket, the kind of bauble a man might buy his sweetheart at a country fair, but the enameled flowers surrounded by tiny seed pearls caught Hattie's fancy. Surely Lady Barbara wouldn't miss such a trifling piece.

Slipping it in the pocket of her cherry striped gown, she straightened the room and went downstairs to find her supper. The murmur of voices in the parlor slowed her step. She was as curious as Lieutenant Morgan as to Lady Barbara's business with his mother and would dearly love to put an ear to the keyhole. The heavy tread of footsteps forced her to continue on her way to the kitchens.

She wouldn't eat with the other servants for long,

she vowed. One day—and soon!—she would sit down to dinner with the lieutenant and his family and take her tucker from gleaming silver trays.

6

Barbara sipped the wine her hostess had pressed on her and gave silent thanks she'd decided to wear her sapphires. Harry had always insisted they must never appear at a disadvantage before their prey, and anything less than the sparkling stones would have put her at a *distinct* disadvantage before this particular prey.

Louise Morgan, too, had changed her gown for dinner. The elegant amber satin with its over-drape of gold gauze might have been fashioned by one of London's finest modistes. Unless Barbara had lost her eye for gems, those were yellow diamonds encircling the woman's throat and dangling from her earlobes.

As the two women savored their wine, they indulged in a polite exchange. Her hostess asked how Barbara had fared during her journey. She responded with a few amusing anecdotes she invented on the spot. She knew the time for chitchat had passed when Louise set aside her glass and turned a look of cool inquiry on her guest.

"My son said you traveled from London to seek me out. Why?"

Barbara, too, set aside her glass. She'd prepared for this moment for weeks, had rehearsed a dozen times or more the devious mix of fact and fiction she and Harry had concocted. Unfortunately, they'd believed then that Barbara would be dealing with an uneducated aborigine. Instead, she faced a shrewd, sophisticated businesswoman. Hiding her clamoring nerves behind a small smile, Barbara spun a web of half truths and lies.

"I've come in search of you, Mrs. Morgan, because it appears we may be related."

The older woman's eyes widened. "What do you say?"

"I believe you are my great-aunt."

Astounded, Louise Morgan stared at her. "How can this be? My mother was of the Osage. My father of the French."

"I, too, have French ancestry."

That much at least was true. Barbara and Harry's grandmother on their mother's side had fled France at the start of the Terror. From that point on, however, Barbara stole her ancestry from the man who'd died in chains next to Harry.

"My grandmother's last name was Bernay. She

was the younger sister of Julianne Bernay, who married the third son of the Duc d'Argonne. The son's given name was—"

"I know his name," her hostess cut in. "It was Henri. Henri Chartier. He is man I marry before Daniel Morgan."

"Yes, he is. Or was. I understand he died some years ago."

"*Many* years ago." Frowning, she struggled to trace the convoluted lineage. "Let me be sure I understand this. When Henri comes to America, he leaves behind a wife in France. She dies, and he marries me. You say this woman was your grandmother?"

"My grandmother's sister. That makes Henri my great-uncle, and you my aunt by marriage."

Barbara smoothed her gown over her knees, caught herself, and silently cursed the nervous gesture. Harry had taught her never to betray nerves.

"I only learned of your marriage to Henri Chartier a few months ago."

In a dark, dank cell, with her brother's chains rattling as he paced. Shoving aside the wrenching memory, Barbara proceeded carefully.

"The connection between us is tenuous at best and exists only through marriage. You may well choose not to acknowledge it."

The older woman took her time replying. Really, she had the most unnerving stare. So intense and direct.

"You must tell me why would *either* of us wish to acknowledge this connection you speak of."

The blunt question hit right at the heart of the matter. Both women knew there was only one reason an English lady would admit a tie, however slight, to an American commoner of mixed Indian and French blood. Barbara didn't even try to deny her motives.

"When I learned of your marriage to my great-uncle, I also learned you inherited the fortune he amassed during his years in Louisiana Territory."

"Yes, it occurs to me you must know of Henri's fortune."

The dry comment sent heat spearing in Barbara's cheeks. She was more used to playing the role of smiling seducer than supplicant. It scratched her pride to sit here and all but beg.

"I make no bones about it," she said flatly. "I find myself in desperate need of funds."

"How much do you want?"

All of it.

Every shilling she'd inherited from her first husband.

The urge to lay the demand on the table rose in Barbara's throat. Ruthlessly, she suppressed it. If she'd learned nothing else from Harry, it was to avoid overshooting her mark. The bishop's document was her trump card. She'd play it only if necessary.

"I require five thousand pounds sterling."

Louise Morgan didn't so much as blink. She must have many times that amount in the bank to take the demand so calmly!

Relief coursed through Barbara. One of the most serious flaws in the wild scheme Harry had devised was a lack of knowledge as to how much of Henri Chartier's supposed fortune remained, if any remained at all. Sallie Nicks's offhand remarks had given Barbara some assurance. The fine furnishings in this house had provided more.

Now she knew without the slightest doubt this woman's wealth was great indeed. Allowing none of her relief to show in her face, she was ready for the question she saw forming in the woman's remarkable eyes.

"For what purpose do you require these funds?"

"To secure the release of my brother," she answered. This time the truth served better than any lie. "He fell victim to a fraudulent scheme and was sent to prison."

It didn't matter that he'd devised the scheme himself. She waited, half expecting the older woman to refuse and thus force Barbara to play her trump card. Her answer was slow in coming and surprising.

"I know how it is to see someone you love thrown into prison. My husband—my second husband, Daniel—languished in the *cabildo* in New Orleans for months."

The older woman's glance drifted to the window.

The deepening twilight outside must have been filled with images from her past, for the face she turned back to her guest held haunting shadows.

"I make a bargain with the devil to secure Daniel's release."

Barbara held the woman's gaze. "I would do the same to secure my bother's."

"Yes," she said slowly, "I can see you would."

The moment stretched for an awkward length before Louise Morgan broke it.

"I must speak with my husband about this. And you must speak to Zachariah," she added. "Tell him of your brother's plight if you have not already done so and let him put his mind to this matter of unjust imprisonment."

"I would prefer not to involve another lawyer in the matter. The last one cost me a pair of ruby earbobs and left my brother to rot in prison."

The stiff reply won a smile from the older woman.

"I, too, have had sour dealings with lawyers. Why do you think Daniel and I send Zach East to read the law? He's the only one we trust to manage our affairs."

Which meant Barbara might yet have to go through the son to reach into the mother's pockets. Oddly, the prospect didn't disturb her as much as it had a few days ago. She was discovering the lieutenant to be a man of many talents, but he was still a man. She didn't doubt her ability to bring him to his knees.

She didn't have much time to accomplish the task, though. The lieutenant had been released from his military duties for only a few days. She'd have to begin her campaign soon, she decided, as Louise Morgan rose and shook out her skirts.

"Shall we take dinner now?" her hostess asked politely. "We will speak again tomorrow."

With a nod, Barbara rose and followed her to the door. The wooden panels slid open and caught the attention of the two men deep in conversation at the far end of the hall.

"There you are."

The older of the two came forward to greet his wife and guest. Barbara recognized him at once as the lieutenant's father. He was every bit as tall as his son and carried himself with the same square-shouldered erectness. The resemblance went deeper than mere physical traits, though, and had more to do with his calm, confident air. This was a man who recognized his strengths and compensated for his failings, she thought.

She had only to see the light that came into his eyes when they caught his wife's to know Louise Morgan held his heart in her hands. Suppressing an unexpected pang of envy for the older woman, Barbara returned Daniel Morgan's warm smile.

"Welcome to Morgan's Falls, Lady Barbara. I confess, I'm as eager as my son to learn the reason you've journeyed so far to meet with my wife."

His tone was cordial and the words polite, but neither fooled Barbara. Like his son, he would allow no one to harm the petite, black-haired woman who slipped her arm in his.

"She comes because she and I share ties by marriage. Lady Barbara is Henri's great-niece."

"The devil you say!" her husband exclaimed.

Her son, too, expressed astonishment, but it was obvious from the glance the two men exchanged they didn't believe Barbara had journeyed all this way simply to visit with a long-lost relation. Louise forestalled the questions she saw in their faces.

"We must feed our guest or she will think we mean to starve her. Zach, take the lady's arm."

"Please, call me Barbara," she urged as Zach stepped forward. Like his parents and their guest, the lieutenant had dressed for dinner. He'd shed his well-worn buckskins in favor of a green velvet jacket with claw-hammer tails and a double row of brass buttons. His gray wool trousers were tucked into knee-high Hessians polished to a shine that would raise instant envy in the breast of any dandy on the strut in Hyde Park.

Every time she thought she had his measure, Barbara reflected wryly, he changed his stripes. First the rough woodsman, then the officer. Now it was a sophisticated gentleman who escorted her into the dining room.

The noisy chatter that had been emanating from

the room stilled instantly. No fewer than ten people turned in their direction. Three were servants who caught their mistress's nod and scrambled to remove covers from the silver dishes on the sideboard. Four were the children of the house.

The others were introduced as Mr. Harris, a young missionary who taught the school on the Morgan property; Singing Bird McRoberts, a broad-cheeked woman in braids and a stunning necklace of silver and turquoise; and Jeremy, her husband. McRoberts was a little raisin of a man with reddish hair, clacking wooden teeth and a cast in one eye. Squinting at Barbara, he pronounced her pretty as a goose and promptly demanded his dinner.

"Yes, yes," Louise said, not the least perturbed by this breach of etiquette. "First let me introduce Lady Barbara to the children."

Chubby-cheeked little Sarah giggled. A scrubbed and clean-suited Theo made an awkward bow. Urice turned out to be a merry-eyed miss of eleven or twelve. Her sister Vera, Barbara discovered, was a serious-minded scholar recently returned from a convent school in New Orleans. A fourth daughter was mistress of her own home in the Carolinas, Louise informed Barbara, and the other Morgan sons were away at university or off on various business pursuits.

Dinner turned out to be a lively affair. Barbara was unused to sitting down to table with children, but found herself smiling at Sarah's infectious giggles and replying easily to Urice's eager questions about everything from India muslins to the new dropped shoulders and epaulette collars. Vera's questions were somewhat more daunting.

"My mother says you are but lately come from abroad, Lady Barbara. Has the debate over Mary Wollstonecraft's treatise on the education of women lost some of its heat?"

"I, er, have not heard it mentioned of late."

Or at all!

Her delicate face assuming serious lines, Vera lowered her soupspoon. "Do you agree with the basic tenets of the treatise? That women debase themselves by exercising the power of their beauty instead of their reason?"

Barbara was saved by Urice, who'd obviously heard the same question posed before.

"Oh, pooh! You're not going to go off on another lecture about how a gentleman shouldn't jump to pick up a lady's handkerchief for her, are you?"

"Not at all. I merely hope our guest would agree a woman is capable of picking up her own handkerchief."

"I do indeed," Barbara said. "But why should she, if she has a handsome swain to do it for her?"

Urice sent her sister a smug look, which disappeared when their guest continued calmly.

"Beauty can be as potent a force as intellect. A

woman would be a fool not to employ both to achieve her ends."

"The same way a man would be a fool not to appreciate both," the lieutenant put in with a smile.

"Just so."

Spooning her soup, Barbara sipped at the delicately flavored pumpkin bisque. It was quite good, as were the saddle of beef and pork tenderloins in wild mushroom gravy that followed. She reserved judgment on the squash soufflé, but decided she'd never tasted a more delicious syllabub. Rich with raisins, nuts and cinnamon, the pudding-like dessert swam in a puddle of sweet, thick cream.

After dinner, the family repaired to the parlor where Urice gave an astonishing performance on the piano. Her nimble fingers flew through selections from Mozart, Handel and an Italian composer Barbara had never heard of before switching to lively country airs. When the tinkling notes of "Greensleeves" faded, the girl slowed the pace and began a piece with an odd rhythm. Every third or fourth beat she stuck a chord at the lower end of the keyboard, almost like a drumbeat. In between, the notes trilled swift and sweet, like a lark on the wing.

"What an unusual piece," Barbara commented when she finished.

"Do you like it?"

"Very much."

Pleasure stained the girl's cheeks. "It's my own

composition. I based it on one of the songs my mother's mother taught her. The Osage are quite noted for their musical ability, you know."

"No, I didn't. I must confess I've not met anyone of Osage descent before."

Truth be told, she found the girl's pride in her mixed heritage somewhat surprising. The Americans she'd met so far had displayed a wide range of attitudes toward the native population, but here in Indian Country the mix of cultures and bloodlines appeared to occasion little concern or comment.

The concert ended, Zach rose and issued an invitation. "Are you up to a stroll? There's a harvest moon out tonight. It's a sight to see rising over the river."

Barbara started to demur, but the knowledge that the lieutenant must soon return to Fort Gibson changed her mind. If he had questions or qualms about Barbara's claim of kinship to his mother, she'd best hear them now.

Making her excuses to her host and hostess, she went upstairs to fetch her shawl. Hattie wasn't in the room, Barbara saw with a dart of annoyance. Nor had she turned down the bed or laid out a nightdress. Wondering what the woman was about, Barbara draped the elegantly fringed Norwich shawl over her elbows and descended the stairs to find her absent maid in the hall, engaged in conversation with the lieutenant.

Their discussion broke off with Barbara's arrival, and her somewhat tart suggestion that Hattie might attend to her duties sent the maid on her way. Not without a last adoring look at her lieutenant, though.

"You've made a conquest," Barbara commented as they stepped out into a night bathed in bright moonlight. "The woman quite worships you."

"She would worship anyone who rescued her from the brute she was in service to."

"Hattie says you shot him cleanly between the eyes."

"Since I was aiming for his shoulder at the time," he said dryly, "I don't take a great deal of pride in the hit."

"What's that? I was given to understand you rangers are all crack shots. Was I wrong to trust you to keep me safe during the journey to Morgan's Falls?"

"Not at all. Until I hear your business with my mother, though, I make no promises for the return trip."

The threat came accompanied by a smile, but it was still a threat. The view of the moon above the river could wait, Barbara decided. Coming to a halt, she faced the lieutenant.

"Very well, sir. The long and the short of it is that my brother was unjustly convicted and transported to Bermuda, where he rots in the prison hulks. I need five thousand pounds to free him. I came to play on our admittedly loose connection to your mother and borrow or beg the money from her."

She thought he might gape in astonishment at her outrageous demand. Or perhaps make a show of sympathy for her brother's plight. She did *not* expect him to slap his leg and burst into laughter.

"You thought to put a hand in my mother's pocket and pluck out five thousand pounds? Damnation! I wish I had been present to hear her response."

"She has yet to give it to me," Barbara informed him icily.

Still chuckling, he shook his head. "You should have told me what you were after. I would have warned you. My mother is the shrewdest horse trader and financier west of the Mississippi. If she gives you five thousand pounds, you'll pay it back with interest, I assure you."

No, Barbara would not.

She was tempted, so *very* tempted, to stalk inside, march up the stairs and retrieve the document hidden in her valise. Lieutenant Morgan would find little to laugh about then. Only the certain knowledge that he would challenge the contents of that paper in court and tie up his mother's inheritance for years kept her from doing just that.

Harry didn't have years.

"Tell me again how it is you're related to my mother?" Zach asked when he'd recovered from his mirth.

Barbara wove once more the same web of truth and lies she'd spun for Louise Morgan.

"So the two of you share no blood tie at all."

"That is correct."

"Thank the Lord for small blessings," he muttered.

Barbara went stiff as a poker. "I understand you might be reluctant to acknowledge the connection, sir. You're a barrister, after all. And a military officer. Your family is much respected in this area. I, as you've just learned, am the sister of a convict."

"We'll get to the matter of your brother in a bit," he promised. "My most pressing concern at the moment is making sure there's no obstacle to collection of the debt you owe me."

"What debt?"

"You promised to recompense me for the cost of the second canoe."

She'd forgotten about her rash offer. He had not. Smiling, he curled a finger under her chin and tipped her face to his.

"I've been waiting for the right time to collect on the debt. I'm thinking this is it."

Barbara sucked in a swift breath. Evidently Zach Morgan had been orchestrating a campaign of his own while she was laying out hers. They were like Wellington and Napoleon, each jockeying for position on the battlefield. He might wear the uniform, she thought as he bent his head and blocked the moon's wash, but she intended to leave this field the victor.

* * *

Inside the house, Louise Morgan drew her gaze from the pattern book Urice had pulled from the cupboard and glanced through the parlor window. The wavy glass threw back only distorted shadows, yet there was no mistaking the tall figure of her son or the glint of moonlight in Lady Barbara's gleaming hair.

As Louise watched Zach draw the woman into his arms, a primal instinct stirred deep in her belly. In the same manner as a wolf sniffing the air, she sensed danger.

Unbidden, the legend that had haunted her for most of her life leaped into her mind. She'd lived with the curse of the blue-eyed maiden for as long as she could remember.

Did Lady Barbara bear the same curse?

Her eyes weren't a deep indigo, as Louise's were. More a shimmering turquoise, like the waters that lapped the shores along the Gulf of Mexico. Yet Louise couldn't help but wonder whether this English beauty would bring disaster to those who loved her, as had the blue-eyed maiden of legend.

With a little shiver of unease, she turned away from the window.

7

Barbara had been woefully unprepared the first time the lieutenant kissed her. This time she intended to control matters.

Her palms rested on his chest. Her head tipped to a better angle. Her mouth moved seductively under his. She'd long ago mastered the art of heating a man's blood to near fever pitch with little more than a kiss. It required style, not vulgar grunts and gasps. A sensual promise of more to come, redeemable at an unspecified future date.

So it was with some surprise Barbara felt a sudden heat race through her veins. The rush brought with it the overpowering urge to press her breasts and belly against the lieutenant's powerful frame. She leaned closer, intending only a little more contact, but he took instant advantage of her nearness. Widening his stance, he tightened the arm he'd slipped around her waist and deepened the kiss.

She was crushed against him. The woman in her thrilled to his strength and the play of his muscles under her fingertips even as the seductress experienced a frisson of alarm. The heat between them flared too fast, too intense. Reluctantly, she moved to douse the sparks before they fully ignited.

Drawing her head back, she broke the kiss. Her senses screamed an instant protest. With some effort, Barbara ignored her hammering heart and lifted her gaze to the lieutenant's.

He looked thoroughly bemused. Grateful she wasn't the only one so affected, she struggled to find her voice.

"I hope…I hope that is adequate recompense for any and all debts owed you, because it is all I intend to pay."

"Then it will have to suffice."

The very real regret in his reply acted as a balm to her agitated senses. She hadn't lost her touch. Reassured, she eased out of his arms and permitted herself only a small shiver of delight when he rearranged the drape of her shawl over her bare shoulders.

"Shall we continue our walk down to the river?"

"In a moment."

Zach wasn't sure he could stand upright, much less trek down to the river. He couldn't remember the last time a woman had tied him in so many knots.

"Why don't you tell me about your brother first. Why was he imprisoned?"

"It's rather complicated. And difficult to explain to a man schooled in the law."

The touch of bitterness in her voice suggested she had lost faith in the courts. Zach wasn't surprised. Her brother had been convicted, after all.

"Just tell me what you will."

She turned away and took a moment to gather her thoughts. When she faced him again, Zach sensed she was choosing her words with care.

"Harry has something of a reckless nature, but he's watched over and protected me for as long as I can remember. Our mother died when I was only a babe, you see, and our father when I was five. Harry was heir to the title, an empty estate, and the responsibility of his sister."

"Was there no one else to take on that responsibility?"

"A cousin," she said with a lift of her shoulders. "He resented the expense of our upkeep and did his best to break Harry's spirit. We left his household as soon as Harry reached his majority and made our own way after that."

A tug of sympathy for the unknown Harry stirred in Zach. As the eldest in a large and lively brood he would have shaved pennies and picked pockets if driven to it to provide for his siblings. He suspected Barbara's brother had done the same.

"Fortunately, Harry was always lucky with dice. Less so when it came to certain business ventures."

"Taken for a ride, was he?"

Barbara bit her lip. As much as she hated painting her brother as an unsuspecting dupe, she certainly couldn't admit he was the one who'd taken any number of unsuspecting gentlemen for a ride.

"Harry invested heavily in a railroad that was to be laid through the Swiss Alps," she said instead, "and convinced a number of his friends to do the same. When the firm that was to have engineered the project went bankrupt, the uncle of one of the investors accused Harry of enticing his nephew into the scheme."

He'd also produced evidence that Sir Harry Chamberlain had printed the fictitious engineering firm's prospectus himself. Had his nephew not become so besotted with Chamberlain's beautiful sister, the angry lord had charged, he would never have fallen victim to the scheme.

"My brother demonstrated to the court that he'd lost his investment as well, but his loss was insignificant compared to the thousands of pounds others had invested. He was held responsible and sentenced to ten years in prison."

She turned to the lieutenant again, wanting— *needing*—him to see her anger at her brother's fate.

"As we lacked sufficient funds to bribe the superintendent of prisons and assure Harry a comfortable cell in Rams Head or Millbank, he was transported to Bermuda. He's there now, worked like a field slave by day and confined in a filthy cell by night. I won't leave him there to rot! I cannot!"

"No, of course you cannot. Do you think to demand a new trial? Is that why you need five thousand pounds, to hire a team of barristers and attempt to reverse your brother's conviction?"

She needed the money to hire a boat and crew, bribe the prison guards and spirit Harry away from that damnable island in the middle of the Atlantic.

Whatever funds were left must go toward establishing a household in Italy or Spain. As an escaped convict, Harry couldn't return to England. But if the lieutenant wanted to think Barbara intended to work within the law instead of outside it, she wouldn't disabuse him of the notion.

"I've consulted any number of lawyers," she said. "They all indicated such an effort would require both time and money."

"Yes, it would. And the outcome is very much in doubt. From what I've heard of British courts, they are as slow and ponderous as the courts in this country."

"Will you add your voice to mine, then? Explain the circumstances to your mother and suggest her funds would not be misspent?"

"I'll tell her what you've told me. *She* must decide whether to expend funds on your brother's behalf."

She might have known he'd respond with the slippery ambiguity she'd come to expect of all men trained to the law. She was suddenly out of patience and tired of acting the supplicant. Deciding she'd eaten enough humble pie for one day, Barbara hitched her shawl higher on her arms.

"The air has taken on a chill. Shall we return to the house?"

"Yes, of course. Here, let me wrap my coat around you."

Before she could protest, he shrugged out of his frock coat and draped it over her shoulders. It carried both his scent and the heat from his body. The blend of fragrant tobacco and lye soap lingered on Barbara's shoulders long after she'd trimmed the candle and tugged his sisters' down-filled comforter up to her chin.

She woke to a spill of sunlight and an annoying clatter. Struggling up on one elbow, she squinted through the slanting sunbeams at her maid.

"Whatever are you doing?"

The irritated query spun Hattie around and caused the porcelain pitcher in her hand to rattle again against its matching, rose-painted washbowl.

"I'm pouring your hot water," she said, obviously confused by the question.

"Didn't you see I was sleeping?"

"Yes, but…"

"In the future, you will wait for me to wake before drawing back the curtains and clumping about in my room."

"But it's going on to ten o'clock. The family all took breakfast hours ago."

"Indeed?"

Barbara supposed it would do no good to inform the woman she rarely rose before noon. She wasn't in London or Vienna, but in the wilds of a country where the inhabitants evidently sat down to breakfast before dawn.

"Mrs. Morgan said I was to bring you a pot of hot chocolate when you woke. Or there's coffee, if you prefer."

"Chocolate will do."

Still sleepy and irritable, Barbara shoved the coverlet aside. A porcelain chamber pot took care of her most immediate need. The hot water washed away the last of her grogginess. She was feeling more alert and composed by the time Hattie returned with a tray containing a china pot painted with feathery pink roses, a matching cup and saucer, and a puffy, honey-coated bun.

The chocolate was dark and rich and foamy. The bun melted in Barbara's mouth. She savored every bite while she debated between the hunter-green traveling dress she'd worn the day before and the lavender kerseymere she'd snagged on the pea vines at Fort Gibson. Deciding on the kerseymere, she sipped a second cup of chocolate while Hattie brushed out her hair and wove it into a smooth, shining coronet atop her head.

"Your bruises are beginning to fade," she observed as Hattie placed the last hairpin. "The lotion must have helped."

"And it smells so sweet, too. The lieutenant commented on it this morning when I walked back from the kitchens with him."

"Did he?"

Her eyes took on a dreamy, faraway look. "He's a fine man, the lieutenant."

Barbara started to issue a sharp warning to the woman not to overreach herself, but bit back the words. What did it matter to her, after all, if Lieutenant Morgan chose to dally with the mistress in the moonlight and chivvy up the maid in the morning? He certainly wouldn't be the first man to do so. Still, Barbara was in a somewhat pettish mood when she descended the stairs some time later.

She found Vera awaiting her in the parlor. The girl could be quite a beauty, Barbara thought. She had her mother's blue eyes and lustrous black hair. How unfortunate she insisted on scraping it back in a tight bun. And her keen mind might well put some men off. Barbara herself found it just a bit daunting.

"Mama's with Mr. McRoberts at the counting shed," she informed her guest. "She asked me to bring you down, if you should like to see it. I thought I might also show you the mission school."

Mr. McRoberts, Barbara recalled, was the wizened little man with the wooden teeth. She had no idea what he or Louise Morgan did in their counting shed, but professed herself agreeable to a visit.

"I'll just fetch my parasol."

When she returned a few moments later, Vera acted the proper hostess.

"Do you wish breakfast before we take our tour? We kept some ham and griddle cakes warm for you."

"Thank you, but I'm not hungry. I just devoured two cups of chocolate and the most delicious bun."

"Did you like it? That's fry bread. Singing Bird, Mr. McRoberts's wife, taught us to make it. She's from the Navajo tribe, you know."

"No, I didn't."

She followed the girl through the house and out the back door. The sun beat down with surprising warmth for late October. So unlike the cold, rainy Octobers in England.

"You'll think me appallingly ignorant," Barbara said, raising her parasol, "but I must confess I'm unfamiliar with the various tribes who inhabit Indian Country."

"The Navajo don't live in Indian Country. Their lands are far to the west, in Spanish territory. Although…"

A troubled look came over Vera's delicate face.

"It's hard to say anymore *who* lives in Indian Country. My mother's people used to roam this whole area. The tribes being relocated from the East have pushed them far to the north. Not without considerable bloodshed, I must tell you. We were never allowed to stray far from the house when I was younger. Papa still insists we carry a rifle whenever we go down to the river to fish or swim."

Barbara had heard the issue of Indian Removal hotly debated during her long riverboat ride and again at Sallie Nicks's table. Listening to the issue discussed over wine and braised mutton chops was one matter. Learning the fine-boned girl beside her carried a rifle when she went down to the river put another face on the matter altogether. Barbara had been lulled by the gentility of this plantation into forgetting it sat in an as yet unsettled land.

The hair on the back of her neck tingled as she swept the vista before her with a keen glance. Her gaze darted past the cluster of whitewashed outbuildings to the tilled fields beyond. Most of the fields were still dotted with stubble left from the fall harvest, but a bright patch of pumpkins grew in one.

At the far edge of the fields stood the orchards. What looked like apple and peach trees had already begun to lose their greenery, but the nut trees were weighted almost to the ground with a rich harvest of pecan and hickory.

It was the tangle of oak and ash beyond the orchards that drew Barbara's nervous glance. The dense greenery seemed to stretch forever, covering the undulating hills, shrouding the mountains that loomed to the east and south. Anything—or anyone!—could hide in that impenetrable wilderness.

"Should you like to see the school first? It's on the way to the counting house."

Nodding, Barbara tore her glance from the seemingly endless vista of sky and earth. Vera escorted her past the kitchens and smokehouse, circumvented a henhouse and swine pen, and led the way to a cluster of whitewashed buildings set on a slight rise.

"You'll find the school and dormitories empty right now. Our students have gone to help with the harvest and participate in the fall buffalo hunt. They'll return next month."

"Who are these students?"

"Mr. Harris's church holds a charter from Chief Walter Webber of the Cherokee to instruct their children. Their principal mission is some miles from here. My mother donated land for an additional school. She funds it on the condition that it accept *any* student wishing to attend. Mr. Harris and I teach a very diverse group, I will tell you."

Barbara wondered why a young woman with Vera's beauty, education and family wealth would choose the spinsterish occupation of teacher. She had her answer when they entered the school and spotted the young Reverend Harris at the table toward the front of the room.

"Good morning, John."

The missionary looked up, and a look of utter adoration came over his face. "Good morning!"

An answering blush tinged Vera's cheeks as she stood aside to allow Barbara to precede her. "I've brought you a visitor. Will you show her about?"

The young missionary eagerly agreed. He gave her a tour of the schoolhouse and the dormitories while describing in great detail his students' course of instruction. The breadth of the curriculum surprised Barbara. She herself had been schooled in little more than watercolors, music and the literature deemed acceptable to young women of breeding. She'd certainly never studied mathematics or the use of globes. Not formally, at least. She'd learned a great deal about geography from jaunting about Europe with Harry. And she'd developed the very useful ability to count cards while sipping champagne and smiling bewitchingly at the gentleman seated across from her. Neither Vera nor Mr. Harris, Barbara suspected, would appreciate that particular skill.

The next stop on her tour was the counting house. This turned out to be a large warehouse filled almost to the rafters with barrels and bales. Barbara's nose tingled with the scents of fresh sawdust, hides, tallow, molasses and pepper.

Louise Morgan was poring over a ledger when her daughter ushered Barbara inside. The silk-gowned sophisticate of the night before was gone. In a skirt of sensible wool, a loose-sleeved blouse with modest lace trim and a canvas apron, Louise looked more like a shopkeeper than a woman of substantial wealth.

Mr. McRoberts was with her but left it to Louise to show her guest around the counting house. As she pointed out the various goods she traded in, she gave Barbara a glimpse of her intriguing past.

"I trapped the rivers in Indian Country for some years with Henri—your great-uncle. He teaches me to catch the beaver, the mink, even the polecat."

"Skunk," Vera supplied at Barbara's blank look.

"After Henri dies, I go to New Orleans with Daniel to meet the merchant who buys our furs." A fond smile played around Louise's lips. "Monsieur Thibodeaux is dead now, but we did business together for many years."

"Now Mama does business with so many different merchants even she has trouble keeping them all straight," her daughter put in with a teasing smile.

Somehow Barbara doubted that. The shrewd trader taking her through the warehouse knew the precise contents of every barrel and bale. By the time they'd finished the tour, Barbara's head reeled from so many pennyweights of this and hundredweights of that.

She hoped Louise might use this time to reveal her decision regarding the five thousand pounds, but the subject had not arisen by the time a bell clanged to announce the noon meal. Accompanied by Vera and her mother, Barbara once again stepped into the bright sunlight. She had raised her parasol and was about to join the other two women on the path to the house, when the sound of male laughter brought all three women around.

Zach and his father were coming up from the fields, accompanied by several field hands. The two Morgan men carried axes and were, Barbara saw with a sudden leap in her pulse, shirtless. The sight of Zach's naked chest and roped muscles gleaming with sweat was like a swift, hard punch to her belly.

But when the men stopped at the well to sluice away their dirt and sweat, it was Daniel Morgan's back that had Barbara biting back a horrified gasp. The man had been whipped. Whipped horribly. Every inch of skin from his neck to his waist showed a tortuous pattern of old, crisscrossing scars.

8

The image of Daniel's tortured back remained in Barbara's mind long after he'd poured a bucket of water over his head, swiped away his grime and dragged on his shirt. The horrific scars battled for precedence with the equally disturbing picture of his son's naked, sweat-glistening chest.

Barbara couldn't erase either during a midday meal taken at trestle tables set out under the trees behind the house. The family occupied a table set apart from the others. Still, Barbara felt more than a little odd sitting down to luncheon with servants and field hands at the next tables.

Their ranks appeared to include a wide variety of nationalities. Elaborate tattoos decorated the cheeks and chin of one tall, muscular African. Next to him was a sturdy German plowman, his face brick red from the morning's exertions. On the German's other side was a girl of obvious Indian descent with thick black braids looped over her ears and a slashing scar across one cheek.

Hattie sat with the house servants. As befitting their more exalted status, they kept somewhat apart from the field and farm hands. The Morgans' butler presided over their table. The man spoke a mix of English, French and Spanish with a musical accent that Barbara couldn't begin to identify.

"Joseph's from New Orleans," the lieutenant explained when she inquired about the man. "My mother acquired his services when she visited there some years ago."

"Ah, yes. I saw a number of slaves being marched to market when my ship docked in that city."

"Joseph isn't a slave. None of the people who make their home at Morgan's Falls are. Nor do we buy any indentures."

"Why so? I understand slave-holding is a common practice in Indian Country, as it is elsewhere in the Americas."

And in Britain, although perhaps not for long. The abolitionist movement was growing more strident every day. Its proponents had succeeded in passing a law prohibiting British sea captains from transporting slaves, and Parliament was even now considering an act to abolish the institution of slavery itself.

The practice was not as deeply rooted in England

as it was in the colonies, though. When the Americas were first settled, Britain had shipped boatload after boatload of convicts and indentured servants to work the tobacco plantations. The white laborers had proved too susceptible to illness and disease, however, and a booming African slave trade had followed.

Now, Barbara thought with a tightening in her stomach, England shipped her convicts to Bermuda and Australia and chained them in rotting hulks. Haunted by the memory of Harry's ravaged face the last time she'd seen him, Barbara wrenched her attention back to the American beside her.

"Slave-holding is common enough in these parts," he agreed as he offered her a fresh-baked loaf. "My mother's people make slaves of the captives they take in raids. Many of the eastern tribes purchase them at auction. The Cherokee and Choctaw migrating to Indian Country have brought their slaves with them. My father doesn't hold with the practice, though. He was once in chains himself and won't keep any man against his will."

Tearing off the end of the loaf, Barbara set the crust on the edge of a pewter plate filled with rich, steaming stew. Her glance drifted to the man seated at the end of the table. Louise Morgan had mentioned that her husband had once languished in prison, and that she'd made a bargain with the devil to secure his release. No doubt that was when he'd acquired those horrific scars on his back. His experiences might well make him more sympathetic to Harry's plight. Barbara wanted very much to know how he came to endure such an ordeal, but hesitated to probe too deeply in such a public forum.

His son gave her the opportunity she sought after they'd finished their meal. While the servants cleared the table and dismantled the trestles, the lieutenant proposed an afternoon excursion.

"I'll show you a bit more of the property. And if you're up for it, we can ride to the south and give you a glimpse of the prairies I mentioned."

"I seem to recall you also mentioned the frightening sight of a herd of buffalo thundering across those prairies."

"I'll make sure we steer well clear of all thundering herds," he promised gravely.

"Very well, then. I'll go upstairs and change."

"My sisters ride astride but there's a sidesaddle in the barn. I'll dust it off for you."

Having sailed from England to Bermuda with only her brother's rescue in mind, Barbara had not anticipated afternoon jaunts about the countryside. She'd left her dashing Hussar-style riding habit behind, and would have to make do with her serviceable green gabardine traveling dress. The short jacket buttoned in the front, so she wouldn't need Hattie's assistance to get into it. Just as well, she thought wryly, as the woman was nowhere to be seen.

Ingrained habit made her reach for her straw-chip bonnet to protect her complexion. She settled the crown on her hair and fashioned a bow under her chin. As quickly as she tied the ribbons, she untied them. With a perverse urge to feel the sun on her face, she tossed the bonnet aside.

The lieutenant was waiting with two mounts when Barbara rejoined him. She was no connoisseur of horseflesh. She and Harry had moved too often to maintain a stable and usually relied on rented hacks. But even her untutored eye could see the horses he'd saddled lacked any claim to noble bloodlines. Grinning, he answered the question she was too polite to ask.

"They're a cross between Narragansett Pacer, English Thoroughbred and Indian pony. We're working toward the perfect mix of gait, temperament and stamina."

Dubious, she eyed the rough-coated bay he backed to the mounting block. "How close are you to attaining your goal?"

"You'll have to determine that for yourself."

He held the bay steady while she found her seat, then swung into the saddle of a sturdy roan. A half hour later they reined in on the crest of a low hill and Barbara was ready to pronounce judgment.

"You are indeed close to achieving the perfect mix." Bending forward, she patted her mount's neck. "This fellow is the sweetest stepper."

"My father will be pleased to hear that. He's negotiating with Colonel Arbuckle now to supply mounts for the additional ranger companies the colonel hopes Congress will authorize."

Straightening, she sat back in the saddle. The lieutenant had provided just the opening she sought.

"Your father appears to be a man of many talents. Soldier, surveyor, horse breeder. Yet you say he once wore chains. How did that come about, if I may ask?"

"He was accused of murdering his first wife so he might marry my mother."

Dear Lord! She hadn't expected anything quite so dramatic. "I assume he was innocent of the crime, since he didn't go to the gallows."

"No, he didn't go to the gallows. Shall we dismount and stretch our legs?"

He was out of the saddle and coming around to assist Barbara before she realized he'd evaded the question of his father's innocence or guilt.

No wonder he'd shrugged aside her suggestion he might refuse to acknowledge the Chamberlains' connection to his mother because Harry was a convict! The Morgan family also harbored a few skeletons in their closets.

Certain that must make them sympathetic to Harry's plight, Barbara raised her knee over the pommel and allowed Morgan to lift her from the saddle. He brought her down easily, lightly.

And neglected to remove his hands.

Caught between her mount's warm, solid haunches and the lieutenant's equally solid frame, Barbara tipped her head. She saw herself reflected in his brown eyes. Saw something else, as well. Something that set her pulse to skipping.

"I couldn't sleep last night for thinking about our walk in the moonlight," he told her.

"I had hoped you would think about my brother's situation."

"He figured in my thoughts. Not as much as his sister, though. Not anywhere near as much."

The edge to his voice sent a thrill through Barbara. Excitement fluttered in her veins, along with a heady sense of victory. She'd played the game too often, though, to show anything of her triumph.

"From what you've told me about your father, surely you understand Harry must be foremost in my thoughts. I asked you last night if you would add your voice to mine and press my brother's cause with your mother. I ask you again."

"No need." Bending, he brushed his lips against her temple. "I spoke with my mother on your behalf this morning."

The five thousand pounds were as good as in her hand! And without resorting to the document hidden in her valise. Giddy with relief, Barbara threw her arms around the lieutenant's neck.

"Thank you!"

Thrilled by her victory, she ignored all Harry's strictures against giving way to emotion. Her arms locked around the lieutenant's neck. Her mouth was eager and greedy as it sought his.

When she felt him go taut against her, desire and a jubilant sense of power fired her blood. Zachariah Morgan was just a man. Sharp-witted and damnably attractive, to be sure, but a just a man. Elated by her success in bringing him around, Barbara pressed closer.

His reaction was immediate and intense. Shifting his stance, he dragged her against him. His tongue danced with hers. Every touch, every searing dart of flesh on flesh sent fire through Barbara's veins. She forgot all Harry's cautions and strictures, forgot as well the painful lesson she'd learned from the one other man who'd dragged her into his arms like this. That experience had been unpleasant in the extreme. This one set her blood to singing.

When she opened her mouth to his, the lieutenant took his cue from her. His mouth came down harder. His thigh thrust between hers. The angle of his hip against her belly caused the muscles low in Barbara's womb to clench. A damp heat formed between her legs.

"Barbara. Sweeting..."

He dragged his head up. Red stained his cheeks, and his breath rasped hard and fast.

"You'd best have a care. I'm close to forgetting all that is civilized in me."

The warning set off a clanging alarm. She wasn't in some private drawing room, with her brother just a scream away. She was alone in the wilderness with a man whose arms banded her like tempered steel. Part of her knew she should pull away while she still could. The other part of her, the woman who'd spent her life taking one risk after another, thrilled to his hoarse admission that he was teetering on the edge.

"So am I," she whispered with an honesty that surprised them both.

Zach sucked in a sharp breath. He knew damn well she had no inkling of the danger she was in. She couldn't guess how close the beast in him was to breaking free of its chains.

He wanted this woman so bad he hurt with it, had wanted her from the first moment he'd spotted her by the river near Fort Gibson. Until this moment, though, he'd kept his lust on a tight leash. Now…

Now his blood pounded and her whisper screamed in his ears. Savagely, he beat back the urge to shove her against her mount, lift her skirts and take her right where she stood. She was a lady, for God's sake! Not some trollop eager to spread her legs for a few pennies.

He tried to control himself. He loosed his hold, intending to put her away from him. But the heavy-lidded desire in her eyes drove a spike through every one of his noble intentions.

Training and a survival instinct too deep to ignore made him loop their mounts' reins over a low branch before he swept an arm around her waist and dragged her against him once again. She came readily, her face flushed. Her mouth was eager under his, her breath sweet and hot.

Almost doubled over with wanting her, he put enough distance between them to strip off his shirt. He heard her breath hiss in and felt the fierce satisfaction of a man who knows himself strong and well muscled enough to pleasure his woman. Dropping to one knee, he spread the shirt on the tall, fragrant grass and caught her hand to tumble her down. She landed atop him in a flurry of skirts and breathless laughter.

He rolled over, taking her with him. She lay framed in cloud-white linen surrounded by a sea of green. Zach's stomach clenched at the sheer perfection of her features. No poet himself, he began to understand what drove bards to pen such flowery lines as those describing the face that launched a thousand ships and toppled the towers of ancient Ilium. Swooping down, he claimed Barbara's mouth with his.

When she arched to meet him, all thoughts of poetry and ancient legends fled. The last of Zach's restraint went with it. Pressing her into the earth, he dragged up her skirts and wedged a knee between hers. His hand found the slit in her drawers. With a low growl, he slid a finger into her wet heat.

Her eyes flew open and she bucked like a startled colt. Zach gentled her the way he would a skittish yearling.

"Easy, sweeting." His finger slid out, then in again. "We'll take this easy."

Trapped beneath his weight, Barbara fought a sudden sense of panic. Only one other man had touched her so intimately, and he'd been drunk as two wheelbarrows at the time. What followed had left her bruised and no little disgusted with herself for allowing matters to get so out of hand.

Harry had raked her over the coals for weeks after that sorry incident. The fact Barbara had lost her head angered him a great deal more than her lost virginity. He'd relented enough, though, to assure her she'd eventually enjoy the act of copulation. Harry certainly did, judging from the frequency with which he took women to his bed.

The truth of his offhand assurances came home to her with each slow, tantalizing thrust of Zach's fingers. Barbara's panic subsided. Pleasure swirled deep in her belly. The sensation spread to her limbs and stirred the hunger that had seized her earlier.

It leaped to life when he used his knee to pry her legs farther apart. And when he settled his weight between her thighs, Barbara knew without doubt this time would be different.

Pleasure already had her in its grip. She waited in a fever of impatience while he fumbled at the flap of his trousers. Hungry and just a little nervous, she felt him ease into her. Slowly, deliberately, he eased out again.

This was not so bad, she thought with a mix of pleasure and relief. Not bad at all. Relaxing her tense muscles, she let him pull her into the rhythm. When he punctuated his thrusts with low, hoarse growls and nipping kisses, she lifted her legs and wrapped them around his calves.

The thrusts grew stronger. Faster. Barbara's breath came in sharp pants now, and every muscle in her belly clenched tight. She opened her eyes to the bright sky and brilliant sun, then squeezed them shut again as shudders wracked her.

Her head went back. With a cry, she gave herself up to the pleasure spiraling through her.

The intensity of it stunned her. So much so, it was some time before she realized Zach hadn't shared it. She opened her eyes to find his skin stretched tight across his cheekbones and his mouth clenched in what looked very much like pain.

He was still lodged deep inside her. She thought perhaps he was waiting for her to bring him to the same shattering release he'd brought her. Gathering her strength, she clenched her thighs.

His lower body jackknifed. With a muttered oath, he jerked away from her. Only afterward, when he used his shirttail to cleanse himself, did Barbara understand that he'd spilled his seed on the grass.

With understanding came relief. This stolen hour had erased the awful memory of her one other coupling, but that's all this was. A brief, passionate interlude. She'd never see the lieutenant again once she departed Indian Country. She certainly couldn't leave here carrying his child.

Yet the oddest sense of regret tugged at Barbara as she straightened her clothing. She couldn't help but wonder what it would be like to hold her child in her arms. Or raise it in a home filled with love and laughter, such as the Morgans had built here in this wild, untamed land.

With a man such as Zachariah Morgan to share her days and nights.

Really, she was being quite ridiculous! One tumble in the grass, and she started weaving the most absurd fantasies. She had to remember why she was here and why she would leave as soon as Louise Morgan handed her a bank draft for five thousand pounds.

9

The fall afternoon had taken on a nip by the time Zach and Barbara rode up to the stables. Neither of them noticed the small figure at the window of his sisters' room, nor the woman who stood in the doorway of the counting house.

Her expression troubled, Louise watched her son reach up to help their guest dismount. He was besotted with the English woman. Louise saw it in his smile as he lifted her from the saddle. In the way his hands caressed her waist.

A heaviness settled in her chest. She should take pleasure in the knowledge Zach had lost his heart to a woman of such beauty. Most mothers would, she supposed. Yet there was something about the lady that stirred the deep, primitive instincts of a she-wolf determined to protect her cubs.

"It's her eyes," Louise muttered to her husband as they dressed for dinner that night. "Each time I look into them, I see disaster."

Daniel had learned long ago to respect his wife's intuition. He'd also learned to step warily around the legend that had haunted her from her birth.

"Vera's eyes are as blue as yours," he reminded her. "So are Urice's. Do you see disaster when you look into them?"

"No! Only in those belonging to this English-woman."

Daniel said nothing as he pulled a clean linen shirt over his head and tucked the tails into his breeches. A grimace crossed his face when he eyed the coat laid out on the bed. All these years out of the army and he still felt more comfortable in a roundabout jacket than a cutaway with all these brass buttons.

"I see them when they return this afternoon," his wife continued, crossing the room to help him tie his cravat. Her nimble fingers arranged the linen in neat folds.

"The lady's gown was stained with grass. So, too, was Zach's shirt. And he wears the most foolish face."

"I don't doubt it. The lady could knock any man off his pins…if he wasn't already married to the most beautiful woman in Indian Country."

The outrageous compliment won him a smile, but

it was fleeting at best. As Louise gave the linen stock a final twitch, her face settled into glum lines.

"Me, I think they lie together."

"What?"

"Zach and his lady. I think they lie together this afternoon."

"You're jumping a mighty big creek here, and all because of a few grass stains."

"I jump this creek you speak of because Zach comes home with a so-foolish look. I know this look," she insisted stubbornly. "It is the same one you wear after we roll in the blankets."

The notion that his son had lifted Barbara's skirts was surpassed in Daniel's mind by the notion of doing the same to his wife. After almost twenty-six years of marriage, this small, fierce female could still tie him in knots.

"It's been a while since we rolled in the blankets," he commented.

"Oh, yes! A great while. Six...no, five days."

With a lazy smile, he moved a step closer and backed her against the mattress. "I'm thinking dinner can wait."

"Daniel, we have a guest!"

"I'm thinking she can wait, too."

When Daniel escorted his wife downstairs some time later, he was in a decidedly mellow humor. He had yet to accept the idea Zach had breached the virtue of a guest staying under their roof, but it didn't take long to convince him Louise had the right of it. His son didn't look as smugly satisfied as Daniel himself felt at this moment. He came damn close to it, though, whenever his glance rested on the stunning blonde seated across from him.

The sergeant major couldn't decide how best to probe his son's intentions toward the English beauty. Or whether he should ask at all. Zach was a man, not a boy. He was long past the point of needing or wanting advice from his father. Yet Daniel couldn't let the matter slide. He knew damn well Louise wouldn't let him. He'd have to speak with his son about Barbara.

The right opportunity didn't present itself until the next morning. As he had the previous day, Zach accompanied his father and a crew of hands to the south fields, where they were clearing a stand of scrub oak.

Morning mist drifted like witch's breath above the river and the first touch of frost sparkled the grass. Winter was only weeks away. Daniel repressed a shudder at the thought. If he lived to be a hundred, he'd never forget his first winter in Indian Country. He and a bumbling lieutenant had led a ragged band of starving, snow-blind soldiers down the river known then as the Arkansaw.

They spelled it Arkansas now, like the territory the white settlers had staked claim to in what had once been Indian Country. Shaking his head, Daniel tramped along the path.

Arkansas Territory. Missouri Territory. Most of the state of Louisiana. All carved from the land Tom Jefferson had promised would belong to the red man forever when he first proposed the Indian Removal Plan way back in '03. Daniel had believed the promises, had spent years helping the Corps of Topographical Engineers chart these rivers and mountains.

Louise had looked at matters through different eyes. She'd watched the Osage force the Quawpaw from their traditional hunting grounds, then seen the Osage in turn forced north. She hadn't trusted Jefferson any more than she now did Jackson.

And with good reason. Old Hickory was bent on resettling the eastern tribes. The long-standing enmity between the Osage and Cherokee had erupted into violence often enough in the past. With the Creek, Seminole, Choctaw and Chickasaw now being added to the mix, the situation in Indian Country was dangerously unsettled.

Frowning, Daniel picked out a tall white ash and lifted his ax from his shoulder. He could think better when his hands were busy at some mindless task. Zach took up a position on the other side of the scaly trunk. Within a few swings they'd established an easy rhythm.

"You say this commission Jackson's appointed will…"

Daniel grunted as his blade bit into trunk.

"...arrive at Fort Gibson soon?"

"Any day now."

"Who mans it, do you know?"

"Colonel Arbuckle mentioned Governor Stokes of North Carolina. Also Henry Ellsworth, from Connecticut."

Zach swung hard, widened the cut and pulled his ax free.

"The third is a Reverend Schermerhorn, of New York."

"You'll need to keep an eye to your mother's interests when these politicians start playing with boundaries."

"You know I will."

"If you're not too busy bundling with your bit of English silk and lace, that is."

Zach's ax halted in midswing. His eyebrows snapped together.

"Don't scowl at me, boy. I wasn't the one who came home with grass stains on his backside."

Slowly, Zach lowered his blade. He swept the other workers with a quick glance, saw none of them had broken their swing. The steady whack of blades rang through the woods.

He admired and respected his father as much as he loved him. Daniel Morgan had never spoken a falsehood that Zach knew of, was always ready to put his back to any labor and kept careful rein on both his strength and his temper. Yet he would allow no man, even his father, to speak ill of Barbara.

"I think you should know I've got my sights set on that bit of English silk and lace."

Daniel leaned an elbow on his ax handle. "It's like that, is it?"

"It is."

After yesterday, how could it be anything else? Zach had bedded his share of women. Warm and willing tavern wenches. A saucy eastern miss or two. The sloe-eyed Cherokee maiden he'd tumbled head-long in love with some years back. She'd chosen to marry a man of her own clan, and Zach had been a long time recovering from his bitter disappointment.

He'd never taken advantage of a woman as alone and vulnerable as Barbara Chamberlain, though. By her own admission, she had no money and no family except a brother in prison. She'd come to Morgan's Falls for help, and Zach had used her urgent need to satisfy his own.

A long night's reflection had bred a disgust of his actions, a determination to do the right thing, and a pulsing sense of anticipation whenever he thought of taking her in his arms again.

Adding to the lust she stirred in him was an in bred sense of urgency. Back East, a man might take months to properly court a lady like Barbara. On the frontier, he had to stake his claim quickly. Women were as scarce as gold nuggets, good women even scarcer.

Maids hired to accompany officers' wives to a remote posting generally wed within weeks of arrival. Similarly, widows rarely remained in mourning for long. Soldiers had been known to line up five and six deep to offer comfort and security to the wife of a fallen comrade. After yesterday, Zach wasn't about to allow anyone else to get in line for Lady Barbara.

"Have you informed the lady of your intentions?"

"Not yet."

"What makes you think she'll have you? You can look the part of a gentleman when you have a mind to. Even act it at times. But…"

"But I'm not the sort of country bumpkin a woman like Barbara would marry?"

"But you come from a world much different than hers," he finished calmly. "Do you really think you can bridge so wide a gap?"

"You did," Zach reminded him.

"That's right, I did. But not without some cost."

"Whatever the price, I'll pay it and gladly."

His father studied him in silence for a moment. "Well, she's a beauty, for sure. You'll have your work cut out for you to—"

"Zach!"

The breathless shout cut through the whack of the other axes. Both men turned to see Theo racing through the harvested fields. His boots threw up clods of dirt.

"A ranger just rode in," he panted when he

reached them. "He says he has orders to fetch you back to Fort Gibson straightaway."

Zach found the ranger seated on a stump outside the kitchens, wolfing down the coffee, fresh bread and the bowl of suet pudding Zach's mother had provided him. A small crowd had gathered around, eager to hear whatever news he brought.

Zach strode across the yard. Judging by the layers of dust coating the private's fringed buckskins and weary mount, he must have ridden through the night.

"What's happening, Bowles?"

"It's them pesky Pawnee, sir." Shaking his head, the lanky ranger spit out the dregs of his coffee. "A raiding party hit a Cherokee settlement. They made off with a dozen horses and three captives. Colonel Arbuckle's sending Captain Bean and a troop of rangers out to retrieve them. Since you know Pawnee country as good or better 'n any of our scouts, Captain Bean asked for you to go along, too."

"I'll get my gear and be ready to ride by the time you finish your breakfast."

It was still early morning. If they pushed hard through the mountains, they could make the fort by nightfall. He was planning the route in his head when his father stepped forward and offered the ranger a fresh mount.

"I planned to send a string with my son when he

returned to the fort. You can put your saddle on one of them."

His military duties pulled at him, but Zach couldn't leave without taking care of one piece of business.

"Has Lady Barbara come downstairs?" he asked his mother.

"Not yet."

Hattie edged out of the curious crowd. "She told me she rarely rises afore noon. Said I wasn't to clump about and wake her."

The maid looked different, Zach thought. It must be the ribbon she'd woven through her hair. Returning her smile with an absent one of his own, he caught his mother's elbow and drew her aside.

"About Lady Barbara…"

"Do not worry yourself. I will see she has a bank draft for the funds she needs. Your father will escort her back to John Jolly's, where she may catch the next steamboat."

"That's just it. I don't want her to catch the next steamboat."

"What do you say?"

"She hopes to buy a new trial for her brother and reverse his conviction. I know, which she may not, that will be well nigh impossible to bring about without someone trained in the law to assist her."

His mother's eyes narrowed. "And you think to provide that assistance?"

"I do. She has no one else," he reminded her. "That's why she came so far in search of you."

"She came for money. I will give it to her."

"I'll provide whatever funds she needs," he said quietly, "if I can convince her to become my wife."

"Zach!"

A flurry of instant protests rose in Louise's throat. Just in time she gulped them back. For all his lazy smiles and ready laughter, her son could turn as stubborn as any mule when he set his mind to something. Taking a deep breath, she attempted reason instead of the barrage of hot arguments she wanted to loose.

"You must think on this. She is English. Her father was a gentleman."

"Your father was French, and you wed another Frenchman with ties to royalty. Did that stop you from loving an American rifle sergeant?"

Louise clamped her mouth shut. She wasn't about to admit she'd loved her rifle sergeant only last night, and quite lustily. Her thoughts troubled, she could only listen as her tall, handsome son bared his heart.

"This excursion into Pawnee country shouldn't take more than a couple of weeks. A month at most. If Barbara will wait that long, I'll take leave from my military duties and go with her to London."

Shock snapped her head back. "You would do that for her?"

"If I must." His mouth curving, he slipped into her native tongue. "She's bewitched me, Wa-Shi-Tu. Just as you did the warrior you took to your heart."

Louise had no argument for that. There was none. Her son was ever one to walk in a path of his own making. Nor did he hem and haw and debate for weeks or months over every decision, as did so many trained to the law. He'd traded his wig and robes for an army uniform quickly enough, and his uniform for the backwoods garb of the rangers. Now, it appeared, he would alter his path yet again for this woman Louise could not bring herself to trust.

"And you must remember," he added when she remained mute, "you're Barbara's aunt by marriage. Her only relative other than her brother. Have a care to her until I return and can assume that responsibility myself."

For the second day in a row, the noisy clatter of a pitcher against the washbowl dragged Barbara from sleep. Surprisingly, the rude awakening didn't annoy her half as much this morning as it had yesterday.

Curling her arms above her head, she stretched like a cat. Satisfaction hummed through her as she let her thoughts drift. She'd experienced the most indescribable pleasure, the kind she'd always heard hinted at. She had the promise of the funds she needed. She would soon shake off the dust of the colonies, sail to Bermuda and free Harry.

For the first time in months, she felt lighthearted and eager to meet the day. The giddy feeling lasted until she remembered she'd also be shaking off the dust of a certain lieutenant.

Uncurling her arms, she brought them down. Really, there was no need for this sudden drop in spirits. She'd enjoyed a brief dalliance. She couldn't let the desire that seemed to grab at her throat whenever she was in the lieutenant's company distract her or turn her from her purpose.

Despite the stern lecture, she couldn't keep a sharp note from her voice when she addressed her maid. "Didn't I instruct you to wait until I summoned you in the mornings?"

Hattie jumped a good three or four inches into the air. When she turned, her expression was as pettish as Barbara's tone.

"Yes, you did."

"Then perhaps you'll explain why you woke me?"

"Mrs. Morgan sent me up," she said sullenly. "She wanted me to tell you she's wishing to speak with you at your convenience."

"Very well. You've told me. You may leave the water and fetch my chocolate. Oh, and tell the lieutenant I should like to speak with him, too."

Only to arrange transportation back to Fort Gibson. She was *not* contemplating another session in the grass, with her muscles straining and Zach Morgan's body driving into hers. As extraordinary as those hours yesterday had been, Barbara couldn't risk repeating them.

"The lieutenant's not here."

"What's that?"

"He's not here."

Frowning, Barbara shoved aside the covers and pushed upright. "What do you mean? Where is he?"

"A rider came for him, saying he was needed back at Fort Gibson. He left more than three hours ago."

"But… But he didn't say goodbye."

Barbara regretted the foolish words the moment they were out of her mouth. She regretted them even more when Hattie sent her a smug look.

"Yes, he did. To me."

Zach's abrupt departure left Barbara feeling disconcerted. Her interview with Louise Morgan later that morning added a simmering mix of frustration and anger.

They faced each other across Louise's desk in the counting house. The stink of buffalo hides wrinkled Barbara's nose as she struggled to make her feelings clear to her hostess.

"I cannot possibly stay here until your son returns from this expedition."

"Why?"

"Every day my brother remains in prison saps his strength. I must initiate efforts to free him immediately."

"Zach tells me it will take many months to push a petition through the courts for a new trial, and then only if you can present new evidence. With his help, matters will go faster."

Hell and botheration! Barbara had been caught in her own lie. She could hardly admit now she had no intention of petitioning the courts. Tipping up her chin, she answered in her most aristocratic manner.

"I appreciate the lieutenant's offer of assistance, but—"

"I will hear no buts."

Louise Morgan's expression was every bit as cool as Barbara's. She knew she had the upper hand and didn't hesitate to use it.

"My son wishes you to remain at Morgan's Falls until he returns. When he does, you will receive the funds you require."

10

The tough crossbreeds Daniel supplied Zach and Private Bowles proved their strength and stamina. By midafternoon, the two riders had crossed the Arkansas River. They pushed on through early dusk. Night was dropping fast when they heard the distant call of a bugle sounding tattoo, the warning that all stragglers had to return to the post immediately. They made the ranger camp just minutes before lights out.

Zach asked Private Bowles to see to the mounts and reported directly to Captain Bean's tent. Jesse Bean was one of the reasons Zach had traded his regular army uniform for buckskins and a floppy-brimmed felt hat. Past forty and a great bear of a man, Bean had spent most of his adult life on the frontier. He was a skilled woodsman, a keen hunter and a longtime proponent of mounted riflemen. The last had made him the natural choice for commander of the first company of rangers.

"Sorry to drag you away from the English beauty," he boomed in a voice that could shake the acorns from a pine branch a half mile away. "Nate Prescott is still muttering about what a sly dog you are, spiriting the lady off to Morgan's Falls the way you did."

"Yes, and I intend for her to stay there until we track down this Pawnee raiding party."

"We'll be doing more than tracking Pawnee," Bean warned. "Colonel Arbuckle wants us to make a sweep from the Arkansas clear to the Red River. We leave in the morning at first light."

Zach's lips pursed in a soundless whistle. The Red River cut through the plains far to the west of Fort Gibson. He'd trekked to its headwaters with his father years ago, but as far as he knew, no military patrol had ventured so far across the open prairie. No wonder Captain Bean had specifically requested Zach for his second in command for this expedition.

"Our orders are to make contact with the western tribes," the captain explained. "We're to tell them about this Federal Indian Commission the president has appointed and secure their agreement to come in to Fort Gibson to powwow with the commissioners."

"To what end?"

"The hope is the commissioners can convince them to stop preying on the tribes migrating from the East," Bean said dryly.

Zach figured the chances of that happening were about the same as him sprouting wings and flying across the prairie. The Plains Indians were hunters not farmers. They scorned those who plodded along behind a plow and saw no reason *not* to swoop in and steal cattle, horses and captives from the "civilized" tribes now settling on their traditional hunting lands.

He supposed the commission had to make the attempt to negotiate with them, though. President Jackson would never convince Chief John Ross and the Cherokee still stubbornly clinging to their lands in Georgia and the Carolinas to resettle unless he could show them written promises that fierce tribes to the west wouldn't make war on them.

Not that the treaties would mean anything. The Osage and Pawnee and Kiowa would continue to raid and the troops at Fort Gibson would try to maintain a shaky peace. With a tight feeling in his gut, Zach wondered how long this small, isolated outpost could act as a buffer between all those caught up in the turmoil of Indian Removal.

He'd best send a message to his mother—and to Barbara—advising he'd be gone longer than anticipated. His sense of duty ran too deep to take leave of his men or his responsibilities without giving adequate notice.

"I'll go roust the quartermaster from his tent," he told Bean. "If we're to leave at first light, I'll need to draw extra powder, shot and rations."

* * *

Streaks of pink and gold were shooting through the dawn sky when the ranger company rode out the next morning. Led by Captain Bean, Zach and two less experienced lieutenants, the troop was a motley, colorful bunch. Most of the men wore deerskin trousers to protect their legs, but their shirts, footwear and headgear reflected their wildly divergent individual tastes. Bearskin or buffalo robes were rolled up and tied behind their saddles. A string of packhorses carried two-man tents and extra provisions.

The rangers' route took them north through tangled forests, past scattered Indian villages and the occasional cleared fields being worked by slaves. Gradually, the settled areas fell behind. Soon the wild geese honking noisily as they headed south for the winter and the creatures scrambling through the underbrush were the company's only companions.

With each slap of his powder horn and bullet pouch against his hips, Zach felt his thin veneer of sophistication peel back another layer. He could hold his own in eastern salons and enjoyed waltzing a pretty girl around a ballroom as much as any man, but this was the land he'd been born to, the wilderness that had bred him.

He'd slipped completely and comfortably into a different skin by the time the company made camp that night. The men tended to their horses before themselves, of course. With the mounts hobbled and turned in to the forest to graze on the tough, thorny pea vines, Captain Bean set the sentinels. The rest of the troop lit campfires and cooked game they'd bagged during the day.

The private detailed to the officers' mess filled a black kettle with a brace of fat quail, succulent wild onions, slices of bacon and dough balls formed from flour and water. With the hens and dumplings bubbling, he thrust a sharpened branch through a rack of ribs from a buck Zach had brought down. The ribs sizzled and spit and added to the general merriment of men released from the drudgery of garrison duty.

The rangers in particular were quick to shuck off any semblance of military order. Most were high-spirited youngsters who'd enlisted seeking adventure on the frontier. A few were veteran woodsmen who considered their officers more comrades than superiors. Coarse laughter and ribald jokes soon rose from the groups gathered at the various campfires. After dinner, the night was enlivened by the tinny wail of a harmonica and, later, a rousing chorus of hymns led by the tall, lanky lieutenant whose former occupations included schoolteacher, singing master and Methodist preacher.

The troop entered Osage country the next day and spent their second night with Colonel Auguste Chouteau, government agent to the Osage. His agency consisted of a cluster of log huts that included an office of sorts, a powder magazine and a shed for storing the gifts and supplies provided to the tribe by the government in exchange for the lands they'd yielded to the eastern tribes.

Son of a French trapper and a longtime friend of Zach's parents, Choteau provided information on the Pawnee raiders. They were from the Grand Pawnee band, now camped two days' ride northwest.

The company pushed on the following morning. That afternoon, Captain Bean dispatched Zach and two troopers to forge ahead and scout out the camp. The small patrol found the raiding party before they found the main band. Almost rode right over them, in fact.

Damned if the raiders hadn't stolen a keg of raw-grained whiskey along with their captives. The swill was being smuggled into Indian Country by the wagon- and keelboat-load in violation of every sanction the government tried to impose.

Alerted by the sounds of raucous laughter and foot-stomping ahead, Zach and his men dismounted and crawled forward on their bellies. The Pawnee were camped beside a creek lined with tangled underbrush and cottonwood. A single glance showed the keg wedged into the fork of a tree, the three Cherokee captives bound together and the Pawnee dancing and whooping around the glowing embers of their fire.

There were six of them. All young, all wearing war paint, and all dangerously drunk. Using hand signals, Zach sent one of his men left, another right. When they were in place, he'd make the raiders aware of his presence, convince them they were surrounded and demand their surrender. That was his plan, anyway.

Zach had answered to the colonel scant days ago for shooting a white squatter. He didn't relish facing Arbuckle again to report he'd put a bullet into a Pawnee. Particularly with this Federal Indian Commission hoping to bring the plains tribes in for a palaver.

While he waited for his men to get into position, Zach checked the charge on his rifle and primed his pistol. He was ready when he heard the throaty twill of a wood finch. Seconds later, a turkey warbled off to the right. Rising, Zach called out in Pawnee.

"I am Lieutenant Morgan of the long rifles. My men and I have come for you."

The raiders whirled. Some gaped stupidly at the thicket screening Zach from view. Others stumbled toward their spears.

"Stand where you are!"

Keeping his finger light on the trigger of his rifle, Zach showed himself.

"You have raided Cherokee land and taken captives. You must come with me to answer for these actions."

Several of the warriors began to mutter. One with

wavy black stripes on his chin and forehead curled back his lips.

"We answer only to our headman."

"Your headman can come to Fort Gibson and speak for you."

Zach figured that was as good a way as any of getting the chief of the Grand Pawnee in to meet with the commissioners.

"My men encircle your camp. Move away from your spears and rifles and—"

With a snarl that came from whiskey or bravado, Black Stripes yanked at the hatchet in his belt, pulled it free and swung his arm back in a swift arc.

Cursing, Zach fired. The ax head flew off. What remained of the ax shaft splintered in Black Stripes's hand. He dropped the shattered handle, grunted and stared at a bloody palm missing two fingers.

"Move away from your spears and rifles," Zach repeated.

The small patrol retraced their steps with five disarmed and sullen Pawnee and the three freed captives in tow. The Cherokee had to be kept under as close a watch as the Pawnee to keep them from exacting retribution for the raid on the spot.

They found Jesse Bean and the rest of the company already bivouacked in a thinly wooded area beside a running stream. The men had pitched their tents, and several deer carcasses hung from branches.

Additional hides were pegged out for stretching and dressing, while strips of jerked venison smoked over the fires. Since the sun still rode high in the afternoon sky, Zach naturally questioned why the captain had called a halt to the march so early in the day.

"Colonel Arbuckle sent two Creek riders after us," Bean explained. "Seems one of the commissioners has arrived at the fort and wants to join our little expedition. We're to wait for him and his friends to catch up with us."

"His friends?"

Bean's mouth twisted. "Apparently Mr. Ellsworth made several acquaintances on the trip out to Fort Gibson. A Swiss count or some such and his entourage. Invited them along to see something of the West."

Zach swallowed a groan. Traveling through Pawnee and Comanche country presented dangers enough without adding the responsibility of looking out for a group of easterners. Worse, the greenhorns would slow them down considerably. It was beginning to look as though this expedition would take far longer than anticipated.

He thought about sending another message to Morgan's Falls with the squad Captain Bean dispatched to take the Pawnee prisoners and Cherokee captives back to the fort. After considerable debate, he decided to take his chances. Barbara would wait, or she would not.

* * *

With nothing to do but hunt and rattle the dice for the next few days, Zach's thoughts returned with ever-increasing frequency to the lady whose cool smile and haughty airs both amused and delighted him. At night, the memory of her wild, panting cries and silken body moving urgently under his left him hard and aching beneath his buffalo robe.

He managed to hide his frustration at the delay, but greeted the arrival of the Ellsworth party with profound relief. Relief surged quickly into astonishment when the commissioner introduced his three traveling companions. One was a young Swiss count so eager to hunt buffalo that he'd traveled across an ocean for that express purpose. Another was a bluff Englishman by the name of Latrobe. The third was an American—and the very man Zach's younger brother was named for.

Washington Irving's eyes twinkled when Jesse Bean introduced his lieutenant. "So, Zachariah. Finally, we meet."

Dumbfounded, Zach shook the hand of the author whose elegant prose and effusive recommendation had helped secure an appointment to West Point for the son of a sergeant and a woman of mixed French and Indian blood.

"Mr. Irving! What the devil are you doing in Indian Country?"

"Didn't I promise your parents I would one day

visit the land they described in such glowing terms when we met in Richmond so many years ago?"

"That's true, you did. But last we heard you were still junketing about Europe."

"Seventeen years abroad were enough. I had decided to return home when I met with Mr. Latrobe and Count Portales. Since they, too, desired to come West, we immediately formed a company. You can imagine our delight when we chanced on Commissioner Ellsworth in St. Louis. He was en route to Fort Gibson and graciously offered us the sanction of his official government status. When we arrived at the post, we learned of the ranger patrol and immediately decided to join you. So here we are."

"So here you are," Zach echoed, grinning at the author turned adventurer. In his buckskin trousers, red flannel shirt and leather cap, Irving looked almost fit for the role. His jaunty image was somewhat diminished by the fact that he and his traveling companions had brought several servants to see to their needs and a long string of packhorses loaded with the necessary comforts.

The arrival of the commissioner's party considerably enlivened the camp. While their tents were being set up, the newcomers went around to meet the rest of the rangers. Captain Bean sent their cook a side of venison and a couple of wild turkeys. Zach brought over a tin basin filled with honey dug from a beehive nested in a hollow tree trunk. As their supper stewed, he and Irving downed cups of coffee sweetened with the thick honey.

"This is a remarkable coincidence," he told the author. "I was speaking of you only a few days ago with a guest who's staying at Morgan's Falls. Lady Barbara Chamberlain. She says she met you once. Perhaps you recall her?"

Irving's forehead wrinkled. "No, I—"

"Ha!"

The exclamation came from the stocky Englishman, Latrobe. Stepping around a half-unloaded pack, he joined the two men.

"*I* certainly recall the lady, if my friend Washington does not. She swindled an acquaintance of mine out of two hundred pounds."

Zach fixed the man with a cold stare. "You must be mistaking her for someone else."

"Is she a blonde with the most beguiling face and form? Eyes the color of a tropical sea?"

"I remember her now!" Irving put in. "We met on the Continent. In Bohemia, I think it was. She was with someone...her brother, as I recall. That's how they presented themselves, anyway."

11

Barbara was bored to distraction.

October had slipped into November. The nights had grown colder, the days crisper. The mountains to the north and south had lost their bright slashes of color. The fruit trees in the orchards now raised bare branches to an often leaden sky.

With each day that passed, Barbara had begun to appreciate more how Harry must feel. Her prison was a great deal larger and considerably more comfortable than a warship converted to house convicts, but its walls had begun to close in on her nonetheless.

To be sure, the Morgans had attempted to provide entertainment for their guest. They'd hosted a party attended by all neighbors within two days' ride. Louise, Vera and the young Reverend Harris had escorted Barbara on a visit to the Methodist mission that operated their school. Daniel Morgan had even invited her along on a deer hunt. They weren't riding to foxes, he'd explained with the crooked grin so like his son's, but she might find the chase exhilarating.

She hadn't. A mediocre horsewoman at best, she'd barely kept her seat while ducking under tree branches and tugging her skirts free of brambles. After that sorry episode, she'd been reduced to playing with the children when they weren't at the schoolhouse.

She'd pored over pattern books with Urice, provided lace handkerchiefs and bits of ribbon for little Sarah to fashion into dresses for her dolls, and dealt cards with Theo. So far she'd resisted the temptation to palm the cards as Harry had taught her and relieve Theo of his copper pennies, but the urge was growing greater with each hour of enforced idleness.

More than once, she'd come within a hair of producing the document hidden in the lining of her valise and forcing Louise's hand. The promise of the five thousand pounds held her back. She'd learned enough about Louise Chartier Morgan now to know the woman would keep her promise. No need to enter into a legal wrangle with the Morgans if she could line her pockets without it.

Then there was the tantalizing prospect of a few more days spent in the company of Lieutenant Morgan. And a few more hours in his arms. After all her years of playing the role of seductress, Barbara was well and truly caught in her own snare. Zach Morgan had stirred her blood and her passions. As her restlessness grew, so did the itchy urge to experience once again that intoxicating pleasure.

Still, she'd never intended to seduce the Reverend Harris. It was boredom that took her to the schoolhouse, sheer boredom.

A few students had begun trickling back, released by their parents from the onerous tasks of the fall harvest and hunt. Most of them were of Indian blood, interspersed with a few towheaded boys and two freckle-faced girls sporting shockingly red hair. The children sat elbow to elbow on smooth-planed benches. Vera was teaching the youngest simple sums at the back of the room while the serious young schoolmaster labored with the elder students at the front. They all turned and stared with some surprise when Barbara entered.

"Can I be of any assistance?" she asked of no one in particular.

Vera blinked in astonishment. John Harris fairly goggled before stammering out a reply. "Yes. Yes, of course. That is, if you're sure you wish to…"

The choice was simple. She could either putter about in a drafty schoolhouse with a motley collection of urchins or join Louise in the counting house. The children were infinitely preferable to the stink of the half-cured buffalo hides and the constant clack of Mr. McRoberts's wooden teeth.

"What subject should you like to instruct?" young Mr. Harris asked politely.

Barbara hadn't thought that far. She wasn't particularly qualified to instruct anything.

"I could read to them from Shelley or Shakespeare, I suppose."

"We prefer to teach them to read to us," Vera said gently.

"Oh. Yes." She gave the scrubbed faces a dubious glance and searched her repertoire of skills. "I have some knowledge of gemstones. I suppose you might term that a natural science. I might show your students the best cuts for emeralds and rubies."

Too late, Barbara remembered her jewel case now contained only sapphires. Hastily, she backtracked.

"But then, your students would have no use for such knowledge, would they?"

She saw at once she'd said the wrong thing. Vera's chin lifted, and a cool expression came over her delicate features.

"Our students are not such rustics as you might suppose, Lady Barbara, although a knowledge of gemstones is not required in our curriculum."

"How are you with charcoal?" Mr. Harris said a little desperately.

Barbara's glance flew to the potbellied stove in the center of the schoolhouse. Indignation stiffened her shoulders.

"If you're asking whether I'm qualified to carry

coal," she said on an icy note, "I must confess a lack of ability in that regard."

"No, no!" Horrified, the minister made haste to explain. "We're in need of a drawing master. How are you with charcoal sticks and watercolors?"

"I'm told I have a fair hand," she replied, still somewhat stiff.

"Excellent! We're well supplied with drawing paper and colors. Perhaps... Perhaps you might take the middle class on a nature walk. Have them sketch the orchards or a view of the river."

"Yayyyy!"

Theo's whoop of joy rang through the schoolhouse. Spurred by the tantalizing hint of freedom, he and three other lively youngsters scrambled from their seats and danced around Barbara. She was seriously reconsidering her rash offer of assistance when Mr. Harris restored order.

"Children!" he admonished sternly. "Fetch your drawing pencils and sketchbooks and form a single file."

A hasty scramble ensued. Once the art supplies were gathered, the four lined up as instructed. Mr. Harris introduced each.

"Theo, you know. These are Samuel Fulton, Mary Claremont and Che-ko-tah Williams."

Barbara looked them over with some trepidation before starting for the door. The four followed in her wake like eager ducklings.

"You must mind Lady Barbara," Vera instructed the small formation as it passed. "And don't sully her skirts too badly."

Considerably alarmed by that final admonition, Barbara led her charges outside.

In the next few hours Barbara gained a profound respect for schoolmasters. She couldn't imagine how in the world they managed to engage the attention of four rambunctious children, much less an entire classroom.

She led them to a sunny spot on the hill overlooking the river. Once there, her students displayed a lamentable tendency to turn cartwheels, run about and assault each other.

"Theo, do stop whacking Samuel with that branch!"

"I'm not Samuel," the recipient of the whacks replied cheerfully. "I am Che-ko-tah."

"Yes, well, I wish you would sit down. You, too, Theo."

The boys dropped cross-legged onto the grass beside their peers. Barbara then spent an exasperating twenty minutes attempting to illustrate perspective, a concept she vaguely understood but had never been called on to explain before. Five minutes into her lecture, her students were squirming and rustling the pages of their sketchbooks. Finally, she abandoned her professorial role.

"Just draw the scene as you see it."

They attacked the task with abandon. More charcoal ended up on trousers and blouses than on paper. And, as Vera had predicted, on Barbara's skirts. Oddly, the smudges didn't annoy her as much as she would have imagined.

The children's exuberant spirits lifted her own. She was soon smiling at their lively chatter and sketching away with them. She hardly winced when Mary, a small, dark-eyed girl, tugged on her skirt with a grubby hand.

"Yes, Mary? What is it?"

Silently, the girl held out her drawing. The paper contained only a few lines, but the bold strokes captured the river's curve with stunning accuracy.

"Goodness. Wherever did you learn to draw like this?"

"From my grandmother. She paints horses and buffalo and running deer on the tents and tepees in our village."

"Your grandmother should be the instructor here, not I," Barbara observed dryly.

She echoed that same refrain to John Harris when she showed him the girl's drawing later that evening. They were in the parlor, awaiting the others before going in to dinner.

"Look at this," she said, smoothing out the sketch on a piecrust-edged table. "It's really quite amazing."

"It certainly is."

He bent to examine the drawing more closely. Admiration shone in his eyes when he turned them on Barbara.

"And you're a remarkable instructress to have coached Mary to such artistry."

She responded to the flattery with a trill of flirtatious laughter that came as naturally to her as breathing.

"La, sir! You give me more credit than I deserve. The girl has been coached by her grandmother."

"That may be so, but this is the first time she's demonstrated her abilities. No, you must let me sing your praises as an instructress."

Barbara's mouth curved in a smile that was as sensual as it was instinctive.

The young minister's glance dropped to her lips. A flush rose in his cheeks. Wrenching his gaze up to meet hers, he swallowed convulsively.

Barbara hid a smile as his Adam's apple bobbed above his linen cravat. How reassuring to know she hadn't lost her touch after all these weeks of rusticating.

If only the lieutenant were here instead of this gangly young minister. The game would take on a definite spark then. Her thoughts filled with Zach, she had to wrench her attention back to Harris.

"You are, uh, really quite remarkable, Lady Barbara. Or did I say that already?"

"You did. A woman never tires of hearing compliments from handsome gentlemen, however."

She'd play with him for just a while longer, she decided. Tilting her chin to a more provocative angle, she slanted him a smile from beneath lowered lashes. To her secret amusement, his Adam's apple went wild once more.

Gulping, he leaned toward her. Their shoulders brushed. Neither of them realized they'd acquired an audience until a strangled gasp sounded just inside the door to the parlor.

"John!"

Popping upright, the minister turned a fiery face to the young woman standing stiff with shock.

"Vera! I didn't hear you come downstairs."

He scrabbled for the drawing and held it out with all the desperation of a murderer offering evidence that might save him from the gallows.

"Lady Barbara was just showing me Mary's artwork. But look! It's quite, er, remarkable."

Vera's throat worked. As her swain had done just a few seconds before, she swallowed several times before pride came to her rescue.

"Yes," she said, lifting her chin. "It is."

Turning on her heel, she swept out of the parlor.

Dinner that evening was a distinctly chilly affair. Vera refused to look at Mr. Harris and answered every question put to her in a polite monotone.

Louise, who'd evidently had the story from her daughter, favored her guest with disapproving looks. The young minister spooned his soup in silent misery.

Barbara was unused to explaining her actions, but the barrier she'd thrown up between the young lovers nagged at her conscience. She caught Vera alone the next afternoon and attempted to mend matters.

"You shouldn't view what you saw last night in the wrong light," she said with one of her most charming smiles. "Mr. Harris and I were merely indulging in a bit of light banter."

Vera's eyes flashed with something that looked very much like contempt. "You must excuse me if I find such banter distasteful. Not that one should expect more of you, I suppose."

"I beg your pardon?"

"You told us the night you arrived at Morgan's Falls a woman should employ every weapon in her arsenal to get a man to... How did you phrase it? To lift her handkerchief for her."

"Oh, for pity's sake!" Stung by the girl's disdain, Barbara snapped back. "I don't want him lifting my handkerchief. Or anything else, for that matter."

"Don't you?" Abandoning her dignity, Vera poured out her hurt. "I don't know how I could have thought so. Perhaps because you allowed my brother to get under your skirts so easily."

Barbara's breath escaped on a hiss. Reminding

herself that her flirtation had caused this girl pain, she grudgingly conceded the field.

"I may have toyed with Mr. Harris, but he could never care very deeply for a featherhead who hasn't read so much as a page of Mrs. Wollstonecraft's treatise on... on..."

"On the education of women," Vera supplied through gritted teeth.

"It's you he respects. You he admires."

"Ha!"

Out of patience with the chit, Barbara delivered some stern advice. "If you would stop scraping your hair back in that spinsterish bun and indulge in a bit of silly banter with the man once in a while, you'd have him on his knees."

"If he doesn't love me for my mind, I don't want him."

With that ridiculous pronouncement, she marched off.

Barbara spent the next few days enduring the silent displeasure of Louise, the icy politeness of her elder daughter and the embarrassed glances of Mr. Harris. As if that weren't enough, Theo became positively impish and resisted Barbara's every attempt at instruction in the use of colored pencils. So it was with profound relief that she greeted the news that Zach's ranger company was due to return in a few days.

"Colonel Arbuckle's note indicates they'll be back in time for the Cotton Balers' Ball," Louise related to the family that evening.

Urice instantly brightened. Although not yet fourteen, she was desperately eager to taste the delights of womanhood.

"How wonderful! You can't say I'm too young to attend the ball now that Zach will be there to partner me. When do we leave for Fort Gibson? Mama? Papa?"

Louise's glance lingered for a long moment on Barbara before shifting to her husband. "When do we leave?"

Daniel Morgan smiled. "That depends on how long it will take my ladies to pack all their ribbons and bows."

They settled on a date two days hence. With an overnight stop at the Jolly farm, they would arrive at the fort the day of the ball.

The following evening, with the relief of one freed from the worst sort of drudgery, Barbara directed Hattie to pack her bags.

"No, no, I won't take that one."

She stopped the maid before she could fold the much-worn lavender kerseymere into her valise. The hem was almost in tatters from the pesky vines and Barbara's jaunts about the plantation with her rambunctious students.

"Do you wish to have it?" she asked the maid. "You're much shorter than I. You could turn up the hem and take in the waist."

She smiled as Hattie held the gown against her front and peacocked in front of the mirror. The woman's bruises had finally faded and repeated brushings had given her brown hair a lustrous sheen. With her tiny waist and small-boned features, she was quite attractive.

"You might cut the sleeves at the elbow," Barbara suggested, feeling quite generous now that she was all but on her way to Bermuda. Her only regret was that she'd say goodbye to Zach at this ball or very soon thereafter. Those hours in his arms had been the one thrilling diversion in this otherwise endless sojourn.

"Perhaps you should lower the neckline a trifle," she said with another glance at the preening maid. "I understand every female at the post attends the ball. You might well collect a beau or two."

Hattie nodded, her gaze on her reflection. "You're right. The neckline needs to be lowered, but then I'd need a ribbon or bit of jewelry to wear at the throat."

"You may look through my jewel case and borrow a pin or necklace, if you wish. Not the sapphires, though."

Swishing the skirt of the gown, the maid smiled at the image in the mirror.

* * *

A small cavalcade set out from Morgan's Falls the next morning. Daniel and three well-armed men rode guard. Louise, her children and her guest were also mounted, as was a glum Mr. Harris, who'd decided to give his students a brief holiday and accompany the Morgans. Hattie and two other servants occupied the wagon, along with an assortment of bandboxes and valises.

After a night spent at John Jolly's plantation, they arrived at Fort Gibson to find every building crammed to overflowing. As Barbara soon discovered, the Cotton Balers' Ball was the highlight of the social season in Indian Country.

Apparently the soldiers had issued invitations to every female on the frontier. Young ladies from as far away as Fort Smith in Arkansas Territory had stuffed their ball gowns into saddlebags and traveled the ninety miles by horseback with the hope of snaring a handsome young lieutenant just out of West Point. Maidens from the various tribes in the vicinity had also been invited and could be seen walking about the fort on the arms of their beaus. Two enterprising females of questionable character had set up an establishment outside the gates. The wheezy notes of a hurdy-gurdy issued from inside their tent and there were long lines of troopers waiting to get in.

The parade field inside the palisade was a sea of pitched tents. The bachelors, Barbara was informed, had vacated their quarters to make room for guests, while the married officers and sergeants shuffled children and servants to do the same. Colonel Arbuckle had graciously invited the Morgan family to stay in his quarters, but the arrival of another commissioner and his party had taken up every spare room. The Morgans availed themselves instead of Sallie Nicks's generous hospitality.

"I shall have to fit you all into two rooms," the widow apologized as she escorted them up the stairs. "A steamboat docked yesterday and discharged half the unmarried women of New Orleans, I swear. It left again this morning—carrying an acquaintance of yours," she added, addressing Louise and Daniel. "He was most disappointed to have missed you, I can tell you. Unfortunately, the steamboat captain could not adjust his schedule to await your arrival."

"Who do you speak of?" Louise asked.

"Mr. Irving."

"*Washington* Irving?"

"The same." The widow rattled on gaily, unaware that Barbara had almost tripped over her skirts. "He arrived unexpectedly with Commissioner Ellsworth and has spent the past month out on the prairie with the rangers. Zach will give you a detailed report, I'm sure."

12

Barbara spent what was left of the afternoon swinging wildly from nervousness to bravado. Zach sent a message to his parents that his duties kept him at the ranger camp and he'd see them at the ball. He didn't include so much as a postscript for Barbara. Nor did he make any mention of the weeks he'd spent in the company of Washington Irving.

By the time Barbara retired to the room she shared with Vera and Urice to dress for the ball, anticipation of her reunion with Zach had left her a jumble of nerves. Thank goodness neither of his sisters had as yet come upstairs. She had a few moments, at least, to collect her thoughts. Shedding her traveling gown, she wrapped her dressing robe around her and took the pins from her hair. The last one came out just as Hattie returned from the kitchens with oil to heat the curling tongs.

"It's all sixes and sevens downstairs," she announced, pouring the oil carefully into the kidney-shaped lamp pan. Once the pan was full, she closed the lid, lit the wick, and set the curling iron on the U-shaped prongs. The flame danced merrily under the iron.

"Do you want side curls or a topknot?"

"A topknot," Barbara replied distractedly.

She tried to convince herself it was unlikely her name would have come up in a chance conversation between Zach and the American author during the month they'd spent out on the prairie. If it had…

Well, she'd met Irving only that one time in Bohemia. To be sure, the occasion had included some unpleasantness. The furious baroness had flung rather rude accusations at both Barbara and Harry, accusing the sister of enticing a diamond bracelet out of her corpulent husband and the brother of manipulating the cards at the whist table. Both charges had been true, of course, but were vehemently denied.

She'd hold to those denials, Barbara decided. Whatever Irving had told Zach, she would assume her haughtiest air and shrug off the charges as the ranting of a jealous woman, just as she had so many years ago in Bohemia. She couldn't let Zach think Harry a cardsharp. Nor could she allow him to believe her brother guilty of the scheme that had landed him in prison. If Zach knew the truth, Barbara might never see so much as a penny of the money she needed to free Harry.

Absorbed in her turbulent thoughts, she almost jumped out of her skin at the rap of knuckles on the door. Barbara pulled her dressing robe around her while Hattie went to the door.

It was a note written in a bold, slashing hand and requested a few private moments with Lady Barbara. Zach would wait for her by the stables.

Her heart thumping, Barbara crushed the note in her fist. She considered ignoring the request. She was no student of military tactics but knew a wise general would pick the time and place to engage in battle.

On the other hand, perhaps there would be no battle. Perhaps Zach only wanted to steal a few minutes alone with her before the ball. With that faint hope in mind, Barbara tossed the note aside and threw off her dressing robe. Ignoring the damask-covered corset and ivory ball gown with its overskirt of gold tissue Hattie had laid out on the bed, she snatched up the traveling dress she'd removed just moments ago. The gabardine fell in stiff folds over her linen drawers and camisole.

"Help me pin up my hair," she asked Hattie, fumbling with the buttons on the bodice. "I must go out for a few moments."

The maid's curious glance went to the crumpled note. "Why?"

"That's not your concern. Help me with my hair, if you please."

Frowning, Hattie did as she was told. Barbara grabbed her shawl and was on her way to the door, when Vera and Urice entered. The older girl gave her a cool nod. She'd yet to forgive Barbara for those moments in the parlor with Mr. Harris. The younger fell into instant raptures over the ball gown on the bed.

"Ohhh! That gold tissue is the exact shade of your hair. How exquisite you'll look!"

Vera sniffed.

Barbara started for the door. Paused. Turned to the older girl.

"I know you don't wish any advice from me, but I shall give it anyway. Hattie is heating the tongs. Let her use them to fashion some side curls or a topknot. You'll look quite lovely."

"You're right. I don't wish any advice from you."

Shrugging, Barbara brushed past her. She'd done her best by the stubborn creature. She only hoped the brother would prove less difficult to handle than the sister.

Her first glimpse of the lieutenant shattered those hopes.

He was waiting for her by the low log building

that served as barn and livery stables. He wore his regimentals in honor of the occasion. Under other circumstances, Barbara might have taken a moment to admire the dark blue cutaway coat with its double row of brass buttons, lavish gold braid and embroidered epaulets. At the moment, though, all her attention went to the stiff set of his shoulders and the way his gloved fist gripped the hilt of his sword.

He looked up at her approach. The rapidly descending twilight cast his face in shadow. Wishing she could see his eyes, Barbara moved closer.

"You wish to speak with me?"

"I do." Closing the few feet between them, he grasped her elbow. "Inside, where we won't be disturbed."

Her pulse tripped. His hold on her arm was as tight as his voice. She gave fleeting thought to her shoes and the hem of her gown as he yanked open the stable door, but his grim expression drove any worry about muck from her head.

A stable boy was inside, currying one of the horses. He turned a startled face to the intruders, and looked even more surprised when Zach issued a curt command.

"Get out."

Recognizing the voice of authority, the boy scrambled to obey. The stable door banged shut behind him and left a silence broken only by the swish of horses' tails and the restless shuffle of hooves.

Barbara breathed in the earthy scent of warm horse-flesh and fresh-cut straw, lifted her chin and took the offensive.

"I understand Mr. Irving accompanied the rangers on patrol this past month."

"He did."

She could see his eyes now. They held none of the warmth or laughter she'd grown used to seeing in them. Her chin rose another notch.

"Did you mention me to him?"

"I did."

Anger flared, swift and hot. She wasn't one of his troops, to be treated thus.

"Enough of this 'he did' and 'I did.' Just tell me what he said and be done with it."

He stepped closer. Too close. Barbara refused to back away. Not that she could. She was almost up against the boards of a stall.

"He said you charmed an emerald bracelet out of some petty count in Bohemia."

"He was a baron, not a count, and the bracelet was of diamonds."

He accepted her cool reply with a shrug, as if not particularly interested in the details. Barbara discovered why in the next breath.

"Mr. Irving also said you were accompanied on that occasion by your brother…or the man who presented himself as such."

It took a moment for his words to sink in. When

they did, a sick feeling curled in her stomach. Was this what people thought of her? Paramour to a man who might or might not be her brother? For the first time, her past shamed her. Deeply shamed her.

Pride wouldn't allow her to show it, however. Deliberately, she curved her mouth into a smile. "Did he think Harry my lover? How very droll."

"*Is* he your lover?"

"I will not dignify that with a response. You may believe what you will."

He took another step toward her, and it was all Barbara could do not to shrink against the stall.

"Tell me." The demand was a quick, slashing whip. "What relationship is this Harry to you?"

Goaded, she threw the question back in his face. "What difference does it make?"

"Little, I suppose. Except I'd feel less a fool for wanting you the way I do if I knew he *was* your brother and not your lover."

The admission that he desired her despite the doubt that had been planted in his mind should have thrilled Barbara. She waited for the flush of victory, the heady rush of knowing she could add Zach to her list of conquests. Like so many others she'd set out to tantalize and beguile, he'd fallen under her spell.

The exhilaration came…and fled. She had only to look at the grim cast to his face to know that wanting her accorded him little joy.

"Tell me, Barbara. Is Harry brother, husband or lover?"

She didn't understand the new, piercing ache that lodged just under her breastbone. She'd never cared what men thought of her before. Zach's opinion shouldn't matter any more than the others. But it did. For reasons she couldn't seem to determine, it did.

Ignoring the ache, she shrugged. "You won't believe me now whatever I say."

"Which is he, dammit?"

"My brother!"

He gave a small grunt, but she couldn't tell whether the sound was one of satisfaction at having pulled an answer from her or disbelief. His eyes were hooded as he stared down at her.

"Mr. Irving wasn't the only one who accompanied us on patrol," he said after a moment. "Mr. Latrobe was also a member of the party."

"Is he supposed to be of interest to me?"

"You may not recognize his name, but he recognized yours. It seems you and your brother swindled his friend out of two hundred pounds."

"I told you! Harry was as taken in by that Swiss railroad scheme as any of the men he convinced to invest in it."

"This wasn't a railroad scheme. As I recall, it had something to do with a jeweled miniature purported to have belonged to Marie Antoinette."

Sweet Jesus! How much of her past had he uncovered?

"My grandmother was one of the queen's ladies in waiting," she bit out. "Grandmère smuggled that miniature out of France when she fled the country. My brother and I believed the stones to be real."

And so they were, until Harry pried them off and replaced them with paste.

Zach said nothing for long moments. Barbara let the taut silence spin out. If she was to be interrogated like a prisoner in the dock, he could damn well drag the answers he sought out of her.

"Did he send you here?" he asked at last. "Did you and this brother of yours fabricate this connection to my mother to play on her sympathies and extort money from her? Or are you lying about everything, including the business about Harry being in prison?"

"Shall I describe his prison to you? It was once the HMS *Dromedary*. Now it's a rotting, vermin-infested hulk moored to a stone breakwater in Bermuda. I wasn't allowed aboard, of course, but I could smell the stink of tar and sweat and death from the quay. I'm told the ship once carried a complement of fifteen officers and one hundred sailors. More than five hundred convicts are now chained below its decks each night."

"You tell that tale most convincingly," he muttered. "Why should I believe it? Or you?"

"Because you want to. It wouldn't do for you to

desire a liar and a cheat. Or a woman who would whore herself to save her lover."

With a shake of his head, he drew his knuckles down the curve of her cheek. "Whatever else you are, my golden-haired witch, you're not a whore."

"How can you be so certain?" she flung back. "You must know I wasn't a virgin when you… When we…"

"I'm no Johnny Raw, Barbara. I knew I wasn't the first, but my guess is you haven't taken many lovers."

She would die before she would admit there had only been one before him. Or that the drunken bastard had left her bloodied and almost as bruised as Hattie. Harry had avenged her honor—what was left of it, anyway—but the mere memory of that distasteful incident was enough to stiffen her back.

"So, Barrister Morgan. You've weighed the evidence. Do you find me guilty or innocent of the crimes laid against me?"

"Not innocent." His knuckles made another pass over her cheek. "Certainly not innocent. If I'm to judge anyone, though, I would judge this brother who sent you."

They were back to Harry. Always, Barbara thought, it came back to Harry. She struggled to put her feelings for her scapegrace brother into words.

"Don't judge him too harshly, Zach. You grew to manhood surrounded by a large and loving family. Harry and I had only each other."

To her disgust, tears began to well behind her lids.

Furious with herself for such ridiculous missishness, she willed them away.

"If my brother swindled anyone, it was to feed me. If he cheated, it was to keep a roof over my head. You would do the same for Urice or Vera or Theo."

"In a heartbeat."

The response went far toward calming Barbara's tattered nerves. He studied her for long moments, his thoughts unreadable behind his dark eyes.

"How soon can you be ready to leave?"

"Leave?"

"Commissioner Ellsworth negotiated a treaty with the chief of the Grand Pawnee while we were out on patrol. Colonel Arbuckle has deputized me to carry it to Washington."

She stared at him stupidly. "What has this treaty to do with me?"

"I'm thinking you should accompany me to Washington. Once I've delivered the report, we can take a ship to London."

Her jaw sagged. "To London?"

"To see what can be done to aid your brother."

Dear Lord above!

He really *did* desire her. He must, to put aside his doubts and his duties to travel across an ocean with her.

Barbara could hardly tell him now she intended to sail for Bermuda, not England. Nor could she admit her plans included extortionate bribes and a dangerous prison escape. Her thoughts whirling, she stammered a protest.

"How…? How can you travel to England? You have duties here."

"I've requested a leave of absence. Colonel Arbuckle has agreed to it, after I present Commissioner Ellsworth's report to President Jackson."

"But…I thought…"

"Thought what? I promised to help you. The Morgans hold to their promises."

Feeling much like a dog chasing its own tail, she struggled to make sense of this confusing man. "What of the things Irving told you about me? The things *I* told you about myself?"

"They change nothing. I merely wanted the truth out of you."

The truth! A bubble of hysteria rose in Barbara's throat. She couldn't have sorted through her tangled web of half truths and lies now to save her soul.

She had to get away, had to bring some order to her chaotic thoughts. The shrill notes of a fife announcing the start of the ball gave her the excuse she needed.

"I…I must go and change."

"I'll wait for you out front."

"No!" She dragged in a breath. "Lieutenant Prescott came by this afternoon and asked to escort me to the festivities. Since I had no word from you, I accepted."

"The dog! And Nate dares to call himself my friend. Very well. I'll see you there."

Curling his knuckle under her chin, he dropped a swift, hard kiss on her mouth.

"Just be sure to save a waltz for me."

13

Lieutenant Prescott was pacing Sallie Nicks's downstairs parlor when Barbara rushed in.

"There you are!" His eager smile faltered when he took in her tumbled hair and travel-stained dress. "Have you changed your mind about attending the ball?"

"Not at all. I merely had some business to attend to. If you'll be patient another few moments, I'll go upstairs at once and change."

"Of course."

To Barbara's relief, the bedroom she shared with Zach's sisters was empty. Scattered ribbons and tossed petticoats indicated they had already departed for the ball. Hattie, too, was gone. The fire in the grate had been banked, and the wick was trimmed under the curling iron. Barbara's ivory ball gown still lay across the bed. The gold tissue overskirt gleamed in the light of the oil lamp, but she barely gave it a glance. Her churning thoughts were all on Lieutenant Zachariah Morgan.

He wanted her. Despite all he'd heard about her, he still desired her.

Hugging herself, Barbara paced the cluttered room. She should be pleased that she'd added another conquest to her list. Instead, uncharacteristic guilt nagged at her conscience. The guilt annoyed her, but it was easier to deal with than the nonsensical regret that kept tugging at her heart.

She hated the thought of deceiving Zach yet again, but saw no other path to take. She couldn't sail to London. She had no intention of allowing her brother to rot in the hulks for the months or years it would take to reopen his case.

Nor could she allow Zach to accompany her to Bermuda. He was trained in legal matters. What was worse, he wore a uniform. He hunted down those who violated the law or attempted to evade justice. He didn't help them escape.

She'd have to slip away once they reached Washington. Find a ship sailing for Bermuda. She'd best make sure she got a bank draft from Louise Morgan before departing Fort Gibson, though. She couldn't leave that to chance.

The muted trill of a violin tuning cut into her whirling thoughts. Muttering an oath, Barbara shed her traveling dress, dragged on the ivory ball gown and struggled with the buttons at its back. A firm tug at the rounded neckline bared the slopes of her breasts. A few pinches puffed up the sleeves.

Digging pins from her traveling case, she did her best to arrange her hair. Then it was merely a matter of pulling on her gloves, draping her tasseled reticule over her wrist and tossing the silk-lined opera cloak over her arm.

The Cotton Balers' Ball was in full swing when Barbara and Lieutenant Prescott made a tardy entrance.

The dance was being held in one of the enlisted men's mess halls. The men had cleared the long room of its plank table and benches and outdone themselves decorating the whitewashed interior. Oil lamps and bunting hung from the rafters, while the Seventh Infantry's colors fluttered from every post. A massive silver punch bowl and cups held place of honor at one end of the hall. The regimental band occupied the dais at the other end. They were playing a lively reel for the couples dipping and swirling enthusiastically across the dance floor.

"Let me take your cloak."

Lieutenant Prescott lifted the garment from her shoulders. While he searched for an empty peg amid the banks of scarlet-lined military capes, silk shawls and wool redingotes, a sea of blue coats and gold braid swarmed around Barbara. A fiery-haired young subaltern elbowed his way through the crowd to hand her a dance card.

"You've missed the quadrille and the Scotch reel," he said with a blush to match his hair. "A waltz is next. May I beg the honor of taking you to the floor?"

"I've reserved that for Lieutenant Prescott, but you may put your name down for a later waltz."

Almost overwhelmed by his good fortune, he snatched the card back and used its dangling pencil to scribble his name. His comrades were jockeying for the remaining dances when Nate Prescott returned and offered his arm.

"The colonel's compliments, Lady Barbara. He'd like to introduce you to Commissioners Ellsworth and Schermerhorn."

Nodding, she placed her hand on his arm and let him weave a path through the crowd. Her gaze drifted over the dancers as they passed. These Americans! They were so very egalitarian. Captains and corporals alike trod the boards, partnering their chosen ladies. And there was Sallie Nicks hooking elbows with a tall, mustached sergeant.

Suddenly, Barbara's gaze snagged on a delicate beauty in a shimmering green gown. Well, well! Vera had scornfully declared herself above female vanities, yet someone—Hattie, Barbara guessed—had crimped her fringe and arranged her hair in most becoming side curls. She was dancing with a great bear of a captain and looked to be enjoying herself enormously.

Amused, Barbara searched the ranks of men lined up against the far wall. Sure enough, young Mr. Harris stood with arms folded and a glower on his face as he watched the twirling couples.

A swirl of lavender caught Barbara's attention, and her amusement took a sardonic twist. That was Hattie. Bare-shouldered. Bruises gone. Her steps light and her face alive with pleasure as Zach took her left hand and the gentleman to her right took the other to form a chain. The entire line skipped forward, bowed to the line facing them, skipped back.

Well, that was equality indeed. Barbara shrugged aside her pique and turned a brilliant smile on Colonel Arbuckle. He bowed over her hand with old-fashioned gallantry and introduced the commissioners. The Reverend Mr. Schermerhorn was as short and rotund as Commissioner Ellsworth was tall and spare. The former greeted her with a polite bow, the latter with a keen glance.

"So, Lady Barbara, I understand I have you to thank for Lieutenant Morgan's willingness—no, eagerness—to deliver my draft treaty."

"I'm sure the lieutenant is simply attending to his duty, sir."

"He attended to more than his duty out there in Pawnee Country, I can tell you that. Demmed if he didn't shoot the tomahawk right out of the hands of a renegade Pawnee."

"I'm quite impressed."

"So was I," the commissioner said with a chuckle, "particularly when Zach informed me the rogue was the son of Chief Talaman. The chief agreed to come in and powwow quick enough when he learned we were holding his son. We got him to agree to cease all raids on the Creek and Cherokee in exchange for his boy and a generous stipend in goods and cash."

Barbara made an appropriate murmur of appreciation. Colonel Arbuckle's endorsement was considerably stronger.

"I can't tell you how important this treaty is, Commissioner. All of us at Fort Gibson have seen first-hand the anger and resentment building between the western tribes and those resettling from the East. It needs but a spark to set this whole territory aflame."

"We must hope President Jackson agrees. I asked Lieutenant Morgan to add his arguments to those I've put forth in my report, by the way. He certainly knows this country better than I."

"That's one of the reasons I released him to deliver your report. His father served with Jackson at New Orleans. Old Hickory has almost as much regard for Zach as he does for Daniel."

The fact that father and son appeared to have the ear of the American president impressed Barbara. She also noted that Ellsworth had apparently finished his report. Zach confirmed as much when he appeared at her side some time later.

She'd danced with any number of officers, had

gone in to supper on the arm of Colonel Arbuckle, and had drunk a little too much of the artillery punch being ladled out. Barbara blamed the intoxicating mix of champagne and whiskey dusted with black pepper "firing powder" for the sudden hitch in her pulse when she looked up into the lieutenant's eyes.

"I believe the next waltz is ours."

"I'm afraid you're mistaken." She made a show of consulting her dance card. "I'm sure I promised it to a subaltern."

"You did. I outranked him. He's sulking over there, in the corner."

She caught a glimpse of the young officer's glum countenance as Zach took her elbow to escort her onto the plank flooring. When the band struck up a beat that flowed with the seductive rhythm of the Danube, his arm slid around her waist.

He waltzed with the strength and controlled grace he did all else. Barbara couldn't help but note the glances the other dancers sent their way. They made a striking couple, she knew, with Zach so tall and darkly handsome in his regimentals, and she all shimmering in gold and cream.

For a moment she allowed herself a foolish fantasy. Perhaps one day she and Zach would waltz like this at Maxim's in Paris. Or stroll arm in arm through London's Hyde Park. Or sip coffee at a tiny table in St. Mark's Square in Venice while pigeons swooped in to take bits of cake from their hands.

And perhaps not. Sighing, Barbara tipped her head and met his gaze. "I spoke with your colonel and Mr. Ellsworth earlier."

"I saw."

"The commissioner indicated his report is all but done."

"Yes, he told me."

"When do we leave?"

The music rose to a final crescendo. Tightening his arm, he took her into a sweeping pattern. Barbara's heart was pounding against her stays when the last notes trilled. With the crowd shuffling off the floor around them, Zach held her for a moment longer.

"The *Natchez Star* is due to dock at Fort Gibson the day after tomorrow. I'll book passage for us."

Hattie couldn't believe her ears. Fisting her hands in her skirts, she stared at the gilt-haired woman stepping out of her ball gown.

"You're leaving on the *Natchez Star*?" she echoed hollowly. "And Zach's going with you?"

"Yes, he is. If you decide to accompany me as my maid, however, I must ask that you cease referring to him so casually."

Hattie almost choked on a thick, hot bubble of anger. He danced with me! she wanted to shout. With *me!* Not once, but twice.

What's more, he'd smiled and teased her about

how pretty she looked. She'd been so sure he'd finally finished with this…this cow.

Had he paid no heed to the stories being whispered about her? If even half of them were true, the woman was little better than a common thief. She and this brother of hers.

If he *was* her brother. Hattie had heard that rumor, too. It burned like a hot brand in her mind as the woman turned to her, a question in her stupid, watery-pale eyes.

"*Do* you wish to come with me? If so, I'll send word in the morning for the lieutenant to book your passage."

When Hattie only stared at her, stonelike, she shrugged and pulled at the ties of her petticoats.

"I'll understand if you choose not to accompany me. It's a long journey to Washington, after all, and from there…" She chewed on her lower lip. "Well, it's a long journey."

The petticoats fluttered to the floor. Hattie watched them puddle about Barbara's ankles and made no move to pick them up. She could barely think for the bitter disappointment and jealousy eating at her.

One thing was certain, though. She'd be aboard that paddle wheeler when it left Fort Gibson.

"You're still set on aiding her?" Zach's mother's voice rose on a note of disbelief. "After all you tell us about her?"

Unaware she echoed Hattie's doubt and distrust, she paced Sallie's front parlor. Her silk skirts whipped about her ankles as she took another angry turn.

She'd tried to like the Englishwoman. Not because of her thin claim to kinship, certainly. Louise's loyalty lay first, last and always with those she loved. She'd feed anyone who hurt her family to the wolves, Barbara Chamberlain included.

"Me, I do not understand why you insist on continuing with her to England. She is well able to take care of herself, that one."

Zach propped his shoulders against the mantel and shot a glance at his father. Daniel's shrug indicated his son was on his own with this one.

"I promised to do what I could to help her brother," Zach said.

The Russian ruby in his mother's thumb ring flashed angry fire as she flapped a hand. "How do you know he is her brother? Or that he needs help?"

"She says he does."

"Pah! She says many things. To any man who will listen. Your sister still hurts with the pain this woman caused her."

Zach had heard the story. Both versions. Vera had poured out a short, angry tale of betrayal by young Mr. Harris. Urice had offered an equally passionate defense of Lady Barbara, who still shone in the younger, fashion-mad girl's eyes.

"Vera didn't look as though she was hurting too badly tonight," he commented. "She had poor Harris ready to crawl across the floor on his knees."

"That's as may be." The ruby caught the light once more as his mother made another extravagant gesture. "I tell you, Zach, I do not trust this woman. Nor am I at all sure what she will do with money you give her."

"I'll be there to see what's done with it. That's one of the reasons I'm accompanying her to London."

"One? Ha!" Louise tossed her head. "Me, I guess the other."

Zach straightened and pushed away from the mantel. He loved his mother with the same fierce devotion he did his father. Yet whatever it was that drew him so inexorably to Barbara pulled him just as inexorably away from his parents.

"You don't have to guess," he said, holding his mother's scornful gaze. "I admit it freely. The woman is in my head, and in my blood."

"Oh, Zach. I fear she'll bring you grief."

His mouth relaxed into a grin. "I don't doubt she'll try."

The next day passed in a flurry of activity. Zach turned his ranger troop over to his second in command, arranged with the elderly freed slave who served as his groom to see to his horses, went over his financial dealings with his parents and spent a final few hours with Commissioner Ellsworth and Colonel Arbuckle. He left the meeting with the commissioner's sealed report tucked inside his jacket and the colonel's urgent messages for President Jackson about the importance of the proposed treaty burned into his brain.

The following morning the *Natchez Star* steamed up the river and dropped her gangplank a full two hours ahead of schedule. She was one of the newer packets, side-wheeled, white painted, drawing less than eighteen inches under her flat bottom. While Hattie and Barbara threw the last of their things together, Zach checked out their cabins and saw to the loading of their baggage. The paddle wheeler's whistle was shrilling notice of its imminent departure when he arrived at Sallie Nicks's house to collect the women.

"Where's Lady Barbara?" he asked Hattie.

"In the back parlor, with your mother. She said they needed to finalize a few matters before we departed."

Zach started for the closed parlor door. Hattie's nervous twitter delayed him.

"I've never been on a steamboat before. I'm all sixes and sevens."

"So I see."

Amused, he watched her make several unsuccessful attempts to tie the ribbons of her bonnet.

"Here, I'll help you."

Despite his big hands, Zach fashioned a neat bow. "There, you're all set. That's a fetching hat, by the way."

"Do you like it?"

"Very much."

"Lady Barbara said it got too crushed in her trunk for her to be seen wearing it again. She was going to toss it on the rubbish heap, but I asked if I might have it."

She was about to say more when the parlor door wrenched open and Barbara emerged. High spots of color burned on her cheeks.

"Your mother informs me you've assumed responsibility for all financial arrangements relating to this journey." Her glance speared Hattie before slicing back to Zach. "And for the matter that brought me here."

"That's right. I would have informed you myself if I'd had ten minutes to spare these past two days."

"Indeed?"

The scream of the steamboat's whistle snapped her head up. Her jaw tight, Barbara snatched up her traveling valise. "We'll finish this discussion later."

They finished it that same evening, as Zach was preparing to leave his cabin and escort Barbara to dinner in the *Natchez Star*'s opulent dining room.

Like most of the steamboats vying for the lucrative river-passenger trade, this one boasted crystal

An Important Message
from the Editors

Dear Reader,

Because you've chosen to read one of our fine books, we'd like to say "thank you"! And, as a special way to thank you, we're offering you a choice of two more of the books you love so well, and a surprise gift to send you — absolutely FREE!

Please enjoy them with our compliments...

Pam Powers

eel off Seal and
Place Inside...

EDITOR'S
FREE GIFT
SEAL
THANK YOU

What's Your Reading Pleasure...
ROMANCE? _OR_ SUSPENSE?

Do you prefer spine-tingling page turners OR heart-stirring stories about love and relationships? Tell us which books you enjoy – and you'll get 2 FREE "ROMANCE" BOOKS or 2 FREE "SUSPENSE" BOOKS with no obligation to purchase anything.

Choose **"ROMANCE"** and get **2 FREE BOOKS** that will fuel your imagination with intensely moving stories about life, love and relationships.

FREE!

Choose **"SUSPENSE"** and you'll get **2 FREE BOOKS** that will thrill you with a spine-tingling blend of suspense and mystery.

FREE!

Whichever category you select, your 2 free books have a combined cover price of $11.98 or more in the U.S. and $13.98 or more in Canada.

And remember. . . just for accepting the Editor's Free Gift Offer, we'll send you 2 books and a gift, ABSOLUTELY FREE!

YOURS FREE! We'll send you a fabulous surprise gift absolutely FREE, just for trying "Romance" or "Suspense"!

® and TM are registered trademarks of Harlequin Enterprises Limited.

Visit us online at
www.FreeBooksandGift.com

THE EDITOR'S "THANK YOU" FREE GIFTS INCLUDE:

▶ 2 Romance OR 2 Suspense books

▶ An exciting surprise gift

YES! I have placed my Editor's "thank you" Free Gifts seal in the space provided above. Please send me the 2 FREE books which I have selected, and my FREE Mystery Gift. I understand that I am under no obligation to purchase anything further, as explained on the back and opposite page.

PLACE
FREE GIFTS
SEAL
HERE

Check one:

ROMANCE
193 MDL DVFJ   393 MDL DVFL

SUSPENSE
192 MDL DVFH   392 MDL DVFK

FIRST NAME   LAST NAME

ADDRESS

APT.#   CITY

STATE/PROV.   ZIP/POSTAL CODE

▼ DETACH AND MAIL CARD TODAY! ▼

(BB1-04) © 1998 MIRA BOOKS

The Reader Service — Here's How It Works:

Accepting your 2 free books and gift places you under no obligation to buy anything. You may keep the books and gift and return the shipping statement marked "cancel." If you do not cancel, about a month later we'll send you 3 additional books and bill you just $4.74 each in the U.S., or $5.24 each in Canada, plus 25¢ shipping & handling per book and applicable taxes if any.* That's the complete price and — compared to cover prices starting from $5.99 each in the U.S. and $6.99 each in Canada — it's quite a bargain! You may cancel at any time, but if you choose to continue, every month we'll send you 3 more books, which you may either purchase at the discount price or return to us and cancel your subscription.

*Terms and prices subject to change without notice. Sales tax applicable in N.Y. Canadian residents will be charged applicable provincial taxes and GST.

If offer card is missing write to: The Reader Service, 3010 Walden Ave., P.O. Box 1867, Buffalo, NY 14240-1867

BUSINESS REPLY MAIL

FIRST-CLASS MAIL   PERMIT NO. 717-003   BUFFALO, NY

POSTAGE WILL BE PAID BY ADDRESSEE

THE READER SERVICE
3010 WALDEN AVE
PO BOX 1341
BUFFALO NY 14240-8571

NO POSTAGE
NECESSARY
IF MAILED
IN THE
UNITED STATES

chandeliers, linen-draped dining tables, a private salon for the ladies and a smoke-filled poker room for the men. Zach was considering the possibility of a few hands of five-card stud later that night when knuckles rapped sharply against his door.

Barbara stood on the threshold. Her eyes glittered as bright and hard as apothecaries' glass. "May I come in?"

"Of course."

He stood back to allow her entry and closed the door behind her rustling skirts. She still wore her traveling gown, he saw, but she'd put off her hat and gloves.

It soon became apparent she intended to put off her dress as well. She tossed her reticule on the bed, spun around to face him and began, methodically, to push the buttons of her bodice through their loops.

14

With every button Barbara worked free, her anger burned hotter. She didn't so much as glance around the sumptuous stateroom. It matched hers, she supposed, with rich wooden scrollwork, crystal teardrops on the oil lamps and a potbellied stove that glowed with a cheerful heat. Her entire attention was concentrated on the man who stood watching her with an air of polite interest.

Barbara considered herself something of a master at manipulation, yet Zachariah Morgan had outmaneuvered her at every turn. Worse, he'd played her for a fool. Not once, but several times over. By acting the backwoods ruffian. By promising so very earnestly to speak to his mother on her behalf. And, damn him, by feeding her that slop about how much he desired her.

How could she have been so stupid as to believe

him? How could she have imagined he'd really look beyond her face or her past? He was like all the others. Dazzled by her beauty. Excited by her body. Determined to have her. The only difference between Lieutenant Morgan and the Bohemian baron who'd gifted her with a diamond bracelet was the price each was prepared to pay for her.

Barbara supposed she should feel flattered that he thought her worth five thousand pounds. Harry would certainly have chuckled with glee. Lightening men's purses was what they did best, after all. This time, though, she intended to give full service for payment rendered. She couldn't have said whether that rash decision sprang from anger or hurt or the perverse desire to prove what was said about her was true.

Her jaw set, she pushed the last button through its loop. Her hands were clumsy as she peeled off the puff-sleeved bodice and tossed it onto the bed to join her reticule.

Zach followed its course with every appearance of interest. He didn't say a word, however. Instead, he merely folded his arms and propped his shoulders against the oak-paneled bulkhead.

Barbara's chin came up. Her voice could have etched glass. "Shall I continue?"

"By all means."

The lazy drawl set her back teeth on edge. She fumbled at the hooks at the back of her skirt, finally released them, and then kicked the garment aside to form a puddle of green on the cabbage-rose carpet. He let the pile of linen settle almost at the toes of his boots while Barbara yanked at the tapes of her petticoat. It, too, dropped to the floor. She stepped out of it and reached for the strings of her corset.

Still he didn't move.

Her jaw clenching, she gave the strings a tug. Of course they had to knot. She tugged again and snapped one string off at the gusset.

She stood there with the thin cord clenched tight in her fist. For reasons she couldn't begin to fathom, the broken lace seemed to represent everything that had gone wrong these past months.

"How is it you always manage to tangle yourself up in some manner?"

The amusement in his voice brought her head up. "It seems to be a particular talent of mine," she replied with bitter irony.

"Do you want assistance with that knot, or has your fit of temper played out?"

"No, to both."

Hooking her thumb in the strings, Barbara yanked hard. The knot gave. She plucked at the cords and pulled them through the metal gussets. A moment later her corset fell away.

"Do you wish me naked?"

"How could I wish anything else?"

She refused to acknowledge the laughter glinting in his eyes. She was done with games, done with being taken for a fool.

"Very well."

Removing to the velvet-covered corner chair, she perched on the edge of the seat and bent to unbuckle her shoes. Her garters went next. Carefully, she rolled her silk stockings down her calves.

When she stood, she could feel the deck vibrating under her bare soles. And when she pulled at the ribbons gathering the neck of her chemise, Zach at last acknowledged that she was indeed serious. The laughter disappeared from his eyes and from his face.

"What the devil is this about, Barbara?"

"I merely wish to make sure you receive full value for your money."

He pushed away from the wall. "You know damn well I'm not trying to buy you or your affections."

"You can't imagine how relieved I am to hear it, as my *affections* are not for sale."

His eyes hardened. "But you are?"

"Didn't the inestimable Mr. Irving tell you so? Isn't that what your mother and sister think?"

The mark hit home. She saw it in his face even as the bitter truth cut into her with the savagery of a lash.

They were right, she thought on a wave of disgust. Irving. Louise Morgan. Prim, disapproving Vera. Barbara Chamberlain was nothing more than a high-born slut. She smiled. She enticed. She promised. That she'd never before intended to make good on those promises placed her several rungs below the whores who sold themselves on street corners. They, at least, were honest in their dealings.

"It doesn't matter what anyone says of you," Zach bit out. "I told you as much not two nights ago."

"Yes, you did."

She covered the hurt of that with a brittle laugh. "To be frank, I find your nobility rather tedious. I'd rather be done with all pretense and act the strumpet we both know me to be. At least then you'd receive a proper measure of payment for your coin."

"Dammit, Barbara…"

"I want to see it first, though."

"What?"

"The color of your coin. I should like to have a bank draft in hand before we proceed any further."

As angry now as she, he raked her with a withering stare. "You don't trust me to make good on my promise to aid you?"

"I trusted your mother when she said she'd help me. As circumstances appear to change with the wind, I think it wisest to settle the matter of payment now."

He scowled down at her for so long Barbara was sure he'd repudiate her demand. She'd questioned his honor. Refused to accept his word. She was bracing herself for a scathing retort when he turned and strode to the fold-down writing table. As sumptuous as the rest of the cabin, the desk was fitted with a heavy blotter, sheets of vellum and a brass-capped inkwell. A few scratches of a quill later, he returned.

"You can present this at the Bank of Virginia when we reach the capital. They'll honor it."

He'd made the draft out for U.S. dollars. Barbara translated the amount into pounds and felt her throat go dry.

"I didn't ask for this much."

He let his glance slide to the slopes of her breasts. "You underestimate your value."

Heat rushed to her cheeks. He was taunting her, daring her to end this farce here and now.

She wanted to. God knew, she wanted to. She ached to fling the bank draft back in his face. Had she been the only one to consider, she would have done so with great relish. Almost choking on her pride, she waved the document to dry the ink, rolled the stiff vellum and slipped it into her reticule. Her smile was blade-sharp and mocking when she turned to face him.

"I'll try to give you a good return on your investment."

He made no move to stop her when she loosened the ribbons at the scooped neck of her chemise. They'd both crossed the line now. There was no going back.

A roll of her shoulders sent the soft linen sliding to her elbows. From there it drifted to the floor. She stood stiff before him as he took a slow inventory. It was as insulting as it was thorough.

A corner of Barbara's mind registered the whistle of the ship's calliope and rhythmic slap of the paddle wheel on the river. She counted each sharp note, each watery churn, until Zach nodded.

"Continue."

She fumbled with the ties of her drawers and let them fall. This was what she was, she reminded herself once again. What she'd become.

"Turn around. Slowly."

Her hands fisting at her sides, she performed a slow pirouette. Her chin jutted when she faced him once again.

"Well? Are you satisfied with the merchandise?"

"Not yet. But I soon will be."

His hands went to his trouser flap. Spinning on her heel, she started for the bed.

"Not there," he rapped out. "Here."

She swung back, saw the hard set to his jaw.

"You're the one who insists on playing the whore. Any two-penny trollop can service a man where he stands."

She didn't move. Her heart hammering against her ribs, she tried to imagine how she was to accomplish what he demanded of her.

He must have seen, or sensed, her confusion. "You use your hands," he drawled. "And your mouth."

Stone-faced, she moved toward him. Her palm slapped against his trouser front. He grunted, but stood his ground. Barbara stared a hole in his shirtfront as she moved her hand in a tight circle.

He was already rampant. She could feel the length of him, the bulging hardness. His shirt became a blur of white as she pressed the heel of her hand against him.

His breath hissed in. He didn't move, but she felt his stomach muscles coil.

Her mouth. He wanted her to use her mouth. The thought of closing her lips around him made her throat go dry and her heartbeat thunder in her ears. When she slipped a hand inside his trouser flap, the heat of him also stirred a wanton thrill deep in her belly.

The intensity of it sickened her. She was, indeed, no better than a two-penny trollop. She would have quit the field then and retired in ignominious defeat, but she'd pushed him too far.

Muttering a fierce oath, he grabbed her wrist and yanked her hand free of his trousers. A savage twist brought her arm up behind her back and her body slamming into his.

She knew an instant of panic. The memory of that awful night in Naples came crashing back…and was obliterated by the crush of Zach's mouth on her. She was caught between terror and molten heat. Between the stupid girl she'd once been and the woman who'd found a searing passion in this man's arms. Shutting her mind to everything but the prod of his shaft against her belly, Barbara wrenched her arm free and locked both arms around his neck.

Zach knew the moment she yielded her body, if not her heart. He was desperate to have her, to drag her up, hitch her legs around his hips, drive into her. That's what she'd asked for. What she'd demanded. Hell, she'd all but begged him to treat her like the strumpet she believed herself to be.

Zach might well have believed it, too, if not for her clumsy responses that day at Morgan's Falls. She'd been eager, as eager as he, but so unskilled he'd come near to spilling himself before he'd brought her to a panting, writhing peak.

He was perilously close to that state now. Too close to spin this out any longer. Whirling her around, he backed her to the wall. Her shoulders hit the polished oak with a thump. In the next breath, he had her just where he'd imagined her a moment ago, her legs locked around his waist, his rod probing at her wet heat.

"Look at me."

Her head came up. Her cheeks were flushed, he saw with savage satisfaction, and a pulse beat frantically in her long, slender throat.

"I want you. So bad I hurt with it. I won't take you in payment for a debt but..."

"But what?"

"I'll take you every other way I know."

With a flex of his thighs, he thrust into her. She was ready for him. Wet and ready. Gritting his teeth, he pleasured her. When she cried out and convulsed around him, it near killed him to pull away and spill himself.

* * *

Barbara was slick with sweat when Zach tumbled her to the velvet-covered bunk.

Mewling with pleasure when his teeth and tongue stirred her once again to pleasure.

Limp and near boneless with exhaustion when he reached for the coverlet that had fallen to the floor.

"What…?"

The hoarse croak startled her. Her throat was raw from trying to suppress her groans. Wetting her lips, she tried again.

"What are you doing?"

"The coals in the stove have burned out. It's cold in here."

She hadn't noticed the chill or the prickly bumps it had raised on her skin. Both disappeared when Zach dragged up the coverlet and curved her body into his.

"I should go back to my cabin," she protested as he bent his legs and made a nest for her on his thighs.

"Not tonight."

She tried to squirm around, but he held her warm and fast.

"Not any night, I'm thinking."

"Zach…"

"We'll talk about it tomorrow. Let me sleep." His arm was heavy on her waist, his voice a soft rumble in her ear. "You've well nigh killed me, woman."

* * *

Hattie sat alone in the cabin she shared with her mistress. Like a small, rapacious barn owl, she stared unblinking at the wall separating this stateroom from the one adjoining it.

Darkness surrounded her. She'd trimmed the wicks on the oil lamps and hadn't bothered to feed coals into the stove. The gay notes of the calliope and tinkle of glass from the dining salon at the end of the passageway had died away. Faint whiffs of cigar smoke had curled through the louvered door for some time after that, bringing with them the chink of poker chips and a murmur from the smoking salon. Eventually those echoes had died, too. Now there was only the steady thump-thump of paddle wheel against river to break the silence.

With every splash of the wheel, the jealousy and resentment roiling inside her churned and thickened. The mixture was like a rancid stew, heavy as a stone in her gullet, with a foul, disgusting aftertaste. When she added hate to the pot, her throat became so thick and clogged she could scarce draw a breath.

Damn the woman! Her and her haughty ways. She liked to look down that long nose of hers, but lifted her skirts as quick as any round-heeled whore. Small wonder Zach went after her like a hound after a bitch in heat. What man wouldn't? She should rot in hell, right alongside that bastard, Thomas.

That vicious thought gave birth to another.

Accidents happened, didn't they? Particularly aboard steamboats churning through sleeting rain and darkness. People fell overboard and drowned all the time. Mostly drunks who lost their footing, but there were snags aplenty in the river. Who's to say the *Natchez Star* wouldn't hit one? Or bump up against another steamer fighting for space in the narrow, twisting channels? In the resulting confusion, all it would take was a quick shove, like the one she'd given Thomas.

Hattie's heart began to thump. Eyes burning, she stared at the dark, shadowy bulkhead. She could almost see the future unfolding on the oak paneling.

With that blond bitch out of the way, Zach would turn to her. Hattie knew he would. He'd smile at her in that particular way of his and take her hand the way he did the night of the Cotton Balers' Ball. And he'd take her to his bed.

Barbara Chamberlain wasn't the only one with an itch that needed scratching. Swine that he was, Thomas had given Hattie the rare moment or two of pleasure. With Zach, those moments would pile one on top of each other.

All she had to do was find the right chance.

15

Hattie watched and waited. She was sure an opportunity would present itself, but she hadn't counted on the suicidal desire for speed that possessed the captain of the *Natchez Star.*

With so many steamers competing for river traffic, every steamboat company tried to lure passengers with new speed records to augment the luxurious accommodations. Ten years ago, the run from Fort Gibson to Cincinnati had taken twenty-five days. Now the same journey took only nine. The captain of the *Star* seemed determined to best even that record.

Despite the ever-present hazards of sunken stumps, shifting river channels and busy river traffic, he kept the boilers roaring night and day. The boat docked at the major towns along the route only long enough to discharge and take on passengers, but didn't stop between. Not even to take on fuel. The bargemen who supplied wood for the boilers tied their flat-bottom skiffs alongside in mid-channel and tossed cut logs to *Natchez Star*'s crew and passengers, who stacked them willy-nilly on the deck.

A mere sixteen hours after departing Fort Gibson, the *Star* hit the confluence of the Arkansas and the Mississippi. The following day, the boat had docked at Memphis. Sometime during the next night, it left the muddy waters of the Mississippi for the Ohio. Louisville lay behind them now, Cincinnati just ahead. There they'd take another steamer to Wheeling, West Virginia, where Zach intended to hire a coach to convey them over the National Pike to Washington.

With each passing mile, Hattie's hate festered like an open, oozing wound. With each hour the *Star* drew closer to Cincinnati, her frustration mounted. She barely saw Barbara. When she did, the woman was almost always in Zach's company. The two took their meals together in the elegant dining room. Strolled the upper deck in the frosty morning air. Joined the other first-class passengers for cards or a minstrel show each evening.

Worse, far worse, the whore spent every night in the lieutenant's bed. The only occasions she spoke to her maid were when she came to her cabin to bathe or change her dress.

Between times, Hattie prowled the decks. By day she watched Zach with Barbara and ached inside. By night she pawed through her mistress's things. It was during one of those sessions alone in the cabin that she found the folded oilskin. The small packet was tucked inside the lining of the valise Barbara had shoved under her unused bunk.

"What's this now?"

Carefully, she unfolded the oilskin. The parchment inside rustled. Curious as a cat, she smoothed the document out and scanned its lines. She couldn't read or write except to make her "X," but the red wax seal at the bottom looked properly impressive. Frowning, Hattie traced the seal with a fingertip.

Instinct told her the document had something to do with Louise Morgan. Maybe this was proof of the tie between Louise's first husband and the Chamberlain woman. Maybe the English cow had brought it to back up her claim of kinship. And maybe it was something else altogether.

Pursing her lips, Hattie glanced at the stateroom wall. Zach and the whore were on the other side of the partition. If the past few nights were any measure, they'd go at each other for hours before falling asleep in Zach's bunk.

Folding the parchment, Hattie slipped it into her pocket. A moment later, the stateroom door closed quietly behind her. Surely there was someone still roaming about who could read the lines to her.

The task took longer than anticipated. The first cabin steward she approached could read English, but this, he informed her, was written in what he guessed was Spanish or French. Finally she found a farmer's wife among the steerage passengers with Creole blood and a knowledge of both languages.

The steerage compartment on the upper deck reeked of sweat-stained woolens and boiled onions. Closing her nose to the stink, Hattie hovered at the woman's shoulder as she translated the document in exchange for a copper penny filched from Barbara's purse.

"Near as I can tell, *ma cher,* this is written by the bishop of Reims. It's a place in France, you understand. With a big cathedral."

Hattie wasn't interested in the where. "What does this bishop say?"

"Something about another priest. A Jesuit. Ahhh, he was a rogue, this Jesuit. The bishop declares him *défroqué.*"

"What's that?"

She waved a hand. "He loses his sanctity and cannot perform baptisms or marriages. Any that he performed while here, in America, hold no validity. Including the marriage of…"

Frowning, she squinted at the document. Hattie held her breath and guessed the answer before the Creole supplied it.

"The ink is blurred here, but I believe… Yes, it refers to the marriage of one Henri Chartier to a woman of mixed French and Indian blood."

Hattie almost snatched the paper from the other's hand. With a muttered word of thanks, she hurried back downstairs. She didn't fully grasp the import of what she'd just learned, but she knew it must be significant. Why else would Barbara have hidden away this bit of paper?

Alone in the stateroom once again, Hattie debated whether or not to take the parchment to Zach. She'd have to think on the matter, she decided. Be certain showing him the paper would be to her advantage.

Carefully, she wrapped the oilskin around the document and slipped it back into its hiding place. A small, sly smile played at her lips as her glance went once again to the bulkhead separating this cabin from Zach's.

On the other side of the partition, Barbara stretched lazily. Zach lay sprawled beside her, magnificent in his nakedness.

After their first night, he'd taken care to feed the potbellied stove before stripping off his clothes and peeling away Barbara's. The stateroom was now warm and cozy and pungent with the scent of sex.

Idly, she propped her head in one hand and traced a fingertip through the curling hair on his chest. He opened one eye and flashed her a grin.

"Again?"

"No!" she protested, half laughing, half alarmed. "Not yet."

Folding his hands over his naked belly, he closed his eye. "Tell me when you're ready."

She couldn't help but smile at his blatant male complacency. The man had every right to feel smug. In the past week he'd pleasured Barbara in ways she'd never imagined possible.

She found it hard to believe an entire week had passed since they'd boarded the *Star*. The days had flown. And the nights…

Sweet heaven, the nights!

Every one of them was branded on her soul.

The realization they had only one more left aboard the *Star* crept into her mind and slowly pushed aside the pleasure. Tomorrow they'd dock in Cincinnati. Three more days aboard another steamer would bring them to Wheeling, where they'd board a coach for Washington. By this time next week, Barbara would be searching out a ship to take her to Bermuda.

Chewing on her lower lip, she played with the wiry curls on Zach's chest. She could tell him her plans, confess that the evidence against Harry was too damning to overturn his conviction and secure his release from prison by any legal mean. She could also admit the bank draft tucked safely in her reticule was intended to fund outrageous bribes and a dangerous escape.

She *could* tell Zach all, but should she?

He'd sail to Bermuda with her. She knew him

well enough now to accept without question that he'd hold true to his promise to help her and, by extension, Harry.

The problem was she was fast tumbling into love with the man. The thought both thrilled and disturbed her. She wasn't sure quite how to deal with it or the emotions Zach stirred in her.

Should she confess her feelings and draw him further into her schemes? Allow him to risk his reputation, his career, and perhaps his own freedom by helping Harry escape?

For the first time in her selfish, tumultuous life, Barbara found herself worrying more about the prey she'd snared in her web than about her brother or herself.

"Easy, sweeting!"

Zach's mumbled protest startled her out of her thoughts. He snared her wrist, and Barbara looked down to see she'd twirled his chest hair into a tight corkscrew.

"I'm sorry. I didn't mean to hurt you."

"You didn't, but I'm thinking one good pull deserves another."

With a lazy move, he levered up, rolled her onto her back and pinned her wrist to the tangled sheets. His eyes glinted as he dipped his head and took her nipple between his teeth.

Barbara gasped at the small pain and gave a whimper of pleasure when he began to suckle.

Later, she thought. She'd decide later what to tell Zach. When her mind wasn't spinning with delight and her body curling in desire.

Five days passed, and still she couldn't come to a decision.

They'd transferred to the *John Hawley* for the trip upriver to Wheeling. As she had aboard the *Star,* Barbara spent almost every waking hour with Zach. Each night she fell asleep in his arms.

The weather worsened as they neared the end of this leg of their journey. Freezing November rain pelted the upper decks. A stiff wind churned the river. Barbara began to feel queasy well before they docked at the bustling town set on a bluff overlooking the Ohio River and transferred to the coach Zach hired.

The jostling, jolting ride along the crowded National Pike was even more uncomfortable than the boat trip. Barbara soon saw the truth of Zach's assertion that the road was the most traveled highway in the country. Wagons and carts filled with immigrants seeking land in the Ohio or Oregon Territories rolled westward in a line that stretched for miles—so many that the noses of their oxen or horses almost touched the rear of the carts ahead. Almost as many vehicles traveled eastward.

Faster-moving curricles and coaches slowed time and again to inch around wagons with broken axles,

long strings of packhorses or overturned stages
driven too recklessly over the crushed-rock road.
Tollgates every few miles further slowed progress,
as did the ever-increasing climb through the pine-
and mist-shrouded Allegheny Mountains to the
Cumberland Gap.

Travelers crowded every inn and tavern along the
route. Barbara was forced to share accommodations
with Hattie and an assortment of other women, children and female servants while Zach bedded down
with their male companions. He did secure private
dining parlors when he could. Some were richly appointed, others mere cubbyholes off the main taproom. Smoky fireplaces, greasy venison cutlets and
the ripe aroma of unwashed bodies added to Barbara's queasiness.

To her embarrassment, she was obliged to have
Zach halt the coach the afternoon of the second day
so she could toss up her lunch. The same mortifying
event occurred the third afternoon.

Only later that evening, when they stopped at a
busy hostelry, did Barbara begin to suspect the reason for her brief bouts of nausea. Extra coins had secured her and Hattie beds in the large dormitory set
aside for women travelers, but they shared the quarters with a half-dozen other women. One of them
was bent over a bucket of water, muttering about her
monthlies while she attempted to rinse bright red
stains from her petticoat.

With a small frown, Barbara drew the curtain partitioning her cot from the rest of the room. Come to think on it, she should be facing a similar dilemma. When had she last bled? Just before she arrived at Morgan's Falls, she remembered counting back the weeks.

With a sudden, hollow feeling in the pit of her stomach, Barbara dropped down onto the thin straw mattress. Panic followed hard on the heels of dismay.

She couldn't be increasing! She couldn't!

Zach had pulled away before he spilled his seed their first few times together. Of late, he'd taken to using a lambskin sheath.

Even as her mind shouted denials, a traitorous longing crept into her heart. She hadn't been more than five when she and Harry had left Whitestone Manor to live with their cousin. Neither of them had ever been made to feel at home there. In the years since, they'd occupied every sort of temporary quarters.

What would it be like to have a real home again? A child to cradle in her arms and dress in lace-trimmed gowns? And a husband, she thought with a sudden ache in her chest. One who would cherish and protect her. A husband like Zach.

Sometime during this journey he'd slipped past the barriers she'd always maintained around her heart. She was an expert at flirtation. Desire, she could handle. But this aching need, this constant hunger to hear his voice or feel his arms about her, was altogether beyond her experience.

Swinging wildly between the fear she might be pregnant and worry over what she'd do if she was, Barbara shed her outer gown and curled under the covers.

Their hired coach rolled into Washington late the following afternoon. Barbara barely made it to the luxurious suite of rooms Zach had rented for them in the Arlington Hotel before snatching up the chamber pot and rushing behind a screen in the bedchamber. She was too miserable to object when he followed a few moments later and held the pot steady.

After she finished emptying her stomach, he put the pot aside and drew a silver traveling flask from the pocket of his military greatcoat. The drizzle that seemed to have followed them all the way to Washington spotted the wool cape of the coat and added a damp sheen to his lashes and eyebrows.

"Here, drink this."

Mortified, she sat back on her heels. The brandy burned her throat but took away the vile aftertaste. "I'm sorry. I'm not usually such a poor traveler."

"No need for apologies. Do you want me to fetch a physician?"

"Goodness, no! I just needed to empty my stomach of those johnnycakes we had for lunch. I thought at the time they tasted odd. The grease used to fry them must have been a bit rancid."

He helped her to her feet, concern stamped on his strong, chiseled face. "Are you sure that's what caused you to become ill? Rancid grease?"

"That and all these days of jolting about in a coach." She couldn't meet his eyes. "I'm fine now. Truly."

"You'd better rest while I present my credentials at the office of the secretary of war and arrange a meeting with him and the president. I'll return in time to take you to dinner, if you're up to it."

"I'm sure I will be. And while you're gone, I'll wash away all these days of travel." She spoke rapidly, too rapidly, trying to cover her embarrassment and dismay. "Would you ask Hattie to go down to the kitchens and fetch some hot water?"

"Of course."

Zach's face was thoughtful as he crossed the elegantly appointed bedchamber. He had a good idea what had sent Barbara running for the chamber pot and it wasn't rancid grease.

He was the oldest of eight children. He'd seen his mother doubled over often enough, retching up her breakfast or dinner. Unless he missed his guess, Barbara's belly would soon swell with his child. He'd tried to protect her. Done his damnedest to prevent this from happening. But every soldier knew such precautions were precarious at best. If she was with child...

A fierce, primal satisfaction raced through him at

the thought. He'd claimed her body these past weeks. Now it was time to make that claim official.

He didn't deceive himself. He knew she hadn't yet trusted him with the truth about herself or this brother of hers. But she would. She was inching closer to it each day. Each night. She didn't realize that she revealed a little more of herself each time Zach took her in his arms or tumbled her to his bed. There, she held nothing back.

His thoughts filled with Barbara, he strode into the sitting room where Hattie stood amid the pile of their luggage.

"Is she all right?"

"Right enough," Zach answered.

"That's three times now she's lost her dinner."

She darted a glance at the open door to the bedroom. Her tight, pinched expression told Zach she'd hit on the same explanation for Barbara's temperamental stomach.

She would know, he thought. She tended to Barbara's most intimate female needs. He was tempted to ask when her mistress had bled last, if only to confirm his own suspicion, but curbed the impulse. The possibility Barbara might be pregnant was something she and Zach should discuss privately, if and when it proved to be true.

"Barbara wishes to wash and rest before dinner. I'll carry in the luggage if you'll go down to the kitchens and fetch some water."

* * *

Hattie stumbled out of the suite, almost blind with rage.

The bitch was breeding. She'd swell up like a mangy barn dog, drop her whelp and keep the lieutenant tied to her forever.

Hattie should have stuffed a pillow over her face when she'd had the chance. Or found some excuse to lure the whore onto the deck of the *Star* or the *John Hawley*. Now she would pay the price for wasting all these days and nights.

Fury pumping through her veins, she stumbled down the hotel's narrow back stairs. Sounds of hearty laughter and the clink of pewter on pewter came from the taproom at the front of the establishment. She followed the hiss and sizzle of roasting meat to the kitchen at the rear.

After the cold outside and the narrow, drafty stairs, the heat from the roaring fireplace hit her like a blow. She was gasping for breath, when a cook's helper hefted a tray heaped with platters on his shoulder and hurried her way.

"What do you need, missus?"

"Hot water for…" She almost choked. "For my mistress."

"Darcy!" He shouted to the girl basting a spitted haunch of mutton. "Help this woman."

Hattie's lip curled. The girl was a slattern. Her hair hung in greasy tangles. Food stained her apron, and mud crusted the ragged hem of her homespun skirt. Hattie waited in tight-lipped silence while the slut ladled water from the black kettle hanging on the hock.

"There you be, missus."

Hattie took the pitcher without so much as a word. She had one foot on the stairs when she realized she needed more than hot water. She needed a way to rid Zach of the woman who could never love him the way she did.

A kitchen slut like this one would surely know the direction of an apothecary or a midwife. Or, she thought, a rat-catcher.

Slowly, she turned back.

16

≈≈≈≈≈≈≈

"I asked the kitchen maid to make you some chamomile tea. It'll settle your stomach."

Barbara propped herself up on one elbow as her maid entered the bedroom carrying a silver tray.

"Thank you. I'll take the tea and gladly, although my stomach seems to have ceased its acrobatics."

Hattie poured the fragrant brew into a china cup decorated in a delicate Blue Willow pattern. Familiar now with Barbara's tastes, she added milk and two spoons of sugar.

"The heaves will come back," she predicted as she handed her mistress the tea. "They most always do during these early months."

The china cup rattled on its saucer. Barbara's gaze flew up to lock with the brunette's.

"You know?"

"That you're increasing? How could I not? You've not bled since I started to tend to your underlinens. I didn't think to count the weeks until you tossed up your dinner a few times, though."

"Nor did I," Barbara admitted.

She still couldn't bring herself to accept the possibility. She was a few weeks late, that's all. Hardly surprising given the worry that had dogged her since Harry's arrest, not to mention all the plotting and scheming.

"I went to the apothecary while you were resting," the maid said after a moment. Digging a hand into her skirt pocket, she withdrew a twist of oiled paper. "My mam tossed up her breakfast every time she took pregnant. The only thing that helped her was a touch of cowbane in her tea."

Barbara eyed the twist with some misgiving. Cowbane was a common remedy for cramps and other women's illnesses. It was also a deadly poison. Rat-catchers spread it in sewers and garbage-strewn gutters to kill off the ever-present swarms of rodents.

"Don't take more than a pinch," Hattie warned, confirming the herb's lethal power.

"Thank you, but I don't need it now. I'm feeling much better."

"It's best to take precautions. Especially since you're sitting down to dinner with the president tonight."

"What's that?"

"Zach…" Flushing, Hattie caught herself. "Lieutenant Morgan sent a note. The sergeant who delivered it said he was to wait and escort you to the White House for dinner. He's downstairs now, in the taproom."

"Where is this note?"

Hattie retrieved a folded piece of parchment from the silver tray. The lines inside were penned with a bold, slashing stroke.

Barbara—

My apologies for this hastily scribbled missive. I'm still in meetings with the secretary of war. He's informed the president of my arrival…and the fact that I intend to take leave of my military duties to accompany you to London. I fear General Jackson isn't best pleased with the news. He desires to meet you and invites us to join him for dinner this evening.

If you feel well enough, Marine Sergeant Dougherty will escort you. Dinner is at seven. Formal dress isn't required. We'll likely sit down to a dinner of boiled potatoes and a saddle of sirloin served rare and in the company of a few chosen intimates.

Yours,

Zach

The very thought of a red, bleeding slab of beef made Barbara's stomach lurch.

She was in no mood to meet with anyone, much less this homespun president. All she wanted to do was lie back down, draw the covers over her head and cower until she knew how to handle the possibility she might be breeding. Stubborn pride wouldn't allow it. She had her faults—any number of them—but she wasn't a coward.

"Set the tea on the dressing table," she told Hattie. "I'll put in a pinch of cowbane, as you suggest, and sip it while you brush out my hair. First I must decide what to wear."

Almost dancing with glee, Hattie took the tea to the dressing table as instructed. This was better than she'd hoped for. With her back to Lady Barbara, she opened the paper twist. A tap of a finger dumped half the contents into the porcelain cup. Quickly, she screwed the paper tight again and laid it beside the saucer.

That ought to be enough to kill the stupid cow *and* her unborn calf. If it didn't, Hattie wouldn't take the blame. The Englishwoman would add another pinch and suffer the consequences wrought by her own hand.

The first cramp struck Barbara just after her marine escort had handed her cloak to an attendant at the presidential palace. She placed her hand lightly on the arm the sergeant offered and took only a step or two before she faltered.

Pain sliced into her. Gasping, she dug her fingers into the marine's sleeve.

"Ma'am?"

As quickly as it had come, the agony eased. With a shaky smile, she loosened her clawlike grip.

"Forgive me. I feared I'd caught my heel on my skirts for a moment."

He accepted the ready explanation and continued his measured tread down a marble hallway that might have been magnificent if not for the muddy boot prints dirtying its floors.

Despite the advancing evening hour, people of all descriptions lingered in the hall and crowded an antechamber hung with red twill satin. Frontiersmen in buckskin rubbed shoulders with gentlemen in frock coats and snowy cravats. A beefy, red-faced farmer shared an alcove with a barrister in black robes and a powdered wig. Merchants were scattered throughout the rooms, many with cases containing their goods tucked under their arms.

They were petitioners, Barbara supposed, come to see their president just as British subjects did their king.

"The general keeps late hours since his wife died," her escort explained when she commented on the crowd. "Often as not, he'll take appointments until midnight or later."

Her curiosity about the president she'd soon meet grew. She knew little about him, only the bits and pieces of gossip she'd picked up since arriving in America. Like Zach, Jackson was both lawyer and soldier. He'd served as congressman and judge and had commanded the Cotton Balers at the Battle of New Orleans. As president he fought to enhance the power of his office. He was also fiercely determined to remove the eastern tribes to lands west of the Mississippi…despite being an avowed friend of the Cherokee and father to an adopted Creek son.

Rumor had it that he'd fought any number of duels to protect the honor of his late wife, whom he'd married and lived with for several years in the mistaken belief the Virginia legislature had granted her first husband a divorce.

In person, Andrew Jackson proved every bit as intimidating as his reputation. He was a tall man, well over six feet, and whipcord lean. His piercing blue eyes looked out from under bushy white eyebrows as Barbara approached on the arm of her escort. She was unsure whether she should curtsy. American customs were so odd. The president resolved her dilemma by thrusting out his hand.

"So Lady Barbara." He gave her hand a hearty shake. "What's this about you dragging one of my most promising young officers away from his duties to accompany you to London?"

She could hardly admit she had no intention of

traveling to London. "Lieutenant Morgan made the decision to take a leave of absence without consulting me, sir. You must speak to him about it."

"I have. Blistered his ears about it, as a matter of fact."

He leveled his quelling stare on the young officer under discussion, at that moment making his way across the room in their direction.

"Just make sure you send him back to us. Zach has all the heart of his father. Sergeant Major Morgan served under me at New Orleans, you know."

"So I've been informed, sir."

"I need men like Daniel Morgan and his sons. I'm depending on them to keep Indian Country from flaming up like a tinderbox."

"That grows more difficult with each new wave of immigrants," Zach said, joining them. "Both white *and* red."

His glance roamed Barbara's face, as if to verify that she'd thrown off her indisposition. She smiled and accepted the glass of wine a steward offered her. Reassured, Zach gave his attention once again to the president.

"Settlers with false quit-claim deeds are causing almost as much trouble as the Osage and Pawnee."

"I know it," the president grumbled. "As fast as my treasury agents nose out one illegal printing press, another starts turning out counterfeit banknotes and deeds."

"If we don't stem this tide of white immigrants," Zach warned, "none of the tribes will believe we intend to honor the boundaries your commissioners negotiate."

"I'm well aware of that," Jackson snapped. "I appointed the commission, after all, and drafted their charter with my own hand."

He drew in a breath and turned to Barbara with a rueful smile.

"People think me ruthless for being so determined to enforce the provisions of the Indian Removal Act."

They thought him more than ruthless. In her short weeks in America, she'd heard him described as everything from a self-serving politician desiring only to appease his white voters to a cruel despot out to destroy the peoples his government had negotiated countless treaties with.

"Moving the eastern tribes is the only way I can guarantee them freedom to live according to their customs," he explained. "The state legislatures—Alabama, Georgia, South Carolina—are determined to exercise jurisdiction over their populations. Once they do, their indigenous tribes will lose all power and identity. Chief Justice Marshall, damn him, has buried his head too deep in the law books to recognize that bitter inevitability."

Others drifted over to join the conversation.

"The Cherokee might have made the Supreme Court decision stick if gold hadn't been discovered on their land in north Georgia," a rotund general with bushy side-whiskers put in. "Now there are lynchings and burnings every night, and the governor refuses to use the militia to stop the mayhem."

"It'll bode ill for the Union if we're forced to send in federal troops," another murmured. "We'll find ourselves at war with the State of Georgia."

"With the rest of the southern states, as well," Jackson predicted grimly. "They're already threatening to secede if the abolitionists push legislation through Congress outlawing slavery."

Obviously burdened by the responsibilities of his office, the president thrust a hand into his thick white mane.

"Damned if I'm not at point nonplus. To save this cobbled-together Union of ours, I must support slavery, which I abhor, and evict our native peoples from their homes and lands. If anyone knows a better path to tread, I wish they would tell me!"

None of the powerful men present offered an alternative course, and Barbara sensed the destiny of the native peoples Jackson referred to had already been written in stone. Or blood.

It would be left to men like Daniel and Zach Morgan to determine which. The president had indicated as much, and Zach used the moment to push a cause Barbara knew was dear to his heart.

"Honoring the boundaries your commissioners negotiate is the only way to maintain peace in Indian

Country, and we must use all means necessary to keep white settlers from encroaching on those boundaries. That will require more troops. Mounted troops."

"Yes, yes, you rangers have proved your worth out there on the prairies."

Jackson paused and hooked his thumbs in his waistcoat. Rocking back on his heels, he nodded to a bushy-bearded gentleman in a rusty black frock coat.

"I've instructed the secretary of war here to prepare a request for establishment of a regiment of dragoons. We'll submit the request to Congress when it reconvenes in January. That news should please you, Lieutenant Morgan."

Zach gave a whoop of joy. "It does indeed!"

The president's grim expression eased. Even the solemn secretary of war smiled.

"Colonel Arbuckle recommends you be given a captaincy in the new regiment," Jackson said. "I concur. I want you back from your leave of absence in time to help recruit and train these dragoons."

"Yes, sir!"

The confidence the president placed in Zach both amazed and delighted Barbara. She couldn't imagine anyone better suited to the task they'd just given him. As Jackson had pointed out, Zach knew Indian Country. He also understood better than most the challenges the dragoons would face when they deployed to the frontier. More importantly, he brought intelligence and compassion to his duties.

If she *had* to be pregnant, Barbara decided as her gaze slid over his tanned, handsome face and broad shoulders, she could have picked a worse father for her babe. Far worse.

With the thought, some of her worry over the possibility she might be increasing disappeared. In its place came a different emotion, something perilously akin to hope. A babe might bridge the chasm when Zach finally learned the truth about her intentions.

Assuming he believed the child his, that was.

She couldn't discount the distinct possibility he might not. After the stories he'd heard about her— and those disgusting innuendos about her relationship with Harry—how could he not think the worst? Barbara was swinging from hope to despair yet again when another cramp seized her.

The pain sliced into her bowels like a saber. It was all she could do not to gasp or double over. Clenching her teeth, she stared blindly at the portrait hanging on the far wall until the agony lessened.

"Lady Barbara?"

She let out a shaky breath and blinked to clear her vision. "I beg your pardon, sir?"

"I was inquiring whether I may escort you to the table. I believe the cooks are ready to serve."

Lord, yes! All she wanted now was to conclude this evening as swiftly as possible. Forcing a gracious nod, she allowed the president to seat her on his right.

She soon saw Zach had characterized the general's tastes accurately. Servants presented platters of rare sirloin, stewed potatoes and something they called fritters. She choked down two bites of the beef, but the fried corn stuck in her throat.

When had it grown so uncomfortably warm? And why had the president chosen to seat her so close to flames dancing behind the richly embroidered fire screen? Discreetly, she daubed at the perspiration dewing her upper lip and tried to follow the quicksilver changes in conversation.

She thought she'd succeeded in hiding her distress until she met Zach's eyes. A small frown creased his forehead. When he cocked his head in silent inquiry, Barbara couldn't disguise her discomfort any longer. She pressed her napkin to her lips again and sent him a pleading look. Instantly, he pushed back his chair and addressed President Jackson.

"I know you'll understand if I don't stand on ceremony with you, sir. I fear Lady Barbara may still be feeling the after effects of our long journey and is gallantly trying to hide her distress. May I beg leave to take her back to the hotel?"

"Of course, of course!"

Jumping up, Jackson himself pulled Barbara's chair back for her. She rose, took two steps, and clamped both arms around her waist.

She couldn't fight the wrenching pain this time. Caught in its vicious vise, she bent double. The painted canvas covering the floor blurred. She would have fallen flat on her face if not for Zach. His hands steadied her. His voice rumbled soothingly in her ear.

"It's all right, darling. Retch if you need to."

Perspiration stung her eyes. She was hot. So very hot.

"I…I just need air."

Zach scooped her into his arms. She leaned into him, still in the grip of the awful agony. From a great distance she heard the president instruct Zach to carry her immediately to an upstairs bedchamber.

"I'll send for my personal physician. In the meantime, Mrs. Camden, the head housekeeper, can assist you."

By the time Zach laid her on a massive four-poster, the cramps were attacking Barbara with unrelenting brutality. His face was an indistinct blur. The canopy above him spun crazily. She wrapped her arms around her middle and kept trying to curl into a tight ball while he stripped off her outer garments and loosened her corset.

Vaguely, she heard someone else bustle in. Heard, too, a swift, indrawn hiss.

"That's blood on her petticoats, sir."

"I see it."

At that point the anguish consumed Barbara. With an inarticulate sound, she gave herself up to it.

17

Barbara drifted in that half state between slumber and wakefulness. Her mind foggy, her body limp, she tried to pinpoint the faint clicking sound that penetrated her sleepy haze.

It was sleet, she decided after a while. Hitting the windowpanes.

For a moment or two she imagined herself a child again, tucked warm and snug in her bed, while rain danced against the leaded panes of Whitestone Manor.

But Whitestone was gone. Sold to creditors after her father's death on the dueling field. She had no home. Neither she nor Harry.

Harry.

Harry was in trouble. He needed her.

And Zach. Where was Zach?

Barbara tried to open her eyes. Her lids felt as

though they were glued together. She forced them up with a small grunt.

Something stirred at the sound. A pale blur drifted through the darkness and hovered at her side. She thought at first it was a ghost, some specter from the grave waiting to claim her. Dark eyes burned in a face shadowed in shades of gray. She cringed back against the pillows, but couldn't escape.

An arm slid under her neck, raised her up a few inches. Something cool touched her lips. She tried to turn her head, heard a deep voice command her to drink.

The next time she woke, the shadows were gone. Thin slices of sunlight teased their way through drawn drapes and filled the room with weak, watery light.

Barbara stared at the gold tassels decorating red velvet drapes for long moments before dragging her gaze to the portrait hanging on a wall covered in crimson silk. A bewigged gentleman dressed in the style of twenty years ago stared back at her somberly. She didn't recognize him or the velvet drapes, but she was sure those silver-backed brushes on the dressing table were hers. As was the valise sitting on the floor beside the table. She fretted about both until a more pressing concern gradually took precedence.

She tried to throw off her heavy covers, but they weighted her down. The best she could manage was a restless stir. The movement was enough to summon a round, red-faced woman to her bedside.

"Well, then!" Her cheerful countenance matched her bracing tone. "You're awake."

"Who...?" She swiped her tongue along lips as dry as parchment. "Who are you?"

"Mrs. Camden. I'm head housekeeper here at the White House. I've been helping tend to you. You've been quite ill, m'dear. Quite ill indeed. Here, take a drink of this."

Propping Barbara up with a stout arm, the housekeeper held a glass filled with a milky liquid to her lips. The concoction tasted of cool, refreshing mint, but the mere act of swallowing it brought tears to her eyes.

"I know, I know." Clucking sympathetically, Mrs. Camden eased her patient back to the pillows. "Your throat aches something fierce. And no wonder. You retched for hours after Dr. Armbruster administered that purge to empty your stomach."

Bits of it came back to Barbara now. The swirl of unfamiliar faces. The horrid, endless vomiting. The pain. Dear God above, the pain! The mere memory of it popped beads of sweat out on her temples.

"Shall I bathe your face?" her housekeeper asked. "You'll feel more the thing, I promise you."

There was a more pressing concern that needed tending to first. "Chamber...pot," Barbara croaked.

"Yes, of course. Here, I'll assist you."

Her movements were as shaky and awkward as a new foal's. When she flopped back onto the pillows, the room spun. Gulping, Barbara closed her eyes and prayed the awful sickness wouldn't attack once again.

"You were fortunate Dr. Armbruster lives but two blocks away and arrived as quickly as he did."

Bustling about, the housekeeper dipped a cloth in a china washbasin and wrung it out.

"You really should be more careful with cowbane, m'dear. A pinch or two to relieve cramps is fine when you have your monthlies, and you certainly wouldn't be the first woman to use more to rid herself of an unwanted babe. But too much could kill you along with the babe."

Barbara heard only one word. Her babe. The child she'd only begun to suspect she might be carrying. In an instinctive gesture as old as time, she wrapped protective arms across her stomach.

"It's...gone?"

"No, m'dear." Gently, Mrs. Camden drew the cool cloth over her patient's face and neck. "You bled some, but didn't pass it."

Like a bird on the wing, Barbara soared from despair to blinding joy. She didn't understand how the possibility she carried a child had come to consume her in such a short space of time. Or why she felt such relief that she hadn't lost it. She'd sort through these whirlwind emotions later. For now, all that mattered was that the child had remained lodged in her womb.

"It's difficult, I know, you being unmarried and a lady at that," the housekeeper said with another sympathetic cluck. "But such things happen. Take heart that waistlines are still high enough to hide a swollen belly for as long as you've a mind to."

She dipped the cloth in the china bowl and wrung it out again.

"Not that you'd need to hide it. From the way Lieutenant Morgan insisted on helping tend to you, a blind man could see how the wind blows with him. He'll do the right thing by you, m'dear. If that's what you desire, of course."

At the moment, Barbara didn't know *what* she desired, except perhaps another swallow of that cool, soothing drink.

"Whatever you decide, though, don't resort to cowbane again. It's too dangerous."

She wanted to protest she'd put only a pinch in her tea. A mere dusting of the dried, grayish-green leaves. Her throat ached too much to form the words.

"There." The older woman surveyed her handiwork. "I'll just brush your hair and help you into a clean nightdress, shall I, before Lieutenant Morgan returns. I insisted he go down and take some breakfast," she added with a confiding smile. "Other than a quick trip to the hotel to fetch your things, he hasn't left your side for more than a few minutes at a time."

* * *

When Zach rapped on the door to the bed-chamber, Barbara had downed the rest of the mint-flavored liquid and could speak in something more than a croak. With Mrs. Camden's assistance, she struggled to a sitting position in the wide four-poster. The housekeeper propped another pillow behind her before hurrying over to admit the lieutenant.

Barbara's first thought was that he looked as wretched as she felt. Red rimmed his eyes, and fatigue had carved deep furrows on either side of his mouth. He'd obviously shaved, but his uniform coat showed considerable wear and his stock was tied with something less than its usual precision.

He crossed the room to where she lay and took her hand. The warmth of his palm was infinitely comforting. His shuttered expression somewhat less so.

"How do you feel?"

"Disgustingly weak."

"You'll get your strength back fast enough," Mrs. Camden predicted cheerfully. "I'll go down to the kitchens, shall I, and have Cook prepare you a hearty stew."

She left Zach standing beside the bed. Barbara gripped his hand, as if to draw from his strength.

"You gave us quite a scare," he said slowly.

"So I've been told."

"Thankfully, Dr. Armbruster guessed at once

you'd eaten something that violently disagreed with you and purged your stomach."

His eyes were hooded as they searched her face.

"We didn't know what that something was until I went back to the hotel and Hattie showed me the cowbane she'd procured for you."

So that's how Mrs. Camden knew of it. Barbara had wondered, but until this moment hadn't put her thoughts together.

"Hattie said she warned you to be careful with it."

"Yes, she did. It appears I sadly underestimated the herb's effect. I'm…I'm mortified to have caused such a fuss."

He withdrew his hand from hers. She missed its warmth instantly.

"Is that what bothers you, Barbara? You caused a fuss?"

"That, of course, and…"

She picked at the red coverlet, wondering how much he knew, how much he guessed. Mrs. Camden had assumed Barbara had taken the cowbane to abort an unwanted babe. Did Zach think the same? Agonizing over what to tell him, she let the moment for truth slide past.

Her silence heaped coals on the anger burning in Zach's gut. Didn't the woman realize how close she'd come to death?

He'd held her while she twisted and moaned, had forced her jaws open while Armbruster poured that vile purge down her throat. During the torturous hours that followed, she'd drenched him with her sweat and near covered him in vomit.

Neither had bothered him. He was a soldier. A frontiersman. Dysentery and cholera and yellow fever regularly swept through the ranks. Zach had assisted the surgeons treating his troops in garrison and tended to their wounds himself on the march. More than once, he'd pushed protruding bones or spilled intestines back inside gaping wounds. He would have sworn nothing Barbara did could give him a disgust of her.

Then a tearful Hattie had handed him a half-empty paper twist and a folded oilskin packet.

That Barbara would risk her life to rid herself of his child he could understand, if not condone. That she could sit there, look him in the eye and allow more lies to pile up between them drove a sharpened stake right through his gut.

"I brought your valise from the hotel."

Perplexed by his abrupt change of subject, she glanced at the tapestry-covered grip.

"So I see."

"This was inside it."

Reaching into the breast pocket of his uniform coat, Zach withdrew the oilskin packet and dropped it on the coverlet. He refused to feel so much as a flicker of remorse when Barbara's cheeks lost the little color that had returned to them. Like a rabbit confronted by a hissing rattlesnake, she stared at the small square in frozen horror.

After several moments of stark silence, she lifted her gaze to his. "Did...? Did you read it?"

She saw the answer in his face.

"What a stupid question," she said in a low, strangled voice. "Of course you did."

"How did you come by that document?"

When she looked away, Zach's fury slipped its tether. Curling his hand under her chin, he brought her face back to his.

"No more lies, Barbara! I want the truth, if you have it in you."

Her face was paper white, her eyes wide. The spark of defiance that kindled in their turquoise depths killed any regret Zach felt at handling her so roughly.

"Where did you get that affidavit, woman?"

"Harry lifted it from a corpse."

"Christ!"

He might have known. Harry. It always came back to Harry. Zach was close to hating the man.

"Did he kill for this bit of parchment?"

"No!"

The denial was instantaneous, the shock behind it convincing enough for Zach to ease his hold on her chin. Ruthlessly, he suppressed a twinge of conscience as she sank back against the pillows.

"He took it from a French émigré," she said wearily, "imprisoned for indebtedness. The man was chained next to Harry on the ship transporting them to Bermuda. The man took ill, became delirious and ranted about the...the half-breed savage who'd inherited the fortune that rightfully should have come to his family."

Zach's jaw clenched. He'd needed only a single reading of the bishop of Reims' sworn statement to grasp its import. With a few strokes of his pen, the bishop had invalidated his mother's first marriage and dispossessed her of her inheritance from Henri Chartier.

He said nothing, though. He wanted to hear the story from Barbara's lips.

"Just before this émigré died," she said in a voice that grew hoarser by the moment, "he whispered to my brother that he'd sewn a document into the lining of his coat. One that would prove his claim. Harry stole it that same night."

That's how it had happened. Harry *swore* that's how it had happened. Barbara wouldn't allow herself to doubt it.

"So your brother decided to claim this fortune and appointed you his emissary."

It wasn't a question, but she answered anyway. "Yes."

She should have felt relief that the truth was out at last. Instead, a great weight seemed to have settled on Barbara's chest. She knew the crushing ache had much to do with the coldness in Zach's eyes.

"Enlighten me on one point. You traveled to Fort Gibson armed with what you believed was the means to dispossess my mother. Why didn't you use it?"

"I intended to."

The admission sapped the little strength Barbara had regained. Dragging in a shaky breath, she struggled to continue. "When I learned you'd read the law, I guessed you would fight my claim in the courts."

"You had the right of that!"

"I didn't have time for a lengthy court battle. Harry's situation is too desperate. I decided to play on your mother's sympathies and take what I could get."

She didn't realize she'd given away the rest of her scheme until she saw awareness dawn on Zach's face.

"You couldn't take the time for a court battle," he repeated. "I must assume, then, you never intended to return to London, either."

"No."

Feeling almost as miserable as she had at the president's dining table, Barbara wanted only to finish this ordeal.

"I intended to cash your bank draft, leave you here in Washington and take ship for Bermuda. I thought… I still think…to bribe the guards and buy Harry's release."

"First, though, you had to rid yourself of the annoyance of a pregnancy."

"No! I wasn't...I didn't..."

"Your lies won't wash this time," he snarled. "I saw the paper twist containing the powdered cowbane. It was half-empty."

"But I used only a pinch! I swear, I..."

The anguished protest died in her throat. He didn't believe her. She could see it in his eyes. Why should he? She'd fed him nothing but falsehoods since the first moment they'd met.

Bone-weary and too weak to shield herself against the scathing contempt in his face, she almost sobbed with relief when Mrs. Camden returned bearing a silver tray.

"I've brought you a nice bracing chicken stew."

Her sharp glance went from Barbara to Zach and back again. If she noted the tension that coiled like a living thing between them, she made no mention of it.

"This will put some color back in your cheeks." Setting the tray on a gateleg table, she lifted the lid on a china tureen and sniffed appreciatively. "It's my own recipe. Lieutenant, shall I ladle you out a bowl, as well? Cook said you never got a chance to finish your breakfast."

"No. Thank you."

Without another word to Barbara, Zach strode out of the room. Mrs. Camden noted his stiff-shouldered exit with raised eyebrows and busied herself with the ladle.

* * *

When Zach returned late in the afternoon, Barbara was fully dressed and sitting in an armchair. Two bowls of hearty chicken stew, some dry biscuits and a long, if troubled, nap had restored her strength and a good measure of her spirit.

She'd make Zach understand. She hadn't deliberately set out to hurt him. Nor had she intended to fall in love with him. He *must* see she'd done all she had out of sheer desperation.

He didn't give her the chance to make him understand anything. Politely dismissing Mrs. Camden, he turned a look on Barbara as hard as slate.

"I rode down to the docks at Alexandria and hired a sloop."

The unexpectedness of it took her breath away. He'd hired a boat to take her to Bermuda. Despite all, he'd done that for her.

"I suspect it's a rumrunner," he warned. "You'll find the accommodations something less than elegant."

"That doesn't matter. If you'll just take me to get my bags…"

"Hattie packed them. I sent them on to the sloop just before I put her in a coach."

"A coach?"

"She's on her way back to Indian Country. I would have sent her to her home in Georgia, but she said she had no one there. In any case, I won't have her involved with bribery and prison escape."

Barbara chewed on the inside of her lip. Of course he couldn't allow Hattie to take such risks. Nor could he take them himself. Fighting the weight of the stone pressing against her heart, she tried to thank him.

"I don't want your thanks," he said coldly. "I want only one thing from you, and I'll claim that after we return from Bermuda."

"We?" she echoed, stunned.

"We. I'm sailing with you."

"You...? You would do this for me?"

"I gave my word I would aid you," he ground out, "but there's a price attached to my services."

"I understand. I'm to destroy the bishop's affidavit."

"I don't give a damn about that scrap of paper. You have as much chance of making it stand in the courts as you do convincing me you would destroy it."

She flinched at that. "What price do you want me to pay, then?"

"If you *are* carrying a child—and if I can bring myself to believe it's mine—you'll return with me to Indian Country and remain there until you birth the babe."

Her chin lifted. She guessed the answer he would give, but had to ask the question.

"And after the babe is born?"

"The child stays at Morgan's Falls. You…"

He rolled his shoulders in a shrug that cut almost as deep as his words.

"You can take yourself to hell for all I care."

18

Palm Cove, Bermuda
December 1832

God was punishing her for her sins.

Barbara was sure of it.

He was also seeing she paid mightily for them.

Cold, shaking and miserable, she huddled under a scratchy blanket in her bunk aboard the *Chesapeake* and fought the bile that kept rising in her throat. The sloop had dropped anchor in this secluded cove hours ago, but the accursed waves continued to slap against the hull.

Moaning, she rolled over and buried her face in a lumpy pillow smelling strongly of old sweat, saltwater and mildew. How could her stomach continue to torment her? She'd put nothing in it for close on to two weeks except brackish water and dry ship's biscuits.

There was no question in her mind now. She was pregnant. Miserably, wretchedly pregnant.

As if the nausea that struck her at unexpected times both day and night wasn't torture enough, the voyage from Washington to Bermuda had turned into a howling, horrific hell. Winter storms had churned up the Atlantic and tossed the *Chesapeake* about like a child's toy. Barbara had spent almost the entire voyage with her arms wrapped around a wooden slop bucket.

Little enough penance for her sins.

Or so Zach had suggested the first time he'd found her, green-faced and miserable. Cursing, he'd shoved the slop bucket at her, told her they were in for some weather and slammed out again.

He'd returned later. As he had throughout this hellish voyage, he'd forced Barbara to down fresh water and dry biscuits. He'd emptied the slop bucket. He'd even roped her to her bunk when the seas grew particularly vicious.

Not because he cared whether she wallowed in her own mess, she knew. Because of the babe.

Another wave knocked against the hull. The bunk tilted. Her stomach tilted with it.

"Ohhh, God!"

Where was Zach? Why hadn't he returned from reconnoitering the Royal Dockyards, where the convict hulks were moored? When would he deem it safe for them to show their faces in St. George's or Hamilton Township?

She understood the need for caution. She truly did. They intended to engineer a felon's escape, after all. She hadn't needed Zach's curt reminder they could both end up in the hulks beside Harry if they made a single misstep. She'd keep her head about her. She would! If only she could get off this damn boat.

To her infinite relief, she heard the thump of boots hitting the boards above her a short time later. The heavy tread had to belong to Zach. The motley crew of the *Chesapeake* wore rope-soled shoes to keep their footing on the slippery decks.

Throwing off the damp blankets, Barbara swung off the bunk onto shaky legs. She straightened her coat and dragged her fingers through her hair to put it in some sort of order. She could only imagine the rat's nest it must resemble. She didn't have a mirror—or a maid, for that matter—to set the tangled mass to rights.

A moment later, Zach shoved open the door to the cubbyhole that passed for her cabin and cut right to the heart of things.

"I've word of your brother."

"He's…? He's alive?"

"Yes."

Her knees went weak. She dropped onto the unmade bunk, fighting a rush of hot tears.

All these months Barbara had clung stubbornly to the belief Harry would survive the filth and pestilence and exhaustion that claimed one of every three prisoners sentenced to the hulks. Only now did she realize how thin and tenuous her belief had been.

"Did you speak with him?" she asked around the lump in her throat.

"No. He's out on a work gang. But I've arranged a meeting with the prison superintendent. The intelligence I've gathered suggests he may well be our most likely candidate for a bribe. We'll see if he'll accept one from Lady Barbara Chamberlain's lawyer."

That was their plan, such as it was. Zach had stashed away his uniform and donned civilian clothes. He would play the role of the barrister Barbara had hired to help her plead her brother's case. He would also provide the necessary funds for a bribe.

Given the rampant corruption, thievery and brutality in the British penal system, it was only a matter of finding a guard or warden willing to accept the bribe. Zach certainly hadn't wasted any time doing so.

"We're to be at the superintendent's office in an hour," he informed her.

"An hour! However did you arrange a meeting so soon?"

"I sent my card tucked inside a twenty-pound

note." His mouth took a sardonic twist. "An appropriate entrée for a lawyer, don't you think?"

"Quite appropriate."

"I've hired a carriage. It's waiting for us ashore. Wear your blue silk gown."

She blinked at the abrupt command. "The blue silk is evening dress. A smart wool walking dress and warm coat would be more appropriate."

"Wear the blue silk, and pull the neckline low." He raked a mocking glance over her bedraggled face and figure. "I'm counting on the seductive Miss Chamberlain to distract the superintendent during our negotiations."

Her chin came up. "I won't mistake that for a compliment."

"Very wise of you."

Zach left her standing stiff with anger. Good, he thought. At least she was on her feet. God knew she'd spent most of this damnable voyage on her knees.

He, on the other hand, had spent most of it topside, with the rain and salt spray lashing his face. The wild winter storms had suited his mood exactly. They'd also whipped away most of his anger and disgust at himself for thinking he could win Barbara's trust.

Or her love. That she reserved for this brother of hers, and only for him. Zach knew now she'd let nothing stand in the way of winning Harry's freedom.

Well, she'd pay the price for that freedom. He'd see she held to her promise to return to Indian Country until she birthed the babe. After that, she could go wherever the winds took her.

Ducking his head to avoid the low crossbeams, he entered the dark, dank area that served as galley, crew quarters and main cabin. The one-eyed seadog who went by the name of Captain Jiggs Throckmorton greeted him with an offer to share the contents of the rum keg lashed to the masthead.

"Something to warm your insides, Morgan?"

Nodding, Zach shrugged out of his wet greatcoat.

"I'll have a tot, too," the first mate put in.

The two were a scurvy pair and not above using their fists on the four other crewmen to keep them in line. Zach wouldn't trust any of them farther than he could spit, but they were just the sort of rogues he needed for this venture.

Straddling a bench, he tossed back the tot Throckmorton passed him. The potent rum went down with a fiery warmth. Welcoming its heat, Zach studied the navigational chart rolled out on the greasy planks of the mess table. The focus of his attention was Ireland Island, a narrow finger of rock at the westernmost tip of the island chain that constituted the Crown Colony of Bermuda. Ireland Island lay directly across the Great Sound from Hamilton Township. More to the point, the island housed the Royal Naval Base and Dockyards.

The base served as the headquarters for the British Atlantic Fleet—the same fleet that had sailed up the Chesapeake and sacked Washington during the War of 1812. Zach had been little more than a boy at the time, just old enough to remember the final Battle of New Orleans and share his father's fierce dislike of lobsterbacks.

He might dislike them, but he didn't underestimate their military skills or their firepower. His brief foray into town had yielded the information that civilian guards administered the convict hulks and assigned the prisoners to work gangs. Royal marines guarded the gangs when they labored at the naval base. If bribes didn't work, Zach might well have to snatch a convict out from under the noses of those well-trained sharpshooters.

"While Lady Barbara and I are gone, I want you to move the *Chesapeake* and anchor her here."

He thumped a finger on Mangrove Bay, close to the small drawbridge connecting Ireland Island to neighboring Somerset Island.

"That's on the Atlantic side," Throckmorton protested. "If we anchor there, we'll take a battering from wind and waves for sure."

"I scouted the bay. It's riddled with small coves and ringed by thick stands of mangrove. They'll protect you from the wind and waves. How long will it take you to make the anchorage?"

The puckered skin covering Throckmorton's right

eye socket squeezed into tight lines. His left eye studied the chart. "The tide's running and the wind's from the east. I'd say we'll drop anchor easy by nightfall."

"Good enough. Wait for us there."

"How long?"

"Until noon tomorrow. If all goes as planned, we'll come aboard before then."

"With this extra cargo you said we'd be haulin' back with us?"

"That's my intent."

Letting the chart roll up with a snap, Zach shoved it aside and dug into his greatcoat pocket for his pistol. The Damascus-etched steel barrel gleamed in the light that filtered through the open hatch.

While the two interested seamen looked on, he extracted the ebony ramrod and used the iron worm at its tip to clean the barrel. That done, he rammed home a shot and added powder to the pan. The pistol went back into his coat pocket, along with a leather cartridge case containing extra powder and shot.

Throckmorton rubbed a finger alongside his nose. "Lookin' to have a bit of sport tonight, Morgan?"

His mate answered before Zach could. Whistling through the rotten stumps of his teeth, he dug an elbow into the captain's ribs and jerked his chin toward the narrow passageway.

"More than a bit, I'd say."

Zach followed the two men's glances and took a roundhouse punch to the chest.

Barbara was making her way down the passageway. Sick and wretched, she still put every other female he knew in the shade. Combed, corseted and gowned in shimmering blue silk, the blasted woman knocked the breath back down his throat.

The silk clung to her lush curves. She'd pulled the sleeves so far down her bare shoulders, her breasts almost spilled from the bodice. She'd also rouged her cheeks and lips. The bright spots of color stood out in stark relief against skin still wan from the tortuous crossing.

She saw Zach's eyes on her. "You wanted a tart," she said icily. "You have one."

"So I do."

A half hour later, the carriage Zach had hired in town drew up at the gates of the naval base. An iron portcullis hung suspended above the narrow entry. Royal marines manned the sentry box. Zach noted both while he waited for the marine guard to verify his credentials and his appointment with the prison superintendent.

Once cleared, they were directed to a squat building apart from the naval offices and warehouses. Zach climbed out into the blustery winter afternoon and snatched at his top hat before the wind took it. Hanging on to the beaver with one hand, he reached with the other to assist Barbara from the carriage.

She put one foot on the step and froze. Her gloved hand fisted in his. "Dear God," she whispered raggedly. "They're worse than I remembered."

He followed her stricken glance to the hulks moored alongside a long stone quay. The *Dromedary* lay there, along with two other ships whose names he couldn't make out.

The great, gray behemoths bore little resemblance to the proud warships they'd once been. Their masts were gone, and pitched roofs covered their decks. They reminded Zach so vividly of the engraving of Noah's ark in his mother's Bible, he half expected a pair of giraffes to poke their heads through the roof vent.

Unlike Noah's ark, however, these converted hulks weren't intended to save or rescue. They were floating charnel houses, filled to overflowing with the refuse tossed out by the British courts. Men, women, mere children, all transported for their crimes.

The lawyer in Zach understood the expediency of using vessels no longer fit for sea duty to relieve overcrowding in prisons. The landowner in him also understood the necessity in previous years of using convict labor. America's early economy had depended on that labor. For decades tobacco planters desperate for hands to work their fields had begged the Crown to transport all able-bodied prisoners to the colonies.

The British government had responded by emptying its prisons of old, young and in-between. Zach's study of law cases had included records of a nine-year-old chimney sweep transported for pinching a bit of bacon. A twelve-year-old clog-maker sentenced to ten years for stealing her mistress's linen apron. An eighty-four-year-old widow shipped across an ocean for taking an ax handle to her feeble-minded son. The widow had hanged herself the day before the ship transporting her docked in Annapolis.

Not all those sentenced to the hulks were petty criminals, Zach reminded himself grimly. Their numbers also included dissidents who spoke out against the government, agitators and rebels.

Particularly rebels. More than ten thousand Americans captured during the war for independence had been confined to hulks anchored off New York, Charleston and Savannah. Twenty years after the war, workers constructing the Brooklyn Naval Yard discovered mass graves filled with the scattered bones of prisoners off the notorious hulk *Jersey*. Captain John Jackson, proprietor of the neighboring property, had arranged for the bones to be reinterred at his own expense. Later, public ceremonies were conducted over their common grave.

Looking now at the *Dromedary,* Zach understood

part of his reason for agreeing to help Barbara in her desperate attempt to free her brother. No man or woman should endure such filth and degradation. Not even a man such as Sir Harry Chamberlain, who'd set his sister to thievery to save his own neck.

Grasping Barbara's elbow, he turned her away from the hulks and steered her to the building housing the offices of the superintendent of prisons. A potbellied stove glowed in the corner of the outer office. A guard in a uniform with shiny buttons bearing the insignia of the prison police showed them into Superintendent Davenport's office.

The intelligence Zach had gathered during his earlier scouting expedition had pinpointed Davenport as their most likely target. Formerly warden of Newgate Prison, the man had lost that post amid some sort of scandal. He'd accepted what was apparently a demotion, had left a wife and twelve children behind in England, and arrived in Bermuda a scant six weeks ago. Judging by his watery eyes and the steady drip at the end of his brick-red nose, he had yet to acclimate to the Atlantic winds that swept across the island in winter.

"Good afternoon, Miss Chamberlain." Sniffling, the warden rounded his desk and bowed over her hand. "Have I been informed correctly? This is your second visit to Bermuda on behalf of your brother?"

A drop hung suspended from his left nostril for long seconds before splatting onto Barbara's thumb. She slid her hand free of his.

"Yes," she replied, surreptitiously swiping her thumb against her coat skirts, "it is."

"Such sisterly devotion. I'm quite impressed." His glance shifted to Zach. "And this time you bring a barrister with you."

Making a show of it, Davenport produced Zach's card from an inside uniform pocket. The twenty-pound note was still wrapped around it.

The warden tapped the card against his palm. "Do you know the penalty for attempting to bribe a prison official, Mr. Morgan?"

"That," Zach replied with a careless shrug, "is merely a token of our appreciation that you agreed to see us on such short notice."

"Indeed?"

"If I were to offer you a bribe, it would be considerably more substantial."

Another drip fell from Davenport's nose. His glance slid to the closed door. His voice dropped to a mere whisper.

"How substantial?"

Barbara's heart thumped against her stays. They were treading dangerous ground here. In an effort to control the corruption so prevalent in the British penal system, the Crown set spies to watch the gaolers who in turn watched the prisoners. The guard in the outer office might well have his ear to the door.

Zach understood the dangers as well as she did.

With the skill of a fencer dodging a thrust, he refused to let Davenport lure him into making the first offer.

"You must tell me," he murmured. "What would it take for you to assign a certain prisoner quarry duty on Somerset Island tomorrow morning?"

Scrubbing his nose with his sleeve, Davenport darted another look at the door. He was dithering, Barbara realized. Or trying to calculate how much he could squeeze out of them. She didn't need Zach's sardonic glance to know it was time she slipped into her assigned role.

"It's rather warm in here." She lifted a casual hand to the buttons at her throat. "Do you mind if I remove my wrap?"

"Not at all. Allow me to assist you."

"Thank you."

Turning, she let the warden lift the coat from her shoulders. She heard his breath catch, and a disgusting dribble landed on her bare shoulder. Hiding a grimace, she angled her head to give him ample view of her half-naked breasts.

When they emerged from the superintendent's office some time later, Barbara's skin crawled where the man had dripped on it. But she clutched a signed authorization to visit her brother and her head whirled with the details of a whispered agreement.

They were to take rooms at the Somerset Arms on the neighboring island. A note would be delivered later tonight specifying a hidey-hole. Zach would stash three thousand pounds in that place before midnight.

Tomorrow, prisoner number one thousand twenty-six would march out with the quarry detail. The normal three-man squad guarding that gang would be one short. Zach would deal with the remaining guards when the detail rattled across the wooden drawbridge.

It sounded so simple. So dangerous.

"How can we trust Davenport?" Barbara murmured as she and Zach waited in the same fetid visitors' chamber where she'd last seen Harry.

"We can't."

The careless reply scratched on nerves strung as tight as piano wire. He was so cool about this whole venture, she thought with a mix of admiration and resentment. So damn deliberate.

That was the soldier in him, she supposed. He'd scouted the enemy stronghold, selected the weakest point in their defenses, laid out his plan of attack. Gripping her gloved hands in her lap, Barbara tried not to think of everything that could go wrong between the planning and the execution of that attack.

The clank of shackles spun her around. The door opened, and a scarecrow in canvas work pants and a ragged coat stumbled inside.

They'd fetched the wrong prisoner, she thought in dismay. Surely this cadaverous, hollow-eyed wretch with the festering sores couldn't be her brother.

Doubt riddled her until the scarecrow let loose with a whoop of joy.

"Babs!"

Shackles clanking, he stumbled across the stones and swept her into a fierce embrace.

"Oh, Harry!"

His stench almost gagged her. His debonair, desperate grin when he gripped her arms and held her away broke her heart.

"I *knew* you wouldn't fail me."

Tears blurred her eyes. She barely heard the jangle of the guard's keys, the scrape of the door closing behind him.

"Tell me, did you fleece that half-breed squaw of her entire fortune?"

"No."

"Whyever not?"

Zach chose that moment to make his presence known. Pushing away from the wall, he strolled across the chamber.

"The pigeon wasn't as ripe for the plucking as you thought she'd be, Chamberlain."

With a rattle of his chains, Harry whirled around. His burning gaze raked the stranger from his top hat to his Hessians.

"Who the devil are you?"

"Zachariah Morgan."

The two men's eyes locked. Zach's were filled with contempt, Harry's with speculation.

"Morgan? Are you kin to…?"

"The half-breed squaw? I am."

The slow drawl lifted the hairs on the back of Barbara's neck. The air between the two men seemed to crackle. She rushed to intervene before one or the other of them set a spark to it.

"Lieutenant Morgan is Louise Chartier's son by her second marriage."

"A lieutenant, is he?"

"And a barrister."

At that, Harry gave a bark of laughter. For the first time since clanking into the visitors' chamber, he looked and sounded like the brother she'd adored and depended on all her life.

"Hell and damnation, Babs. You've made a royal mess of this one, haven't you?"

19

Nervous as a cat, Barbara paced her cozy sitting room at the Somerset Arms.

The inn was situated on a high bluff overlooking Somerset Village, the principal township on the island of the same name. The hostelry boasted weathered cedar timbers, walls plastered in crushed oyster shell mixed with lime and a kitchen reputed to be one of the finest in the colony. When the innkeeper had shown Barbara and Zach to their rooms earlier, leaded-glass windows had provided spectacular views of the gray-green Atlantic. Now, the small square panes showed only blackest night.

Barbara found it hard to believe a mere six hours had passed since she'd seen Harry. Five, since Zach had strolled into the largest bank in Hamilton Township and presented a draft drawn on the Second Bank of the United States.

Barbara's worries that a Bermudan financial institution wouldn't honor such a large draft had proved groundless. As Zach explained, foreign investors—including a number of the same men who backed the Bank of Britain—held a majority of the stock in the U.S. bank.

After that, she and Zach had taken rooms at the Somerset Arms. Every minute had dragged until an ebony-skinned lad of eight or nine delivered an unsigned note. Buried in the note was an oblique reference to a burnt and blackened cedar tree not far from the inn. Zach had gone out to drop the bribe at the cedar tree an hour ago and had yet to return.

Like rats caught in a maze, a dozen different fears chased around and around in Barbara's head. What if Zach had walked into a trap? What if Davenport had arranged for thugs to waylay him and steal the money? What if he'd found a platoon of guards or royal marines waiting at the cedar tree?

She should have insisted on accompanying him.

No! She should have insisted on finding the damn tree herself. Harry was *her* brother. She should have delivered the bribe and taken the consequences if, indeed, Davenport had sprung a trap.

Zach was an officer in the army of the United States. His president placed great trust in him. He would assume a captaincy in the mounted ranger unit he so loved upon his return. The knowledge she'd placed him at risk of losing his career and his life heaped guilt on top of Barbara's remorse and regret.

She and Harry had been alone for so long. She wasn't used to worrying about anyone except herself and her brother. Had certainly never given anyone else the same degree of loyalty and devotion she felt for her brother. Zach was the first, the only, man to stir both passion and this aching sense of loss.

She still loved him desperately, despite the grievous hurt she'd done him. Alone in the dark of night, at this strange inn, pacing and worrying, Barbara could admit the feelings hidden deep in her heart.

It was two hours past midnight before she heard the clip-clop of horses' hooves. Rushing to the window, she almost sobbed with relief when she saw a rider with Zach's unmistakably broad shoulders steer his hired hack into the inn's yard.

The moment his tread echoed on the stairs, she threw back the bolt and yanked open the door to her chambers.

"Are you all right?"

Her anxious gaze swept him from head to foot for powder burns or bloodstains.

"I'm fine."

"Why were you gone so long?"

Nudging her inside, he shot the bolt behind them. "After I deposited the money in the cedar, I circled back, shinnied up another tree and waited to see who came to retrieve it."

He'd shinnied up a tree! And roosted there for nigh onto four hours! She didn't know whether to laugh at the absurdity of a man his size perched like a canary on a branch or to indulge in a healthy bout of hysterics.

She did neither. Instead, she dogged his heels as he crossed the room, withdrew a pistol from the pocket of his greatcoat and placed it on a draped table. Her toe tapped impatiently while he poured a measure of brandy from the bottle he'd ordered up earlier in the evening.

"Well?" she bit out. "Do you intend to tell me or not? Who came to retrieve the money?"

"Mr. Red Nose himself."

Grinning, he tossed back the brandy.

"He scuttled by right beneath me, tucked the money under his arm and scurried off again like the wharf rat he is. I was tempted to drop down onto his back and scare the piss out of him for the sheer fun of it."

"For the fun of it?" she echoed incredulously.

"I might have done it, too, if I hadn't feared he would drip all over me, as he did you."

He made it sound as though he'd been off on a lark. Some schoolboy prank. She'd stewed and fretted and near worn a hole in the carpet with her pacing, and he'd been off having a grand adventure!

She didn't so much as consider laughing this time. Or giving way to hysterics. With one of the wild swings of emotion that seemed to have afflicted her of late, she snatched up the brandy bottle and threw it at his head.

"What the devil…!"

He dodged it just in time. The heavy glass decanter sprayed an aromatic arc before it clattered to the floor.

Infuriated that her aim was off, Barbara groped for another missile. She didn't realize she'd wrapped her hand around the pistol butt until Zach leaped forward. Cursing, he wrenched the weapon away with one hand and jerked her arm behind her back with the other.

She slammed against his chest. Near snarling now, she put all the hurt, all the shame of the past weeks into a solid kick to his shins.

"You little hellcat!" He tightened his hold, pinning her against his length. "Stop this nonsense before you hurt yourself."

She already had. She'd near broken her toes with that whack. The pain brought tears to her eyes and a torrent of angry curses to her lips.

"Damn you, Zachariah! Damn you to hell and back! I wish you *had* dropped out that tree and broken your neck. I wish Davenport *had* pissed and dripped all over you! I wish… Oh, God, I wish…"

He buried his hand in her hair, yanked her head back. As angry now as she was, he snarled down at her.

"What, Barbara? What do you wish?"

A new emotion sliced through her fury. As fierce and sharp as a dagger thrust to the heart, it made a mockery of all else. She had only to look at him, feel the strength and hardness of him, to know the truth. It spilled from her lips before she could stop it.

"I wish you would kiss me."

His jaw clamped shut. His eyes narrowed with instant suspicion. He stared down at her for what felt like an hour, then muttered a derisive "Why not?"

The kiss was meant to punish, and it did. Hard and bruising, his mouth savaged hers. Barbara withstood the assault, accepted the humiliation. She deserved this, she knew. More than deserved it.

Widening his stance, Zach fisted his hand in her hair and thrust his tongue past her teeth. She could taste the brandy on him, the anger in him.

The memory of another night and another man drunk on brandy flickered through her. Sternly, Barbara banished it. This was Zach. He might despise her. He might feel nothing but disgust for her lies and betrayals. But he wouldn't hurt her. Not the way she'd hurt him. Following her instincts, she opened her mouth under his.

Zach felt the shudder just before she surrendered. It shamed him enough to ease the brutal pressure of his mouth, but not enough to release her.

The touch of her inflamed him. The taste of her was like a knife to his gut. He had to have her, had to feel her under him one last time.

She didn't protest when he took her to the bed. Didn't resist when he raised her skirts and found the slit in her drawers. The feel of her slick, damp flesh set his blood to pulsing and his groin to aching so fiercely he could barely work the buttons on his trouser flap.

He wanted to drive into her. Had every intention of leaving his mark on her. He kneed her legs apart and positioned himself between her thighs.

Her breath caught. Her body tensed. But she didn't try to deny him.

Cursing himself for a fool, Zach entered her with a slow, easy thrust.

They didn't speak afterward.

Exhausted by the journey, the bouts of sickness and the tension that had held her in its maw for months, Barbara sank into a deep, dreamless sleep. Zach swaddled her in the heavy coverlet and held her against him while the wind off the Atlantic rattled the windows.

Would he ever understand this woman? Ever stop wanting her? She had the face of an angel and the wild, untamed spirit of a mountain cat. She'd lied to him with every breath, yet could still tie him in knots with a toss of her head or a flash of those turquoise eyes.

He should hate her. The Lord knew he'd come close to it in Washington. It had been hard to maintain his fury those weeks at sea, though, with Barbara so damn wretched. Harder still tonight, when she'd all but demanded he kiss her. Whatever else had passed between them, the heat still flared bright and hot.

Darkness blanketed the windows when Zach eased his arm from under her head. He let her sleep while he went down to the taproom and roused the boy dozing beside the hearth. The boy summoned the innkeeper, whose wife was already in the kitchen setting loaves beside the ovens to rise. She soon served up a hearty breakfast of ale, fried shark and hot honey cakes.

Instructing the innkeeper to have a carriage brought around, Zach requested a tray and a pitcher of hot water be carried up to Barbara, then settled the bill. The innkeeper didn't question the early rising or departure. Ships and the sea were Bermuda's lifeblood. His patrons came and went with the tides.

Barbara was still asleep when Zach lifted the latch and let himself into her room. He stood beside the bed for long moments before brushing back the tangle of gold hair spread across her face.

"Barbara."

Her eyes flew open. She blinked at him in confusion. "What is it?"

"We've but an hour until dawn."

She swallowed. Her face looked paper white against the sheets. To ease the fear that pooled in her eyes, Zach grinned and gave her hair a tug.

"It's almost over."

He kept his tone just as light some time later, when he passed her a small bundle.

"I withdrew some extra funds from the bank, in case you should need them. Tuck them away, with this."

The small, bone-handled knife would hardly protect her from Throckmorton or his crew should Zach not return from his dawn foray. He was counting on the stack of bills to do that.

The darkness to the east was beginning to pearl when the carriage rattled over the wooden drawbridge connecting Somerset and Ireland Islands. The Royal Naval Base and Dockyards lay a mile and a half ahead. To the left, a thick stand of mangrove fringed a wide, restless bay. To the right was the Great Sound, with the lamps of Hamilton Township beginning to wink in the distance.

A thump on the roof signaled the driver to stop. If he thought it strange his passengers would alight on this uninhabited stretch of road, the coins Zach passed him killed his curiosity and kindled his delight. He backed up the carriage, brought it around and drove off whistling.

Barbara stood gazing through the dim gray light at the narrow bridge. Zach joined her, imprinting yet again on his mind the wooden span, the restless waters on either side of it, the thick brush and spiky palmettos fringing the waters.

"Are you sure the quarry detail will pass this way?" she asked in a small, tight voice.

"It must, if the convicts are to work the limestone caves on Somerset Island."

His plan was simple enough. The drawbridge worked on a pulley mechanism operated by massive concrete weights. A single fisherman wanting to take his boat from the sound to the bay could haul on the rope dangling on the bridge's side, raise the ramps, row or walk his boat through the narrow opening, then lower the ramps again by tugging on the rope on the far side.

Zach intended to crouch beneath the bridge. When the lead elements of the quarry detail had tromped over the boards, he'd slice the pulley rope and send the heavy concrete weight splashing into the channel. The wooden ramps would shoot upward and divide the work detail. In the resulting confusion, Zach would disable the rear guard, use the man's keys to unlock Harry's shackles and make for the *Chesapeake*.

Where Barbara would be stowed safely aboard.

He'd left strict orders with Throckmorton. If anything should go wrong, if there was so much as a hint of trouble, the captain was to lay on all sail and depart Bermuda immediately. Barbara would not birth her child in a rotting prison hulk.

He let his glance roam over her a last time. In the gray light, her face looked pale and worried and so beautiful he could almost forget the conniving self-interest behind it.

"It's coming on to dawn," he said, taking her arm. "We'd better find the *Chesapeake*."

Jiggs Throckmorton had anchored the sloop exactly where Zach had instructed, in a small cove at the north end of the bay. The strange trees that gave the area its name almost shielded the boat from sight. The mangroves rose from great humps of roots that looked like islands floating in the silvery water.

Throckmorton's rum-running days had made the captain cautious. Despite the secluded location and early hour, he'd kept a watch posted. Zach whistled softly to alert the sailor. Moments later, the captain and his mate climbed into the sloop's dinghy and rowed it to the muddy spit of land where their passengers waited.

"Take Lady Barbara aboard," Zach told the captain, "and be prepared to depart as soon as I return. If all goes as I've planned, I'll be back within the hour."

The captain pursed his lips. "Don't you be wantin' some help with this plan of yours, Morgan?"

"It depends on surprise and speed, not strength of numbers."

Standing off the side of the dinghy, Barbara caught

the look Zach aimed at the captain. She understood well enough the message behind it. Throckmorton and his crew were to remain poised for flight and wait.

Zach didn't know it, but Barbara was done with waiting, done with wringing her hands and standing by while he went about the business of saving her brother. She'd drawn him into this dangerous scheme. She'd not leave him to carry it off alone.

She knew better than to argue with him, however. He was an officer used to command. He'd not take kindly to having his orders questioned or his sacred plan meddled with.

She said nothing while he exchanged his greatcoat for a canvas jacket that allowed him more ease of movement. Nor did she comment when he tied a kerchief around his neck, dragged it up to cover the lower half of his face and tipped her a two-fingered salute.

Only after he'd disappeared among the mangroves did she turn to Throckmorton. "Have you a pistol on you?"

"I've a brace of 'em, missus."

Hooking his thumbs in the lapels of his coat, he pulled them back to reveal the butts of the two weapons thrust into his belt.

Barbara held out a gloved hand. "I'll take one, if you please."

"You don't need a pistol aboard the *Chesapeake*. You can trust me."

"I wouldn't trust you with my pet monkey, had I

one, but that's neither here nor there. It's Mr. Morgan I'm concerned about. I'm going after him."

"If I put a pistol in your hand and let you stumble along after him, Morgan will carve a hole in my gullet."

Calmly, Barbara reached into her pocket and drew out the knife Zach had given her less than an hour ago.

"I'll carve one if you don't."

A measure of respect glinted in Throckmorton's good eye. Rocking back on his heels, he rubbed a finger against the side of his nose.

"Well, now, I'll admit it goes against the grain of my pirate's soul to miss out on this bit of fun."

Fun! Dear God, fun! Gritting her teeth, Barbara battled a touch of near hysteria.

"I'll tell you what, missus. You stay here at the boat and I'll sneak along after Morgan. My mate here can steer a straight course back to Washington, if it comes to that."

Out of patience and fast running out of time, she didn't bother to reply. She swung around and started through the mangroves.

"Here now! You can't go off by yourself."

Her jaw set, Barbara marched on. Throckmorton scrambled after her.

They heard the crack of rifle fire while still some distance from the drawbridge. Barbara's heart jumped straight into her throat as she counted three shots. Four. A near fusillade.

Davenport had betrayed them!

Or been betrayed himself!

Picking up her skirts, she broke into a run. The marshy ground sucked at her half boots. The palmettos sliced at her with sharp-edged stalks.

Throckmorton raced along beside her. Over the pounding of her heart, she heard the snick of his pistols being cocked. She threw a quick glance sideways, saw he held one in each beefy fist, and ran on.

She heard the shouts. Saw the fan-shaped palmettos ahead sway madly. Cursing, Throckmorton shoved her behind a clump of mangrove roots and dived in after her.

A mere heartbeat later, Zach charged through the brush. He carried a cocked pistol in one hand and Harry slung across his shoulders.

Barbara's heart seemed to stop in her chest. "Dear God!"

From the way her brother flopped about on Zach's shoulder, she couldn't tell if he was alive or dead. She started to rise, but before she could get her feet under her, another crack of rifle fire split the air.

Grunting, Zach went down. Harry tumbled to the marshy earth with him.

"No!"

With a small, animal cry, Barbara scrambled up and ran toward the two men. She didn't see Throckmorton pop out from behind the tangle of roots. The weapon went off behind her, almost deafening her with its roar.

There was a flash of red. A royal marine crashed through the brush. Stumbled forward. Fell onto his face.

"Over there!"

The shout came from somewhere off to the right. Close. Too close.

"We're in for it now," Throckmorton muttered.

Keeping his head low, the captain scurried after Barbara.

Harry was alive, she saw with a sob of relief. Cursing and kicking and fighting the leg irons that still shackled him, he struggled to free himself from Zach's sprawled body. He shoved to his feet just as his sister reached his side. Whipping around, he spared Zach one swift glance.

"Well, he's done for."

Barbara heard him as if from a distance. Horrified by the red stain spreading across Zach's back, she sank to her knees beside him.

"For God's sake, Babs!"

Harry wrapped a fist around her arm and yanked her up.

"We've a whole platoon of marines after us. Where's this sloop Morgan said he'd have waiting?"

Throckmorton was already charging back toward the boat. "This way!" he yelled over his shoulder.

Harry dragged Barbara two short, shuffling hops before she wrenched free.

"We can't leave Zach! He's still alive!"

"He won't be for long," Harry snarled. "He's done for, I tell you."

He grabbed for her arm again, but she whirled away and rushed back to the fallen man.

"Dammit, Babs!"

Swooping down, she snatched the pistol from Zach's outflung hand. Her heart pounded with fear and desperation as she leveled the barrel at her brother's midsection.

"Pick him up and carry him, Harry."

20

When Barbara broke out of the brush and ran onto the muddy spit, Throckmorton and his mate had already shoved the dinghy into the water and were fumbling for the oars.

"Wait!"

"Here, missus. Get aboard."

She splashed into the water and scrambled for a hold on the slippery gunwale. The captain reached for her arm to drag her in. She whipped it free and dug in her heels. She'd hold the boat on this spit by the sheer force of her will, if necessary.

"My brother's right behind me," she panted. "He's bringing Zach."

Throckmorton threw a doubtful glance at the palmettos, as if expecting a wave of red-coated marines to pour through them at any moment.

"Please! Help him."

Muttering a curse, the captain jumped over the side and disappeared back into the scrub.

He reappeared long, agonizing moments later with Zach slung over his shoulder. Harry short-stepped behind him. Both men splashed into the shallow water. Throckmorton dumped his burden into the dinghy, shoved Barbara in almost on top of Zach and hooked a leg over the gunwale. Harry flopped belly first over the side.

"Row!" Throckmorton barked to his mate. "Row!"

The marines broke through the scrub when the dinghy was still a good hundred yards from the sloop. Running out into the shallow tide, the marines took aim.

Gunfire rattled across the bay. The gray-green waters around the dinghy began to dance. Barbara heard the soft plunk of a bullet thudding into wood, saw the plank just inches from Zach's head splinter. With the blind instinct of an animal protecting its mate, she threw herself forward and covered his body with hers.

Throckmorton's arms pumped. His mate blued the air with curses. The two sailors skimmed the dinghy around a tall mangrove and used the tangle of its roots as a shield. Long, agonizing moments later the boat careened into the *Chesapeake*'s hull.

Barbara could never think back on the horrific hours that followed without shuddering.

The *Chesapeake*'s crew laid on every inch of sail in the ship's locker. The sloop picked up speed in the relatively calm waters of the bay and plunged into the Atlantic. Timbers creaking, she plowed through troughs and crested waves. Barbara paid little attention to the frantic activity of the crew, still less to Throckmorton's warning to keep a sharp lookout for pursuit by British warships. Her wet skirts wrapped around her like a shroud, she crouched beside Zach and tried desperately to staunch the blood running in pink rivulets from the bullet hole in his lower back.

She couldn't imagine how the bullet had missed Harry, slung over his rescuer's shoulder the way he was. She could only pray it had missed Zach's spine.

"Still breathing, is he?"

Her brother hunkered down beside her. His matted blond hair lay plastered against his skull. Hollow-eyed and gaunt, he looked like the angel of death waiting to claim another soul.

"Yes," Barbara ground out, "he's still breathing."

"Well, he'll be feeding the sharks before dawn."

"Not if I can help it. We need to get him below-decks and see about removing the ball. Find someone to help us carry him."

Harry's careless shrug said she was wasting her time, but he went off as instructed. He returned a short time later with the short, bandy-legged seaman who went by the nickname Ropes. To Barbara's intense relief, the man had served as a surgeon's mate in the British navy before jumping ship and throwing in his lot with the rumrunners. He helped carry Zach down to the main cabin, stretched him out on the plank table and put a tin bucket of tar on the galley stove to heat.

"I know more about sawin' off limbs than digging out spent cartridges," Ropes warned.

He used a long-bladed knife to cut through Zach's jacket and shirt. When he saw the wound, his breath whistled through his teeth.

"Blimey!"

Using the tip of his knife, he probed the hole. Fresh blood poured from the wound. Zach jerked and contorted his body.

"Hold 'im still!"

Barbara gripped Zach's ankles, Harry his wrists. Ropes dug deeper. Sweat dripped from his forehead. Using the blade, he pushed aside skin and muscle to expose white, glistening vertebrae.

"Bloody ball's caught between the bones," he muttered. "Can't get the knife under it."

He dug deeper. The blade scraped bone. Zach went still. Horrified by the blood pouring from the wound, Barbara called a halt to the torture.

"Leave it!"

"It could poison 'im. Lead balls like that have made more 'n one man swell up with gangrene."

She couldn't worry about gangrene now. Zach was bleeding to death right before her eyes.

"Leave it, I said!"

Shrugging, Ropes tossed aside the knife and reached for the rum bottle.

The amber liquid he splashed into the wound must have set Zach afire. He jerked and writhed and kicked free of Barbara's hold. She made a grab for the flailing leg and tucked it under her arm as Ropes retrieved the tar bucket from the stove. The thick black pitch inside bubbled and spit. The stink of it stung Barbara's nostrils.

"Is that really necessary?"

"It is if you want to seal the hole and stop the bleedin'," the surgeon's mate said. Stirring the pitch with a wooden paddle, he issued another warning. "This will make him dance some."

He tipped the paddle. Boiling pitch streamed onto the open wound.

Zach's flesh sizzled. The shock of it ripped a shout from his throat. He jerked his arms and legs and almost knocked the tar bucket from Ropes's hands.

Between them, Barbara, Harry and the sailor managed to keep Zach pinned until his frenzied thrashing stilled and he dropped into unconsciousness.

"Hell and damnation." Harry wrinkled his nose. "He's got the stink of a roast pig."

"Carry him to my cabin," Barbara snapped, near to tears and thoroughly out of patience with her brother. "I'm going to fetch a bucket of seawater."

* * *

When she lugged in a sloshing bucket, Zach lay facedown on the narrow bunk. Barbara dropped to her knees beside him and tore a strip from her petticoat. Trying not to gag at the stench of burnt flesh and tar, she began to bathe his face.

Her stomach rolled rebelliously with every pitch and yaw of the boat, but she refused to give in to it. She wouldn't be sick. She couldn't. Not with Zach swimming in and out of delirium.

Harry shuffled in once to bring her a mug of tepid tea. He returned again, late in the day. This time he walked with a full stride.

"The captain struck off the irons," he said with a delighted grin. "It took some doing, I'll tell you, but Master Throckmorton knows his way around a set of shackles."

Hitching up his ragged canvas pants, he displayed bleeding ankles. Barbara gave them a cursory glance.

"You'd better pour some rum over those scrapes."

"I already did. Poured a good measure down my throat, too." He took a couple of turns about the small cabin. "Ah, Christ, it feels good to walk like a man again."

Shoving back her bedraggled hair, Barbara sank onto her heels. The thrill she should have felt at seeing Harry shed of his leg irons after so many months of imprisonment couldn't make it past her desperate fear for Zach.

Her brother didn't fail to note her lack of joy in his newfound freedom. Joining her on the floor, he propped his back against the bulkhead and stretched out his legs.

"What happened, Babs? How is it I sent you off to fleece a woman of her inheritance and you return with her son in tow?"

"It's a rather complicated tale."

"Tell me."

With a weary sigh, she dipped the rag in the bucket and dabbed at the sweat beading Zach's forehead.

"Louise Chartier wasn't the ignorant half breed we thought she'd be. She's shrewd and sophisticated and not about to be taken in by the sudden appearance of a long-lost niece by marriage."

"She didn't buy your story?"

"Not entirely."

"What about the affidavit from the bishop of Reims? Did she challenge its authenticity?"

"I never showed it to her."

Harry sent her a sharp glance. "What's that?"

"By the time I came face-to-face with the woman, I'd already tangled with her son."

Her touch gentle, Barbara drew the damp cloth over the stubble darkening Zach's cheek. He hadn't taken a razor to it this morning. There hadn't been time.

"He's fiercely protective of his mother, Harry, and well versed in the law. I knew he'd challenge the affidavit in the courts. I couldn't spare the time for that. *You* couldn't spare the time for that. So I smiled and pouted and seduced him into providing the funds I needed to buy your freedom."

"How much did you get out of him?"

She turned then, fury licking at her veins. "Did you hear me? I said I whored myself."

"It wouldn't be the first time, would it?"

The utter callousness of the reply stunned her. Her brother's months in the hulks had toughened him, she realized with a sense of shock, then immediately berated herself. He'd spent months in leg irons. He'd nourished his tall, once-muscular frame with one watery bowl of stew and a few crusts of moldy bread a day. He'd fought to stay alive while the men around him dropped from starvation, exhaustion or disease. The wonder would be if he *hadn't* grown hard.

Or perhaps the coldness had always been there, and she'd never seen it. The awful truth of that became apparent when he gave a careless shrug.

"Why do you look so stricken? I avenged your honor the first time a man abased you, didn't I?"

Icy dread spilled through her veins. Those footpads in Naples… She'd always wondered, always suspected. Now she knew.

"I would avenge it this time, as well." Harry flicked a glance at the man in the bunk. "Fortunately, a royal marine has already done the job for me."

Dear God! It wasn't enough she'd lied and cheated and drawn Zach into danger in an effort to save her brother. Now she'd set him up as a target for the vengeance of the very man he'd taken a bullet for.

"Listen to me, Harry! Zach didn't abuse or abase me. I accomplished that entirely on my own. Despite my lies, despite everything I tried to steal from him and his family, he stood by his vow to aid me. He's a good man. An honorable man. If he survives…"

Her voice cracked, her fury with it. She stared at her brother with wide, frightened eyes.

"He *will* survive," she whispered hoarsely. "Tell me he will, Harry."

Shrugging, he pulled her into his arms. As effortlessly as that, they slipped into their old, familiar roles. She leaned her cheek against his bony ribs, seeking the security and comfort he'd always provided, finding it in his grudging admission.

"He's a tough one, I'll give him that. When those marines came charging down the road from the naval base, Morgan threw me across his shoulders like a slab of beef and took off at a dead run."

"Why did the marines appear so suddenly?"

"I'm damned if I know."

He fell silent, reliving his desperate escape, Barbara guessed. Moments slid by undisturbed except for the rasp of Zach's labored breathing.

"Tell me something," Harry said at length.

"What?"

"When you aimed that pistol at me, would you have pulled the trigger?"

She eased upright and looked into the eyes so like her own. "I'm damned if I know."

He gave a hoot of sheer delight. "By damn, Babs. You've grown into a woman worthy of the Chamberlain name."

Indeed she had. Unlike her brother, she took little joy in the fact.

"You may as well know the rest of it," she said. "There will soon be another to bear the Chamberlain name. I'm breeding."

The amusement left Harry's face. Anger chased across his gaunt features. "So Morgan dropped a bastard on you, did he? Well, that can be attended to easily enough once we reach dry land."

"No!" Barbara crossed her arms over her belly. "I promised I'd return to his family's home until the babe is born. I intend to keep that promise."

His forehead creased in a frown. She could almost see the moment his anger gave way to cold calculation.

"Are you set on that course?"

"I am."

"Then we'll make them pay. Handsomely."

"They've already paid! Zach financed your rescue from his own funds. I can't… I won't take any more from him or his family."

"Very noble, my dear sister, but what about your child? Do you intend for it to scrabble for its dinner as you've had to so many times?"

With everything that had happened, she'd all but forgotten the package Zach had slipped her at the Somerset Arms.

"The child won't have to scrabble for anything."

Her coat still lay in a sodden heap where she'd dropped it hours ago. Snagging one of the sleeves, Barbara dragged it across the deck and rooted through its deep pockets. The package was still there, right where she'd shoved it. She passed it to Harry without bothering to unwrap it.

"I suspect there's more than enough here to keep a body clothed and well fed."

He yanked on the strings, rifled through the stack of banknotes and let out a low whistle.

"*Very* well fed, indeed. I'd better keep this safe for you."

He tucked the package inside his canvas jacket and shot Zach another glance. It was tipped with respect and the envy great wealth had always engendered in him.

"You hooked a ripe one this time, Babs. If Barrister Morgan here becomes shark bait, as I suspect he soon will, we'll give the bishop's affidavit a try. Between that document and the child you're carrying, we should be able to milk the Morgans of most of their worth."

His good humor restored by the prospect of another scam, Harry lifted the latch and left the cabin.

Barbara sat on the floor, unmoving. She felt a

hundred years old, with a body as withered as the Egyptian mummies on display at the British Museum. Her glance lingered for long moments on the cabin door before shifting to the traveling valise stashed in a corner.

On hands and knees, she crawled across the tilting deck. The oilskin packet was in its hiding place. She'd tucked it back inside the lining after Zach had tossed it at her in disgust. She'd held some vague thought of presenting it as a gift when they said farewell.

Unwrapping the oilskin, Barbara extracted the document and tore it into tiny pieces. She dropped the bits into the slop bucket and watched them settle to the bottom before crawling back to the bunk.

"Hush," she murmured to her restless, delirious patient. "Hush, Zach. I'm here."

Once more she dipped the rag in seawater and wrung it out. The bitter irony of her actions didn't escape her. Not three weeks ago, Zach had bathed her face and held her while she retched and heaved. She'd been certain she was dying and in her darkest moments had wanted only to end the agony.

Now Zach lay dying. She could shriek at Harry and deny it all she wished, but she couldn't shut out the sight of that horrific smear of black pitch. The skin around it was burned and seared. Blood still seeped from under the tar.

"I'm here, my darling." Gently, she drew the damp cloth over his face. "I'm with you."

The voices drifted in and out of Zach's head.

He heard them above the burning agony that consumed him. Clung to them through the darkness that spun madly, dragging him into its vortex.

One voice returned again and again. Always calm. Always gentle. With it came the blessed relief of a damp cloth moving over his burning body and a few drops of water or rum dribbled onto his parched lips.

Every once in a while he could see the face that went with the voice. In his most agonized moments, it was that of a golden-haired angel, soothing him, smiling at him. In his rare, all too brief moments of lucidity, it was that of a hollow-eyed, tangled-haired hag.

There were other voices, too. Some raised in excitement. Some in anger. Some with bluff, hearty tones he almost recognized. He tried to make out the words, but the mere effort sent waves of fire leaping up his back to eat at his brain.

The hag was there the next time he fought his way out of the flames. He could see her sagging against his bunk, one arm curled under her head, her hair straggling over her elbow. He lay still, breathing as shallowly as possible, and studied the face just inches from his own.

Slowly the tired, wan face took on the features of the woman who'd come to both bedevil and bedazzle him.

How long had she sprawled like that? How long had he? Zach couldn't separate the hours from the days. Not that it mattered. Whatever time he had left was slipping away as steadily as his strength.

He was a solider. Despite the pain clouding his mind, he understood why he was lying flat on his face, his guts afire. He'd taken a ball to the back. He didn't know what the bullet had hit or how much blood he'd lost, but the fact that he couldn't so much as lift his head told him all he needed to know.

"Bar…bara."

The mere effort of whispering her name sent black waves sweeping over him. He longed to let them take him, to sink back into the darkness forever. Sweat beaded on his temples as he forced another hoarse whisper.

"Barbara."

She jerked her head up, her eyes wild and staring.

"Dear God! You're awake!"

She flopped onto her knees and scrabbled for something on the floor. A crudely fashioned rag teat, Zach saw, sopping with some liquid. She held it to his lips, but he didn't have the strength to suckle.

"Just a few drops," she begged. "There's sugar in it, and a powder Throckmorton swears cures every one of his crew's ills."

"Fetch…him."

"The captain?"

"Yes."

"But why?"

He couldn't explain. He didn't have the time or the endurance.

"And…another," he got out through gritted teeth. "To serve…as witness."

The blood drained from her face. She stared at him with wide, haunted eyes before struggling to her feet.

"I'll fetch Throckmorton and one of the crew straightaway. Hang on, Zach. Just hang on."

Barbara stumbled into the passageway. She knew why he wanted the captain. He'd guessed he was dying. He wanted to make a last will and testament, with a witness to swear to it. Someone he trusted. Someone other than her.

Her heart as heavy as stone, she brought Throckmorton and his mate back with her. They crowded into the small cabin. Barbara pressed her back to the bulkhead as Throckmorton bent over Zach.

"I'm here, Morgan. Want me to hear your will, do you?"

"Not…will." Zach raised his head a few, tortured inches. "Marry Barbara…and me."

Throckmorton's jaw dropped. Barbara felt her own sag in sheer astonishment.

The captain recovered from his shock first. "Here now! I never married no one afore, not even the three women what call themselves my wife. And if there's anything resembling a Bible aboard this vessel, I'll eat my vest."

"You're...captain. Just say...words."

"No, Zach!" Barbara dropped down beside him. "You don't have the strength for this."

He drew in a shallow breath and let it out in slow, agonized pants.

"Won't be...bas...tard."

"What?"

She could barely hear the mumbled words. She stooped closer, her ear almost to his mouth.

"The...child. Not...bas...tard."

Barbara Chamberlain and Zachariah Morgan were married aboard the sloop *Chesapeake* as it pitched and rolled through the Atlantic.

Word of the ceremony had raced through the boat like St. Elmo's fire. Every member of the crew except the watch crowded the passageway outside the cabin, tossing wagers back and forth as to whether the groom would cock up his toes before old Jiggs figured out what words to say.

The bride's brother shouldered his way into the cabin as well. Arms folded, eyes alight with speculation, he watched the proceedings with something that could have been a smile playing about his mouth.

To the intense delight of those who'd wagered on him and the bitter disappointment of those who'd bet against him, Zach survived the ceremony. Throckmorton left the cabin sweating from the ordeal of finding words with a matrimonial ring to them. Once in the companionway, he and his second in command exchanged glances.

"You'd best dig some canvas from the sail locker," the one-eyed captain advised. "You'll need to start sewing a shroud."

21

Looking back, Barbara could never quite pinpoint the hour or the day she began to believe Zach would survive his horrific wound. Certainly not while the *Chesapeake* cut like a blade through the green waters of the Atlantic. Nor during those first hellish days in Charleston, which Captain Throckmorton had made for with all speed.

Harry took rooms for them in the city and Barbara hired a succession of surgeons to attend Zach. The physicians' admission they could do nothing for him sent her tentative hopes plummeting. Zach's bad-tempered snarl when the last one poked and prodded his wound set them soaring again.

Every day she forced liquids down his throat. Every night she stretched out on a pallet beside him.

As December gave way to January, the festering skin of his back began to heal.

Barbara barely had time to exult over her patient's slowly improving condition before he began to test both his fragile strength and her threadbare nerves. Ignoring her strenuous objections and the grinding pain in his back, he attempted to sit up...and promptly pitched over onto his face.

When he regained consciousness, he began to push himself mercilessly. He would sweat and strain and exhaust himself trying to force his lower body to move. Barbara hovered over him until he snarled at her, too, and told her to get out. Harry stalked into Zack's room, then, and slammed the door shut behind him.

Barbara didn't know what was said. She suspected she never would. But Harry emerged with fire in his eyes and Zack's face was masked with fury when she reentered the sickroom. Thinking he wished for someone other than a Chamberlain to attend him, she offered to write his parents and advise them of his condition.

Zack almost bit her head off. "No!"

"They should know about the injury to your spine."

And about his marriage. Although both she and Zack knew the arrangement to be temporary, she suspected Louise Morgan would not take the news well.

"There's no need to worry them," Zach growled. "When we're ready to start back to Indian Country, I'll write to tell them we're coming home."

Home.

She refused to let the word unsettle her, but the bargain she'd struck with Zach weighed more heavily on her mind with each passing day. He'd held to his promise to help free Harry. She'd hold to hers and return to Indian Country until the babe now swelling her belly was born.

After that…

She and Harry would go the way they always had, she supposed. Without her baby. In her heart of hearts Barbara knew the child would be better off with the Morgans, raised in a home filled with love and laughter. Yet the idea of walking away from Zach and her child filled her with almost as much dismay as the thought of returning to her harum-scarum life with her brother.

Bit by bit, Zach built up his strength. By early February, he'd regained some use of his lower limbs and could drag himself across the floor. By the end of the month, when he, Barbara and Harry boarded the train that would take them from Charleston to New Orleans, he could stump along on crutches.

Midway through the steamboat trip upriver from New Orleans, Zach tossed the crutches overboard and began to shuffle with a cane. Despite his best efforts, though, he still couldn't manage the steep gangplank. At each stop, he remained on board rather than submit to the indignity of being carried off the boat on a crewman's back.

So when the *Memphis Wheeler* steamed up the Grand River and arrived at Fort Gibson the first week in March, Barbara made her way down the gangplank on Harry's arm. Her bonnet strings blew about her face as she stepped onto the rock shelf that constituted the fort's riverboat landing.

The outpost looked little different from the first time she'd seen it five months ago. Fingers of dirty snow lay in the shadows of the palisade walls and scattered outbuildings, but tender green shoots pushed up through the parade ground. Soldiers detailed to garden duty hacked at the earth with long-handled hoes. Others hewed logs or chinked mud as part of the ever-constant task of maintaining structures at the mercy of rain and rot.

But it was the group in civilian dress waiting at the landing that drew Barbara's intent gaze. Her fingers dug into Harry's sleeve.

"There they are."

His glance swept the small group. "Well, well," he murmured. "So those are the Morgans of Indian Country."

They were all there. Every member of the family had turned out in response to Zach's letter advising them he'd been injured and was coming home. Daniel Morgan standing as tall and rigid as an oak. Louise Chartier Morgan, her skin stretched taut across her high cheekbones. Zach's sisters and young Theo, looking nervous and excited. And Hattie. Even Hattie had turned out to greet her wounded hero.

Fighting the cowardly urge to turn around and dash back up the gangplank, Barbara loosened her hold on Harry's arm. She'd come this far. She'd not turn tail and run now. Swallowing the lump in her throat, she stepped forward.

Louise disdained any words of greeting. "Where is my son?"

"They'll bring him down after the rest of the passengers disembark."

Her narrowed gaze burned into Barbara. "There is a legend, one the old people still sing of. It speaks of a blue-eyed maiden who brings calamities on her people. The first time I see you, I think of this legend and my heart tells me disaster walks with you."

"Your heart didn't lie to you."

"As you did."

"As I did."

Louise's gaze dropped to the swell of Barbara's belly, barely visible beneath her coat.

"Is that, too, a lie?"

"The child is Zach's. Whether you…or anyone else…choose to believe so matters not to me."

They might have been alone amid the bustle that came with a steamboat docking. Passengers streamed past. Mules hitched to the drays waiting to haul military supplies and cargo shifted in their harnesses. Neither woman paid the slightest heed to the milling crowd.

"You say it matters not what we believe. Why have you come back to Indian Country, then?"

"I made a promise to your son."

"Pah!" Scorn flashed in the older woman's eyes. "Promises from one such as you are written on the wind."

Scowling, Harry stepped forward. "I must ask you to watch how you speak to my sister, Madam Chartier."

"The name's Morgan," Daniel drawled, laying a hand on his wife's shoulder. "And I would advise *you* to have a care how you speak to her, sir."

The two men sized each other up. Harry had regained weight in the past three months. He'd also purchased an entire wardrobe from the funds Zach had provided Barbara that last fateful morning in Bermuda. A beaver top hat now crowned his shining gold locks, and snowy linen circled his throat. With his gleaming boots and malacca cane, he looked every bit the English gentleman.

How strange, Barbara thought. Harry carried a title and an air of sophisticated assurance, yet Daniel Morgan seemed so much more the man. His confidence came from someplace deep inside him, and his chiseled features were stamped with the mark of this vast, rugged land. So like his son's, she thought with a little ache.

"I should like to make my brother known to you," she said quietly. "Harry, this is Zach's father, Daniel Morgan, and his mother, Louise Chartier Morgan. They were kind enough to—"

"There he is! There's Zach."

Vera's cry wrenched them all around. A vise tightened around Barbara's heart as a uniformed figure shuffled out of the shadows cast by the upper deck. Leaning heavily on a knobby oak cane, Zach approached the gangplank. Two burly crewmen stepped forward and gripped each other's wrists. With the cautious movements of an old man, her husband lowered himself into the cradle of their arms.

Louise's breath rattled. Daniel's jaw worked. Barbara understood their anguish.

"The bullet lodged in his spine," she explained softly.

Zach had informed them by letter that he'd taken a ball in the back, but had been purposely vague as to the circumstances. He could hardly put into writing the fact that he'd assisted a convicted felon to escape.

Nor would Barbara or Harry allude to the circumstances. It served them best, after all, to let the world believe Zach had negotiated Harry's release and suffered an unfortunate accident in the process.

"He doesn't like to have a fuss made over him," she told the Morgans. "It's best to let him get his feet under him before you…"

Louise whirled on her. "Do not *dare* to tell me what is best for my son."

Rushing by, the older woman made for the gang-plank. Her husband followed, and the rest of his family flocked after him. Hattie cast a look brimming with hate at Barbara and went with them.

The Chamberlains stood alone. As they always had.

They remained apart while the family crowded around Zach. Barbara could share vicariously in their joy and tears. And hold her breath, as they did, when he pushed unsteadily to his feet. But only she knew the agony it caused him to bring his shoulders back and straighten his spine. She admired his courage even as she cursed his soldier's stubbornness.

Chewing on the inside of her cheek, she said nothing when little Sarah threw herself at Zach and wrapped her chubby arms around his left leg. Nor did she comment when Theo rebuked his sister and yanked her roughly away. When she saw sweat begin to bead on Zach's temple, however, she knew it was time to speak out.

"Have you all quite finished?" She made a show of fluffing up her coat collar. "I should like to get out of the chill."

The relief that flitted across Zach's face more than made up for Louise's furious sputter and Hattie's malevolent glare.

"Shall we take this homecoming celebration inside?" Zach suggested. "I don't want to keep my wife standing about in the cold."

"Wife!"

Louise spit the word as if it were venom, but Daniel intervened before she could voice her obvious opinion of the union between her son and the woman who'd betrayed him time and again. He hadn't missed the worry Barbara tried to disguise behind her cool facade. His keen eyes had noted as well the relief buried in his son's response. Whatever else Daniel might think of this unlikely match, it was now Zach's business.

"Barbara is breeding," he reminded his wife. "It won't do to keep her on her feet too long."

"Ha! You say this, yet you trekked through the wilderness beside me right up to the moment of Zach's birth."

"As I recall, you gave me no choice. You were determined your son would draw his first breath here, in Indian Country."

Louise had no argument for that. Scowling, she yielded the ground to her husband. Daniel accepted her acquiescence with a nod and turned to his son.

"I know you can't ride..."

"Yet."

"I know you can't ride *yet,* so I padded the wagon bed with straw and blankets. I'll try not to jostle you too much on the way home."

Leaning heavily on his cane, Zach shook his head. "I'm not going back to Morgan's Falls."

"What's this?"

"I've used up all my furlough time and then some. I'm reporting back to duty."

"I'm sure Colonel Arbuckle will grant you sick leave."

"I'm sure he would, sir, but the long and the short of it is that I promised President Jackson I'd help train the new regiment of dragoons."

"Did you now?"

"I spoke with him about it in Washington. He promised me a captaincy." A smile worked its way through the lines of pain grooving Zach's mouth. "I'm thinking the new regiment will also need mounts. Mounts bearing the Morgan brand."

"I'm thinking the same thing," Daniel replied.

Louise threw up her hands. "This is beyond anything foolish! Zach can barely stand, yet already the two of you speak of horses and drilling a troop of soldiers."

"I may not be able to ride—*yet*—but I can certainly scribble out training manuals and equipment requirements for the new regiment."

"Pah!" Louise took out her frustration on her husband. "He is as pigheaded as you, this one."

"Do you think so? Seems to me he takes after his dam in that regard."

Barbara couldn't imagine a more reluctant ally, but Zach's mother managed to swallow her enmity long enough to appeal to her.

"Tell him he must not do this."

"I'm afraid you fit the peg in the right hole. He is, indeed, pigheaded. He refuses to listen to me on this matter, either."

Hattie had been standing mute to this point. Tugging on a strand of her brown hair, she astonished everyone by voicing an opinion.

"I think Zach has the right of it. He should remain here at Fort Gibson. President Jackson's done named Colonel Henry Dodge commander of the new regiment. The colonel could be making his way to Fort Gibson any day now."

Zach's eyebrows soared. "Where did you hear that?"

"At John Stallworth's taproom. I hired on there after I got back to Fort Gibson."

While she waited for Zach to return, Barbara guessed. She didn't know what he'd told the maid when he'd bundled her aboard a stage in Washington, but two things were now painfully obvious. Hattie's feelings for the man who'd rescued her from her brutish master had progressed far beyond hero worship. Her feelings for her former mistress, on the other hand, now bordered on hate. Hattie blamed Barbara for the bullet now lodged in Zach's spine, as did his family.

They couldn't blame her more than she blamed herself.

With a disgusted shake of her head, Louise gave up hope of dissuading her son. "You're set on staying at Fort Gibson, then?"

"I am."

Lips pursed, she turned to Barbara. "What of you and your brother? Do you return to Morgan's Falls with us?"

Harry replied with a short bow. "I thank you, but I'm heading back to New Orleans on the next steamboat."

His mocking eyes met Barbara's. She'd made Harry *swear* he wouldn't use either her marriage or her child to extort money from the Morgans. They'd paid for his freedom. Zach had nearly died achieving it. That was enough. More than enough.

With great reluctance, Harry had agreed. It went against his grain to let such plump pockets go unpicked, but he'd used their brief stopover in New Orleans to scout out that bustling city. He'd already set his sights on larger, more lucrative marks.

"What of you?" Louise asked Barbara, her blue eyes cool. "Will you stay at Morgan's Falls while Zach goes about these duties?"

That was the agreement. He had held to his promise. She would hold to hers.

"I should like to, if it wouldn't discommode you."

Zach tried to ignore the note of forced politeness in his wife's voice. She'd be better off at Morgan's Falls, with his mother to watch over her and servants to tend to her every need.

The only problem was, he wanted her here. Like a shadow he couldn't seem to escape, she'd become part of him.

He knew damn well Harry Chamberlain would have abandoned him in Bermuda. Throckmorton, too. He'd had the tale from the one-eyed rumrunner himself. The captain had also told Zach about Barbara's refusal to leave his bedside for so much as an hour during the voyage back to the States.

In his dogged determination to get back on his feet during those weeks in Charleston, Zach had used her as nurse, crutch and ranting board. Looking back, he was surprised she hadn't tossed a chamber pot at his head in the same manner she'd tossed the brandy bottle at it in Bermuda.

They'd come this far together, Zach decided, in an abrupt about-face. They should finish things together. Telling himself he was just responding to the desolation in her eyes at the thought of being under his mother's thumb, he offered her a choice.

"If you want to stay at Fort Gibson until the summer heat gets too intense, I could arrange quarters here on post. They're nowhere near as comfortable as my parents' home," he warned. "Only two rooms."

Relief flooded her face. From the smile that came into her eyes, Zach might have given her a diamond necklace.

"Two rooms will be more than sufficient."

Swinging wildly between despair and bitter loathing, Hattie made her way back to John Stallworth's tavern. Zach had told her back in Washington City that he intended to bring Barbara back to Indian Country to birth the child.

He didn't care about the cow. Hattie knew he didn't. He'd only married her to keep his child from being called bastard. Hattie had heard Louise Morgan mutter those exact words to her husband while they waited for the *Memphis Wheeler* to lower its gangplank.

She'd been prepared to quit her job at the taproom and return to Morgan's Falls to help nurse Zach. Her few belongings were packed and ready.

She'd been prepared, too, to endure Barbara's presence at the Falls until the bitch whelped. After that the Englishwoman would disappear from Zach's life.

The fact that both Zach and his wife had decided to remain at Fort Gibson made matters easier. It was a busy post. Frontiersmen, Indians, whiskey runners, mule skinners and mountain men all came and went daily. Who could say what sort of ruffian the blonde might meet up with? Who knew what might happen to her while Zach was busy with his duties?

Briefly, Hattie considered asking Barbara to take her into service again. She'd be close to Zach that way, but *too* close to his wife. She was damned if she'd curtsy or kowtow to the woman.

Her thoughts whirling about in her head, she entered the rowdy establishment just off post that catered to soldiers and civilians alike.

* * *

She was serving tankards of ale to a boisterous gaggle of soldiers when Barbara's brother strolled in later that same evening. She half expected his aristocratic nose to wrinkle at the stench of unwashed bodies, rough-cured buckskins and soot-blackened beams, then remembered the gaol-bird had spent the past months wallowing about in prison muck.

She slanted him a narrow glance as he made his way to the long plank set atop two barrels that served as a bar and ordered a tankard of ale. Eyeing him thoughtfully, she slapped at the hand that reached out to fondle her backside.

"Keep your hams to yourself," she told the grinning, half-drunk soldier.

"Aw, Hattie. When are you going to let me court you proper?"

"When you sprout horns, O'Shaunessy."

"I've already sprouted one for you, darlin'. It's a real boner, too."

His companions hooted and thumped the boards. It had become a game to them, trying to gain her affections, or at least attention. And no wonder. There were only three unattached white females at the fort. One was the widow Sallie Nicks, whose wealth and vivacious charm put her well above these men's touch. The other sported a face eaten half away by the pox. Hattie could have had her pick of any single man on post if she'd wanted anyone but Zach.

Wondering if she could use the Englishman to somehow further her campaign to free Zach from his sister, she sidled up to the bar.

"I saw you at the riverboat landing. You're Barbara's brother, Sir Harry Chamberlain."

His blue eyes swept over her. "I saw you, too. You have the advantage of me, though. I don't know your name."

"I'm Hattie Goodson. I was maid to your sister when she first arrived in Indian Country."

"Indeed?" His arched eyebrow indicated surprise that his sister would hire a tavern wench to attend to her. "How did that come about?"

"I was indentured to a squatter who got taken in by a false quit-claim deed. Zach—Lieutenant Morgan—shot the bastard square between the eyes and brought me back to Fort Gibson. That's when your sister took me into service."

The Englishman raised his tankard and took a leisurely swallow. She thought he might comment on his sister's impulsive offer to employ a stranger, or perhaps Zach's keen marksmanship.

His interest took a different direction. Setting the tankard on the bar, he swiped the foam on his upper lip with a casual hand.

"Enlighten me, if you would. What, precisely, is a quit-claim deed?"

22

Less than a week after her return to Fort Gibson, Barbara said goodbye to her brother. She did so with decidedly mixed emotions. He was her family, the only person who'd ever really mattered to her until recently. She hated to see him step aboard the steamer that would take him back to New Orleans, but the sad truth was that her husband and her brother rubbed each other exactly the wrong way.

One was a sophisticated schemer, the other a blunt-spoken soldier. Neither held the other in any particular esteem. Zach had no use for a man who would involve his sister in fraudulent activities. Harry had even less for a man who professed himself content with the plodding routine of life at a remote military outpost. The tension between them had mounted daily. For the first time in her life, Barbara was relieved to see her brother disappear.

"I'll come back for you in July," he promised, "after the baby's born."

She nodded but didn't speak. He was already looking toward a future she wasn't ready to contemplate.

"We'll decide in July where we'll go from here," he told her. "We might stay in America for a while. From the little I saw of it, New Orleans offers definite possibilities for an enterprising pair with our talents. I'll know better after I spend some time there."

"Be careful, Harry. Please! Let's have no more fraudulent railroad schemes."

"No, no more railroad schemes." Winking, he twirled his malacca cane. "I've something else in mind."

Alarm feathered through her. "What?"

"Just an idea. It may not pan out. I'll look into it while I'm in New Orleans."

Before Barbara could demand more detail, the shrill scream of the steamboat whistle pierced the air. Harry dropped a kiss on her cheek, promised again to come for her in July and sauntered up the gangplank.

Troubled, she stood on the landing until the paddle wheeler pulled away. The harrowing months her brother had spent in the hulks had hardened him but obviously hadn't crushed his adventurous spirit. He was a buccaneer right down to the toes of his polished boots.

Barbara had always been a willing participant in his plots and schemes. Now the mere thought of returning to that precarious life filled her with dread.

She *wouldn't* think of it, she decided. Not for the next four months, anyway. She would spend those months nurturing the child swelling her belly and fill the time with the everyday tasks of a lieutenant's wife.

And her nights, she thought with a sudden tightening of her throat, with Zach.

As it turned out, she spent her nights alone.

Any sudden, jarring movement caused Zach excruciating pain. So did the sagging ropes in the bed frame of the four-poster he'd purchased from Sallie Nicks and had moved into their cramped, two-room quarters. Consequently, Barbara occupied the four-poster while Zach stretched out each night on a bed-roll in the front parlor.

His deep, rumbling breathing wouldn't quite qualify as a snore but came dangerously close. She found the steady rasp both comforting and disturbing. She lay awake those first nights, listening to him, knowing he was so close and yet so very far away from her.

By unspoken consent, they didn't address the future beyond the baby's birth, but it didn't take them long to establish a routine similar to that of other married couples on post. Everyone, Barbara soon learned, lived by the same schedule. The clear, piercing notes of a bugle sounded reveille and woke Fort Gibson's residents at daybreak. Not long after that, a

thundering cannon roar echoed through the surrounding hills and the flag was run up the staff. The
bugle sounded regularly throughout the day, announcing morning mess call, assembly, attention to
orders, work detail, noon and evening mess forma-
tions.

Drums rolled at sunset to sound retreat, and the
cannon boomed again during the ceremony of low-
ering the flag. Fifes accompanied the drums to announce tattoo at nine o'clock. Their shrill notes
warned stragglers to return to the fort before the gates
closed. Taps signaled lights out and an end to the long
day.

Much to Barbara's surprise, she adjusted easily to
the routine. Without card parties and balls and midnight suppers to tire her out and keep her abed until
noon, she began to rise when her husband did. While
she tended to her toilette, the private who supple-
mented his meager army pay by serving as Zach's
batman, cook and general dogsbody helped him
shave and struggle into his uniform. Husband and
wife took breakfast together, after which the lieutenant attended to his duties.

These were necessarily restricted. Since he
couldn't march, much less climb into a saddle, Colonel Arbuckle appointed him military adjunct to the
federal commission now busily engaged in negotiating with the various tribes. With the arrival of Governor Stokes, the commission's chairman, activities

picked up considerably. Zach spent long hours each day providing both insight and advice.

While he labored in the stuffy office given over to the commissioners, Barbara slipped into the role of officer's lady.

It began with a stream of visits from the other wives on post. Most were eastern-bred, determined to cling to their gentility and refinement despite the primitive surroundings. A good number were Cherokee, Choctaw or Osage. Wives of the senior enlisted personnel also came on duty visits to Lieutenant Morgan's new bride.

They were all curious about the Englishwoman who'd snared the dashing lieutenant. The fact that the bride was already increasing didn't seem to raise any eyebrows. Barbara soon found herself immersed in lively discussions about lying-in gowns, swaddling blankets and christening robes.

The women also imparted a great many tips on ways to soften the austerity of army quarters. Armed with their advice, she made regular visits to Sallie Nicks's warehouse to purchase carpets for the hard-packed dirt floors, figured muslin for curtains and such wildly expensive delicacies as tinned peaches and molasses to add variety to the standard army rations of beans and beef.

A variety of social activities enlivened the non-duty hours. To fight off boredom, the soldiers wrote and staged theatrical performances. The post chaplain conducted religious services in the same building used for Indian councils. The regimental band gave rousing concerts on the parade ground. Amateur pugilists took to the ring. Horse racing was a wildly popular sport, Barbara discovered. Soldiers, Indians and traders ran their mounts against each other and the racehorses brought up-river by owners intent on relieving the soldiers of their pay.

In addition, a great many dinners were given and returned. The widow Nicks, Fort Gibson's unofficial hostess, hosted a lavish entertainment in honor of Governor Stokes and the other members of the federal commission. It was at this dinner that Barbara first understood how essential Zach had become to the delegation.

"We could not have concluded that agreement with the Seminole delegation from Florida without your husband's assistance," the wispy-haired governor confided over a glass of sherry. "Lieutenant Morgan and his father had hunted the land set aside for the Seminole. Zach described every river and stream and drew exact maps for the Seminole delegation to follow. When they returned from their explorations, they agreed to sign a statement indicating they were satisfied with the proposed lands. I've forwarded that statement to President Jackson."

"I don't doubt he'll make good use of it," Barbara murmured.

She was familiar enough with the politics of Indian Country now, and her short meeting with the president had convinced her he'd use every possible means to move those eastern tribes that still expressed stubborn reluctance to leave their homelands. Whether he would do so without more bloodshed remained to be seen.

Her gaze drifted to her husband, who was helping craft new territories for those tribes. He stood tall and square-shouldered in his dress uniform. Unfortunately, he could only achieve that pose with the aid of a cane. Biting her lip, she returned her attention to Commissioner Stokes.

"Now if only the soldiers at Fort Gibson could keep these pesky settlers out of Indian Country," he was saying. "They put at risk all we're trying to accomplish here, and there certainly seems to be a sudden influx of them in recent weeks."

"Yes, there does."

Barbara couldn't help but remember the first day she'd met Zach, when he'd arrived back at the fort with a bruised and battered Hattie in tow. She hadn't seen her former maid in weeks and could only be glad of it. The woman had made no effort to hide her dislike that day on the landing, and Barbara had no desire to deal with it.

One by one, the days slipped by. March flowed into a rain-drenched April. The rains gave way to a balmy May. Like a hen going to roost, Barbara took each day as it came and nurtured the life growing inside her belly.

She received two missives from her brother, both sent from New Orleans. He gave no hint as to his activities other than to state he'd found a wealth of opportunities in that most cosmopolitan of American cities. In each, he reiterated his promise to return for her come July.

She also received a visit from Zach's parents. They'd come to Fort Gibson to purchase supplies and check on their son. Some of the animosity Louise Morgan had exhibited during her last meeting with her daughter by marriage faded when she saw the home Barbara had made of their austere quarters, but her eyes were grave as Zach and Daniel saw to the loading of the supplies.

With a sigh, she turned to Barbara. "He makes light of my questions, so I must ask them of you. Is my son still in great pain?"

"Yes."

"Do you think he will one day walk without a cane?"

Barbara hesitated. Zach insisted he would toss away the cane one day soon. He insisted, too, that the regimental surgeon would clear him to remain on active service. Yet she'd seen him grit his teeth when he didn't know she was watching, and heard him grunt each time he tried to turn over at night. Sighing, she answered his mother the only way she could.

"I don't know."

Louise bit down on her lower lip. She looked as though she wanted to say more, but settled for a brief admonition.

"Take care of him, and yourself."

"I will."

Shortly after their visit, the officers assigned to Fort Gibson received word that Colonel Henry Dodge, commander of the new dragoon regiment, had decided to assemble and train his unit at Jefferson Barracks in Missouri Territory. Zach and his fellow rangers voiced bitter disappointment. To a man, they felt the dragoons should train here in Indian Country, where they would be employed.

Barbara shared their disappointment but had already begun to suspect deep in her heart that her husband would never recover enough to assume the captaincy President Jackson had promised him. Zach confirmed her suspicion one evening in late May.

He sent word that he had been detained and not to wait dinner for him. When he hadn't returned when the fife and drums sounded nine o'clock tattoo, Barbara sent the private who served as Zach's batman back to his barracks. Trimming the lamps, she settled a soft lawn nightdress over her swollen breasts and belly and sat on the side of the bed to brush out her hair. She was up to seventy-three strokes when the front door crashed open.

Startled, she jumped to her feet. Her fist closed around the brush handle. Heart thumping, she rushed to the bedroom door and pushed it open.

"Steady, old man. Steady."

Nathaniel Prescott staggered into the front room.

His uniform jacket was buttoned all cockeyed and his gait was unsteady as he half carried, half dragged Zach with him. Huffing under his friend's weight, he made for the one sturdy armchair in the room.

"Got to get you into a chair before we both go down," he muttered.

He dipped his shoulder. Zach dropped into the seat, went rigid and instantly turned the air blue with his curses. A thoroughly crestfallen Prescott quickly apologized.

"Sorry, old top!"

Barbara snatched a shawl from the hook behind the bedroom door and threw it over her nightdress. When she rushed into the front parlor, a wave of whiskey fumes hit her like a slap in the face.

"What goes on here?"

Both men turned around—Nate unsteadily, Zach stiffly. Her heart clutched when she saw the white lines bracketing her husband's mouth.

"Zach, are you all right?"

"Ha!" He gave a hoot of drunken laughter, but whatever he'd imbibed didn't impede his speech. "It appears I'm as right as I'll ever be," he announced. "According to our esteemed regimental surgeon, at least."

"What do you mean?"

"It means, wife, I'm no longer fit for military service."

"What?"

Prescott brushed his hand over his mustaches. His brown eyes held both sympathy and misery.

"Major Parks performed the required sixty-day medical evaluation this afternoon. With that ball lodged in Zach's spine, Parks had no choice but to declare him unfit for continued service."

"Oh, no!"

"Oh, yes," Zach countered in a deep, whiskey-roughened baritone.

Suddenly, he sat straighter. A frown carved deep furrows in his forehead. Barbara hurried forward, thinking the pain was about to take him. He surprised both her and Nate with a gruff dismissal.

"Take yourself off, Prescott!"

"You might show a little more gratitude, old man. I *did* haul your carcass all the way across—"

"Take yourself off. I can't have you ogling my wife in her nightdress."

That, of course, directed the lieutenant's immediate attention to Barbara. His glance dropped like a stone to her middle, then to the skirts of her lawn nightdress. From the tide of red that swept into the man's cheeks, she guessed the sheer lawn provided him an almost unimpeded view of her lower limbs.

Fumbling at his uniform buttons, he made for the door.

"Yes, well, we'll sort this out tomorrow, Zach. Parks isn't the only army surgeon. Colonel Arbuckle might well decide to send you back to departmental headquarters for a second evaluation."

Zach answered with a noncommittal grunt and sat unmoving after the door closed behind his friend.

Barbara had spent enough time with both men now to know they'd graduated from West Point and served at different posts before being assigned to the frontier. Although Nate never tired of ribbing Zach for throwing in his lot with the ragtag rangers, he'd crowed with delight when he heard Old Hickory had promised a captaincy in the new regiment of dragoons to Lieutenant Zachariah Morgan.

Now Zach would not only forfeit his promotion, he'd surrender his commission altogether. Crushed by guilt, Barbara laid a hand on his shoulder.

"Your mother was right. This is my fault."

"I've more than enough whiskey in me to agree with that if I didn't know it to be nonsense."

"It isn't nonsense," she said miserably. "I've brought you nothing but disaster."

Reaching for her hand, he drew her around. Another tug brought her down onto his knee. She perched gingerly, afraid of jarring him.

"I'm a soldier. Or I was. I've taken my share of musket balls and knife wounds. Any one of them could have ended my life or my military career."

"You suffered those injuries in the performance of your duty. This one you took aiding a convict to escape his chains."

Tears burned behind her lids. Her throat raw and aching, she slid her arms around his neck.

"I'm sorry, Zach. So very sorry."

"Here now!" He managed a crooked grin. "There's no need for you to sing that song. I'm sorry enough for the both of us right now."

The grin broke her heart. The long, slow shudder that rippled through his powerful frame when he buried his face between her breasts loosed the tears Barbara had tried desperately to dam. They spilled down her cheeks, silent testament to his searing loss and the guilt she knew she'd always carry.

"It'll be all right," she murmured. "I know it will."

The tears flowed freely while she held him, stroking his hair, soothing him the way a mother would a hurt child.

"Commissioner Stokes sings your praises every time I get within earshot. He'll…he'll want you to continue in your advisory capacity, whether you're in uniform or out. I know he will."

Zach muttered something against her breast. She didn't catch the words, but the inflection indicated exactly what he thought of his advisory role.

"It's not the same," she said with quiet desperation. "I know it's not the same. But what you're doing is so important. Nate says the Cherokee in Georgia and North Carolina are being hunted down like animals and killed for their land. The commission has to negotiate a treaty with their delegation or it will mean the end of them."

He drew back then. "What's this? Are you crying over the plight of the Cherokee?"

She could hardly admit the tears were for him. He wouldn't want them. She was searching for an answer, when the baby pushed against her distended belly.

"Oh!"

Her eyes rounded, her hand went to her stomach, and Zach immediately tensed.

"What is it?"

"A foot, I think. Or a fist. There! There it is again."

He flattened his palm on her belly. She edged it over to the right spot. "Wait a moment. Perhaps he'll move again."

"He?"

"Or she. Does it matter which?"

"Not to me."

His palm was warm against her skin, his breath an aromatic waft. When the baby stretched again, a smile replaced the desolation she'd glimpsed on his face just moments ago.

"If it's a girl, I hope she has her mother's dainty ankles."

Barbara's ankles were anything but dainty at the moment, but she summoned an answering smile.

"I thank you, sir." Dipping her head, she feathered a kiss along his right temple. "If it's a boy, I hope he has his father's heart."

The brush of her lips against his skin stirred something deep in Zach's gut. Beneath the pain of his back, below the wretchedness of knowing he'd not have any part in the new regiment, he felt a tug of desire. It seeped through the whiskey that hadn't dulled either ache and roused a new one.

God, he wanted her. These months of stretching out on his bedroll just yards away from her had all but unmanned him. He went to sleep hurting and woke up feeling like a bear with a sore tooth.

Her advancing pregnancy and his damn back had kept him from assuaging the constant, nagging ache. But now her mouth hovered just inches from his own and the whiskey he'd swilled still heated his veins. He didn't so much as try to stop himself. Curling a hand around the soft skin of her nape, he covered her mouth with his.

After her first start of surprise, she gave a breathless little moan and leaned into the kiss. Her full breasts pressed against his chest, her mounded belly his middle. She was so ripe, so fecund. So incredibly, damnably arousing.

Cursing, Zach jerked his head back. "I'm sorry."

The flush in her cheeks faded. Sadness and regret shadowed her beautiful turquoise eyes.

"So am I," she whispered. "Can you ever forgive me for hurting you as I have?"

He blew out a long breath. "I'm past forgiving," he admitted ruefully, "and well into wanting."

It took her a moment or two to catch his meaning. When she did, her color rose again. Looking embarrassed and more than a little excited, she draped her arms around his neck.

"As it so happens, I'm well into wanting myself. You wouldn't think so with this great belly weighing me down, but the other wives said the…the urge often grips a woman at this stage."

"Did they?" Zach crooked an eyebrow. "Did they also suggest ways to satisfy this urge?"

"We didn't discuss the matter in exact detail," she replied primly. "But if I were to straddle your lap…like this…and you were to sit very still so you didn't jar your back, I think… Yes, I'm quite sure we could achieve a certain friction."

They achieved far more than mere friction. Zach had to grit his teeth against the agony in his lower back, but managed to bring Barbara to writhing, gasping pleasure. When she did the same for him, his pain dissolved in a flash of heat.

They fell asleep in the chair, with Zach propped against the back and Barbara curled against his front. Just before he drifted off, the whiskey in him brought the feelings he'd buried up until now swimming to the surface.

She was his wife. She carried his child. He was damned if he was going to let her go.

23

Zach ended his military career on the last day of May 1833. As he chose not to request a formal ceremony, it was a quiet transition. One day he rose, buttoned up his uniform jacket and buckled on his sword. The next, he reported to Commissioner Stokes in civilian attire.

Barbara's crushing guilt over her role in the abrupt termination of his military career was assuaged by the fact that they seemed to have found some peace between them at last. They shared meals, conversation about the day's events and a companionship that surprised them both.

Zach grew ever more involved in boundary negotiations for the tribes President Jackson was determined to move to Indian Country. Given the federal charter of the commission, the former lieutenant and his wife continued to occupy their quarters on post.

Barbara spent her days in the company of other wives and kept busy readying her nest for the baby's arrival.

One by one, the days slipped by. June rolled in with violent thunderstorms that uprooted trees and blew over a portion of the north palisade. The first week of July brought muggy heat and swarms of mosquitoes. They bred in the cane breaks along the river and made life miserable for both man and beast.

With the low-lying fort steaming in the hot summer sun, Zach tried to convince Barbara to remove to Morgan's Falls to escape the worst of the heat.

"I'd rather remain here," she told him.

"My mother has birthed eight children. She would help you with this one."

"I know she would. But…"

Biting her lip, she looked around their two small rooms. How could she explain to Zach that these whitewashed log walls and rug-covered dirt floors had become a home, her first real home since childhood?

"I should like to stay here," she said simply. "Sallie Nicks has promised to help with my lying in, and the midwife here on post has delivered any number of babies."

Zach, too, glanced around the crowded rooms. He saw them with different eyes, Barbara knew, and no doubt compared them to the spacious, well-appointed house at Morgan's Falls.

"Are you sure?"

"I am."

They'd yet to broach the subject of what would happen after the baby's birth, but the marriage that had begun under such dire conditions was slowly taking on a shape and depth neither had foreseen.

"If I can learn to sew curtains with my own hand," she said with a smile, "I expect I can cultivate a tolerance for heat and mosquitoes. After all, I'm the wife of a rough-and-tumble frontiersman."

In his neat civilian attire he hardly fit that label, but the grin he gave her was all backwoods rogue.

"Yes, you are. And just so you don't forget it…"

Sliding a hand under the heavy knot of her hair, he drew her forward. The kiss he dropped on her mouth left Barbara breathless and clinging to a fragile hope.

Her hope shattered into a thousand pieces the day following the celebrations that marked America's independence from British rule. Barbara was browsing at the sutler's store when one of Sallie's employees rushed in.

"The patrol that went out from Company D last week just marched into view."

The dark-haired widow glanced up from the roll of unbleached muslin she had suggested for swaddling clothes. The return of a patrol always excited interest. In this instance, the interest took a sharp turn into dismay.

"Word is they came under fire," the servant announced. "Lost two men, they did. One of 'em was their lieutenant."

Barbara's immediate reaction was one of relief. For the first time, she was grateful Zach no longer wore a uniform and thus hadn't been detailed to take out this particular patrol.

Hard on the heels of relief came guilt. How horrible to be glad someone else's loved one had gone down.

Guilt didn't turn to grief, however, until she joined the crowd that quickly gathered at the parade ground. Like weary old men, the infantry squad shrugged out of their packs and stacked their weapons. Their sergeant saw to the unloading of the two bodies lashed to the saddle of the lieutenant's mount.

When they stretched the corpses out on the parade ground, groans and soft cries rose from the crowd. Barbara's horrified gaze passed over the body of a small, stocky private and fixed on the one wearing the shoulder pips of an infantry lieutenant. The troopers had wrapped a blanket around his neck and head. The gray army blanket was stained with blood and almost black from the flies swarming about it. Only the tips of blond mustaches matted with gore showed beneath the blanket.

"Oh, no!"

Her hand groped for Sallie's. The widow caught it in a tight grip.

"He was so young," Sallie murmured in genuine distress. "So very handsome."

The hot sun beat down on Barbara's head right through the protective shield of her straw bonnet. Sweat dewed her upper lip. A dozen images tumbled through her head.

Of Nate Prescott, the first time she'd met him, all stiff and starched in his uniform. His silly grin when he'd presented her with a posy of wood violets the night of the Cotton Balers' Ball. His drunken despair the night Zach learned the regimental surgeon's verdict. He'd been a friend to Barbara, and as close as a brother to Zach.

Her eyes burned with unshed tears when Zach strode out of the building given over to use by the commissioners. His knuckles showed white on the handle of his cane as he got his first look at the bodies.

"It was squatters, sir."

The weathered sergeant who'd accompanied the patrol spit out a brown wad. Zach might not wear a uniform any longer, but he still commanded the respect and instant attention of the men on post.

"Damn farmer and his two growed sons. We came across 'em splittin' logs to build a cabin deep inside Creek Country. They kept shoutin' and wavin' their deed at the lieutenant, then things got outta hand and one of the boys snatched up his shotgun. All three o' those land-grubbers is eatin' dirt now," he finished with grim satisfaction.

"Did they have any womenfolk or livestock with them?"

"No sir, it was just them three hotheads. My guess is they was goin' to send for their womenfolk when they got their cabin up."

"How about papers? We'll need to—" He caught himself. "Colonel Arbuckle will need to notify their kinfolk."

"Just a Bible. And this."

Disgusted, the sergeant dug a crumpled, blood-stained scrap of paper out of his pocket.

"If I ever come across any of the bastards what print up these false deeds, I swear I'll put a bullet right through 'em. Just look at this one, sir. It's got gold seals and fancy print enough to fool a judge."

His jaw tight, Zach scanned the document. "It would have fooled me, too. The Whitestone Title and Deed Company certainly appears authentic."

The ground swayed under Barbara's feet. Her fingers clutched tight around Sallie's. For a moment, she feared the heat would take her.

"Whoever printed up this deed will pay. I'll see to that."

She barely heard Zach's fierce promise over the buzzing in her ears. When he returned the deed to the sergeant, the splotchy red spots staining it danced before her eyes. She heard Sallie calling to her as if from a deep tunnel.

"Lady Barbara? Are you all right?"

She couldn't answer, couldn't force so much as a single syllable through a throat that had closed tight.

Sallie slipped an arm around her waist and called out sharply. "Lieutenant Morgan! Your wife is feeling faint. You'd best get her out of the sun."

Hours later, Barbara perched on the edge of her bed. Suffocating heat surrounded her. She could hear Zach in the front room, scratching out a letter to Nate's parents. She'd left him to the grim task and sought a private refuge where she could give vent to her own grief and clamoring fears.

It *had* to be a coincidence!

Surely it was a coincidence.

Whitestone was a common enough name. She knew of at least one other Whitestone Manor in England besides the property her father had lost to a turn of the cards so many, many years ago. Harry *wouldn't* create a fictitious title company and give it the same name as his former home.

As swiftly as her heart issued the frantic denials, her mind scorned them. Of course Harry would. He'd done it before. His fraudulent Swiss railway company had been named for the estate that should by rights have come to him. In his mind, it was only fair turnabout to bilk investors with heavy pockets since he himself had been cheated of his inheritance.

Now, it appeared, he was bilking land-hungry

farmers of their savings and their dreams. And Barbara had provided him the means to do it!

Wrapping her arms around her middle, she rocked back and forth. She should have known Harry would use the funds she'd given him for some new scheme. He'd made vague reference to it in his last letter, but she'd shrugged the matter aside. She'd been too absorbed in the task of arranging her little nest. Too content to simply let the days slide by until the birth of her child.

The thought Harry might have inadvertently contributed to Nate's death appalled her. The very real possibility that Zach might hold her responsible as well made her feel physically ill.

He would never believe she'd had no part in the false deed scheme. Why should he? She'd fed him lie after lie. She'd dragged him into a dangerous plan to bribe Harry's way out of prison. Because of her, he'd taken the bullet that ended his military career. Now Nate had taken one, too, and Barbara might as well have pulled the trigger herself.

Piled on top of her fear about what Zach would think was the vengeance he'd sworn for Nate's death. The Morgans held to their promises. Zach had held to his despite all the lies she'd uttered. He'd track Harry down and bring him to justice, just as he'd sworn he would. The idea that her husband might well be the one to send her brother back to prison— or to the gallows—tore a low groan from the back of her throat.

Oh, Harry! How could you do this?

Burying her face in her hands, she squeezed her eyes shut and tried to blank out the image of Nate's gore-stained mustaches and blood-spattered uniform.

"Barbara?"

Slowly, she dropped her hands. She wanted to run away and crawl into some dark hole, but she forced herself to meet her husband's worried frown.

"I heard you moan. Is it the baby? Have your pains started?"

"No. I...I was thinking about Nate."

Zach blew out a ragged breath. "He died in the line of duty. That's rough consolation, I know, but one those of us who wore the uniform take to heart."

That he would offer her comfort in the midst of his own sorrow was almost more than she could bear. Her guilt was ripping her apart. Guilt, and her love for two very different men.

She owed it to Zach to tell him her suspicions. Yet her loyalty to Harry went bone deep. How could she betray her brother? How could she *not?*

"Nate wouldn't want you to make yourself sick," Zach said gruffly. "You must try to sleep."

"I can't."

Coward that she was, Barbara blamed her distress on grief and heat. "It's too hot, and I'm too overwrought to sleep. Every time I close my eyes I see Nate's mustaches and remember how proud he was of them."

"Vain as a damn peacock, you mean." A smile lightened the sadness in his eyes. "I told him so often enough. He thumped me soundly the last time."

His thoughts turned inward, to a time and place she had no part of. Moving to the washstand, he poured water into the bowl and dipped a facecloth in it.

"Here, this will cool you."

Settling beside her, he drew her hair to one side. The cloth felt blessedly cool against the heated skin of her neck, but the very relief it provided only added to Barbara's misery.

"You're all in knots. Roll your neck and try to relax."

He stroked the cloth over her neck and one shoulder, then moved her hair aside to give him access to the other. His hand lingered on the thick mass. It was lank and lusterless, Barbara knew, and as sweaty as the rest of her.

"Do you want me to wash your hair for you tomorrow?"

"You would do that?"

"I've done it often enough before. I've four younger sisters, remember?"

It was so much easier—so much *safer*—to speak of these mundane matters.

"I may just hold you to that offer," she said wearily. "I've grown so clumsy of late, the simplest tasks are beyond me."

He sponged her neck and back. "I wish you would let me hire someone to attend you. I could speak to Hattie. If I asked her, she would leave John Stallworth's tavern and come back to work for you."

"Oh, Zach, we've discussed this before. You know that won't answer. Hattie loves you, and hates me for the pain that slices into you with every step."

"The pain is bearable." He dropped a feather-light kiss on her nape. "And I consider it a small price to pay for you, sweeting. I'll have to make Hattie understand a certain blond beauty has won my heart."

Oh, God! How she'd longed to hear that tender endearment. She ached to turn and tell him she felt the same. Guilt and remorse held her mute.

"You're too close to your time for me to feel comfortable leaving you alone. I'll speak to her after Nate's funeral."

The reminder that he'd bury his closest friend tomorrow wiped all thought but one from Barbara's mind. Swinging around, she caught his arm.

"Zach."

"Yes?"

"The false deed, the one issued by that company. You said this morning you intended to find out who's behind it."

"And so I will. When I finish my letter to Nate's parents, I'll pen one to my mother's man of business in New Orleans. He'll ferret out who's behind Whitestone soon enough. When he does, I'll track the bastard down. He'll be lucky if he lives long enough to face a judge."

The sick feeling in Barbara's stomach intensified. Harry wouldn't be taken without a fight. He'd already spent seven months in a prison hellhole. He'd kill anyone who tried to send him back.

She would lose one of them, she knew with awful certainty. Unless she sent Harry away forever.

She lay awake while he labored over his letters, watching the shadows cast by the lantern in the front room, listening to the scratch of his pen.

She would pen a letter tomorrow, too. To Harry. She would tell him about Lieutenant Prescott and the others. He should know the tragedy his scheme had caused.

She would also tell him he must leave the country immediately or she would notify the authorities. She couldn't allow him to stay and profit from his blood money.

Tortured by what she knew her husband would consider another betrayal, Barbara fell into a fitful sleep.

24

Lieutenant Nathaniel Prescott and Private Adrian Kaparov were buried with full military honors. The entire garrison turned out in dress uniform for the ceremony. Zach tried to convince Barbara not to attend. The heat was too intense, the mosquitoes too insistent.

She wouldn't be dissuaded. Nate deserved her respect, and attending his funeral was the least of the penances she feared she would pay for contributing unknowingly to his death. Her long-sleeved gown and veiled bonnet provided both suitably somber attire and some protection from the gnats and mosquitoes. The garments also had her swimming in sweat before the funeral cortege was halfway to the post cemetery.

Black cloth muffled the drums. The soldiers marching to the solemn, measured beat sweltered in their tall, plumed caps, high-collared blue roundabouts and woolen trousers. The officers trailed their swords in the dust. The infantrymen, Barbara saw through the screen of her veil, carried their muskets reversed.

"It's an old practice," Zach explained quietly at the start of the formation, "dating back to the Greeks. It symbolizes that the normal order of things is reversed and matters are not as they should be."

Indeed they weren't. She had only to look at the chiseled granite of her husband's face to know matters might never again be as they should.

The post chaplain read several long verses at graveside. Colonel Arbuckle followed with a wrenching tribute to the fallen warriors. As the wooden caskets were lowered into the hastily dug graves, a squad of seven soldiers fired off three rounds. Barbara flinched at the sharp reports and shrank against Zach's side.

"Another ancient custom," he murmured, a muscle ticking in the side of his jaw. "A signal that the warring armies have cleared their dead from the battlefield and are prepared to resume hostilities."

While the rifle shots echoed through the surrounding hills, Barbara said goodbye to handsome, dashing Nate Prescott and knew with awful certainty that Zach did, indeed, intend to resume hostilities. He might not wear a uniform any longer, but he wouldn't rest until he'd fulfilled his promise to Nate.

The thick veil hid her tears as the drums and fifes

sounded tattoo—a final "lights out" for Lieutenant Prescott and Private Kaparov.

Exhausted by the heat and drained by her wrenching emotions, Barbara declined to join the somber gathering at the officers' mess. Zach took her back to their quarters instead. He saw her dressed in a loose gown and installed in their one comfortable armchair before he departed.

"I'll only be a little while. Just long enough to drink a toast to Nate and watch the officer of the mess retire his drinking mug."

"Another tradition?"

"The last one. Can I get you anything before I leave?"

All she wanted at the moment was a pen, an inkwell and a sheet of paper. She intended to write Harry now, while her heart ached for Nate. Maybe, just maybe, she could make her brother understand the consequences of his scheme. Perhaps she could also make him understand that he must leave America immediately. Since she couldn't bring herself to ask Zach for the very implements she would use to betray him yet again, she merely shook her head.

"I'm fine, thank you. I'll just rest while you're gone."

His keen glance skimmed over her face. She had no doubt she looked as miserable as she felt.

"I went to John Stallworth's this morning," he

told her. "I spoke with Hattie. She said she'd quit the tavern today."

"She would quit this earth if you asked her to."

"I'll settle for having her keep an eye on you." Leaning down, he brushed her mouth with his. "I'll return shortly, wife."

"I'll be here, husband."

He left the door open to catch the hope of a breeze. Barbara rested until his footsteps faded, then dragged her unwieldy bulk from the armchair. Zach kept his writing implements in his small campaign desk. She found a sheet of paper and a sharpened nib for the pen.

Drawing out the folding stool from under the desk, she sank onto it clumsily. Her husband's promise to return quickly made her missive necessarily brief.

Harry—
A dreadful thing has happened. Two soldiers and three farmers have died as a result of an altercation over a false quit-claim deed issued by Whitestone Title and Deed Company.

She underscored the company name three times. Dipping the pen into the inkwell, she started on the warning she hoped would keep one of the men she loved from killing the other.

You must cease operations immediately and disappear before…

The thud of footsteps sent her pen skittering across the page. Guilty panic made Barbara grab another blank sheet to cover the first.

It wasn't Zach who appeared at the open door, however. It was Hattie. Letting out a shaky breath, Barbara nodded to her.

"Hello, Hattie. Come in."

The woman who stepped over the threshold looked much different from the one who'd arrived at Fort Gibson battered and bruised all those months ago. Her skin was smooth, if flushed from the heat, and her brown hair neatly dressed. Her calico blouse clung to slender curves that must surely have caught the attention of the men she served at the taproom. As one of the few unmarried females on post, the woman could have her pick of husbands. Unfortunately, she wanted Barbara's.

Her expression held none of the enmity it had the few times she and her former mistress had crossed paths these past months. Still, Barbara could feel the dislike buried under the woman's impassive demeanor. She knew instinctively what she'd told Zach last night held true. This arrangement wouldn't answer.

"Zach sought me out at the taproom this morning," the maid said by way of greeting. "He asked me to come and give you some assistance."

"Yes, he said he intended to speak with you. I told him it wasn't necessary. I've become quite adept at taking care of myself."

Hattie's careful mask slipped. Her lip curled, and she swept her former employer with a mocking glance.

"So I see."

Barbara stiffened. She felt as big and bloated as a dead horse. Her hair still awaited the washing Zach had promised. Worry over Harry's role in the White-stone Title and Deed Company gnawed at her conscience like a pack of hungry wolves. She neither needed nor desired the attentions of a serving woman who seemed to have forgotten herself.

"Thank you for looking in," she said coolly. "I'll tell Zach you did so."

The unmistakable dismissal had Hattie swearing under her breath. Her heart had about leaped clear of her chest when Zach had sought her out this morning. She'd been sure, so very sure, he'd finally grown tired of this overblown blond bitch.

Just look at her! Her hair all frowsy, her tits as big as udders, and that loose calico gown draped over her like a tent.

It had near killed Hattie to watch her swell up these past months with Zach's child. It had hurt worse to watch him limp home to her every night, his knuckles white on the handle of his cane. Barbara had done that to him. She and that handsome, no-good brother of hers. Zach might have been forced to marry the woman to give his child a name, but once she dropped her whelp, Hattie would see he was rid of her.

She'd had months to think on ways to make that happen. Months to ponder and plot. She'd come up with a dozen different schemes and abandoned most of them as too chancy. She'd finally decided on the one with the least risk to herself.

Barbara would die in childbirth. Women bled out all the time after delivering a babe. No one would question matters if this pale, overbred aristocrat never rose from the birthing straw. Cowbane had almost worked before. This time, Hattie would make sure it didn't fail her. She still had the half-full twist she'd purchased in Washington.

To use it, though, she needed to be present when Barbara's pains started. And that meant swallowing her pride. With some effort, she adopted a tone of grudging gratitude.

"I didn't come just because Mr. Morgan asked it. You gave me work when I needed it most. I owe you for that. Why don't you let me help you."

Shaking her head, Barbara laid both palms flat on the desk and started to push up. She rose only a few inches and froze.

"Oh!"

Her startled glance flew to Hattie's. Beads of sweat popped out on her upper lip. She hung there for several seconds before sinking back onto the stool.

Joy leaped in Hattie's breast. Nature just might have arranged things perfectly for her. They were alone, just her and the bitch. Barbara would send her for the midwife, she didn't doubt. Hattie would go after her, but she'd swing by her room at the tavern and get the cowbane first. She hid her excitement behind a spurious sympathy.

"Are your pains starting?"

"I don't know." She put a shaky hand to her belly. "I felt a sharp tug."

"Sounds like it to me. I'll go fetch the midwife, shall I?"

"Yes, please, and Zach."

Hattie started out the door.

"No! Wait!"

Swiping her tongue along her lower lip, Barbara reached across the desk and drew a page with writing on it toward her.

"Before you…" She hesitated, swallowed hard, and started again. "Before you fetch Zach, would you put a letter in the mail pouch for me?"

As curious as a cat, Hattie nodded.

"Just let me scribble a few more lines and add my signature."

Sweat was rolling down her cheeks by the time

she'd folded the page into overlapping quarters, dripped sealing wax onto it, and scratched out an address.

"This is rather important." Her fingers shook as she passed the letter to Hattie. "Please see that it gets posted before you do anything else."

Pigs would fly before the letter made it into the mail pouch. Agog now with curiosity, Hattie almost snatched it from her hand and left the Morgans' rooms.

The moment she turned the corner from the officers' quarters, Hattie stuffed the letter in her skirt pocket. She couldn't read herself, but there were plenty around who'd spell out the words for a snuggle or a kiss. She'd get O'Shaunessy to do just that.

First, though, she had to fetch the cowbane.

To Hattie's bitter disappointment, Barbara experienced only that one sharp tug. The midwife poked and prodded at her distended belly and offered the opinion she had another week to go yet.

Barbara took the prediction with a groan. "A week more in this heat?"

Smiling sympathetically, Zach stroked the sweat-dampened hair off her forehead. "How about Hattie and I take turns pouring buckets of water over you?"

Barbara's glance shifted to the maid. Hattie hoped her expression was suitably bland.

"Don't think I won't hold you both to that promise."

With that wry statement, she sealed her fate. Hattie could barely hold back her glee.

The midwife left with a promise to remain close to her own quarters should Barbara need her. Hattie accompanied Zach to the door when he, too, returned to his duties.

"My thanks for coming to stay with Barbara."

"She didn't want me to."

"I know."

"I think she holds a grudge against me for telling you about the dose she took in Washington."

The reminder of those bleak days took some of the easiness from Zach's smile. Hattie hated to see it go, but didn't want him to forget the pain and worry the woman in the other room had caused him.

She held her own hurt for him deep in her heart later that night. The candle beside her bed flickered as she traced a fingertip over the squiggly lines O'Shaunessy had deciphered for her.

The big Irish corporal had resisted at first. Claimed it wasn't part of his kit to go readin' letters writ by officers' wives. Hattie had been forced to offer more inducement than she'd intended to gain his cooperation. His sweat now stank on her skin and his seed stuck her thighs together.

She hardly noticed either the stink or the stickiness. An excitement that owed nothing to O'Shaunessy's enthusiastic rutting pounded in her veins. As if it were yesterday, she remembered Sir Harry Chamberlain sauntering into the taproom. Remembered as well his casual questions about the false quit-claim deed that pig, Thomas, had got himself shot over.

If Hattie was interpreting this letter right, Handsome Harry had dipped his fingers in the wrong pie. What's more, his bitch of a sister knew just what he was about.

She'd come within a breath of snatching the letter from O'Shaunessy's hands, throwing on her clothes and running back to Zach's quarters. The bitter acknowledgment of Barbara's skill at wiggling her way out of situations every bit as bad as this one had kept Hattie right here, in her small, hot room.

She'd use the letter against the woman. That much she was sure of. She'd have to think about the when and the where of it, though.

Two days later, Sallie Nicks received word the steamer *Arabella* would arrive at Fort Gibson that very afternoon, almost a week ahead of its posted schedule. The usual anticipation of letters, newspapers and visitors rippled through the post. When Hattie mentioned the news to Barbara, her face went chalk white.

"It's too soon!"

Hattie had to strain to catch the anguished whisper.

"The letter couldn't have reached him yet."

"Who was it to go to?" she asked, taking malicious delight in the game.

Barbara turned a haunted look her way. "My brother. You met him, that day at the landing."

Hattie almost danced on her toes with glee. And well Barbara should look haunted. If that brother of hers showed his face at Fort Gibson, he'd have to face three hundred troopers still angry over the deaths of their own.

And one very dangerous former lieutenant. Zach might walk with a cane, but Hattie had seen him in action. If it turned out Harry Chamberlain was behind the false deeds now peppering Indian Country, Zach would put him down without so much as a blink and get a medal for doing it.

Shaking with excitement, Hattie didn't realize fate had handed her the perfect opportunity until Barbara turned to her with a desperate plea.

"Will you go down to the landing this afternoon and watch to see if my brother is among the passengers who get off the *Arabella*? I would do it myself but…"

But she didn't want her husband to see her and question why she was standing about in the hot sun, Hattie guessed.

"I can do that," she agreed. "If he does get off, I'll bring him here straightaway."

"No!"

She drew in a shaky breath and erased the panic from her voice.

"Tell him it's not convenient for me to receive visitors right now. I'm too discommoded to see anyone, even my brother. He'll have to remain on the steamer and depart when it does. I'll write out a note and explain things. You can take it with you."

By the time the *Arabella* steamed around the bend of the Grand, her smokestacks belching and her whistle shrilling, Hattie's fertile mind had devised yet another plot. One that would rid the world of Barbara and leave Zach so disgusted he would never mourn her loss.

Hoping against hope Sir Harry was indeed aboard the steamer, Hattie pushed to the front of the crowd that gathered at the landing. Her pulse leaped when she spotted his guinea-gold curls among the travelers lining the rail. She caught him right as he stepped off the gangplank.

"Your sister sent me. She's in a bad way. She wants me to take you to her."

25

Hattie took Sir Harry straight to the stables behind John Stallworth's tavern. When he surveyed the log lean-to, his sun-bleached eyebrows snapped into a frown.

"My sister is here?"

"No."

With a furtive glance over her shoulder, she drew him into the shade of the log building.

"I couldn't speak of it with all those people milling about on the landing, but word has got around about those false quit-claim deeds you had printed in New Orleans."

He drew himself up to his full height. "I'm sure I don't know what you're talking about. Now take me to my sister. At once, if you please."

The demand scraped Hattie just the wrong way.

What gave this crook the right to look down his nose at her? Or speak to her in the same haughty manner his sister used? Hiding her animosity behind a worried face, she dug Barbara's letter out of her skirt pocket.

"If you don't believe me, perhaps you'll believe you sister."

She thrust the letter into his hand. His scowl deepened when he saw the broken seal.

"What's this? Have you taken to reading the letters your mistress writes?"

"No, I never got taught to read. Your sister gave it to me this way. She said Zach—Lieutenant Morgan—found the letter and read it."

Still frowning, he scanned the few lines.

"Hell and damnation!"

"Barbara says you're in terrible danger. That's why she set me to watching every steamboat, so I could catch you and tell you so. She wants you to hire a horse here at the livery stable and leave the post before someone recognizes you. You've got to get out of Indian Country."

He crumpled the letter in his fist. "I'm not leaving without my sister."

"She doesn't intend for you to. There's a cave about three miles up the Fort Smith road, back in a stand of rock. I tied a bit of cloth around a tree limb to mark the place you turn off. You're to wait for her there. She'll meet you there as soon as she can throw a few things in a valise for herself and the baby."

"She's birthed the child?"

"Not yet. But she's due any day. That's why she's so frantic," Hattie added, inventing wildly. "She knows Zach's just waiting for her to deliver the babe. He thinks she was in on this scheme with you. He'll take the child and let her rot beside you in prison."

His hot blue eyes grew hard and cold. "Barbara said he only married her to give his bastard a name. I should have tossed him overboard when I had the chance."

He slapped the letter against his leg while Hattie waited with near breathless impatience to see if he would take the bait. She could have kissed him when he did.

"I'll tell you this. I'll never wear a set of leg irons again. Nor will my sister see the inside of any prison." His jaw tight, he stuffed the letter in his pocket and drew out a silver card case. "Give her this card so she'll know I've arrived. In the meantime, I'll hire a mount and find this cave. Tell Barbara I'll wait for her there."

It was as easy as that! Hattie almost danced a jig as she watched him stride into the livery stable.

After that, it was child's play to hitch up the neat little buggy Zach had purchased for his wife's pleasure and bundle Barbara into it. All Hattie had to do was wave that bit of cardboard under Barbara's nose and echo her brother's own words.

He'd come for his sister.

He wouldn't leave without her.

He'd wait for her on the Fort Smith road.

Hattie could have laughed aloud when the cow started for the door, then ground her teeth and said she'd have to empty her bladder before she could climb into the buggy. While she squatted over the chamber pot, her onetime maid lifted a long-bladed hunting knife from one of the wall pegs. She would have preferred to use a pistol. A bullet was quicker and cleaner, but also noisier. She couldn't risk someone hearing the shots. The knife was safely in her pocket when Barbara waddled out of the back room.

As Hattie gave her a boost into the buggy, she remembered one last detail. She would have to hurry back and pack a valise to make sure the tale she'd tell Zach rang true. She'd do just that after she saw Sir Harry and Barbara on their way to hell.

26

"Zach?"

Sallie Nicks tapped lightly on the door to the hot dusty room where Zach and the clerk assigned to the federal commission sat sweating over a map of the proposed Seminole boundaries. They'd both shed their coats and rolled up their sleeves, but Zach's white linen shirt stuck to his shoulders and back like a wet rag.

"May I speak with you a moment?"

Anticipation and instant worry leaped like twin tigers inside him. He could think of only one reason why Sallie would need to speak with him. His wife's pains had begun for real this time.

Pushing back his chair, he groped for his cane. "Have you come about Barbara? Is it her time?"

"No. Well, I don't think so."

"What's this?"

The widow pursed her lips. "I merely wanted to ask you why Barbara would go jaunting about in a buggy with her time so near."

"What makes you think she's jaunting about in a buggy?"

"One of my field hands saw her. He said she tooled off down the Fort Smith road at a smart clip."

Zach shook his head. "He must have mistaken her for someone else."

"I don't think so. He mentioned that she had Hattie with her. The maid was handling the reins."

"This makes no sense. Barbara said nothing to me about traveling anywhere today."

Or any day. In fact, she'd protested vigorously when he'd tried to send her to Morgan's Falls to wait out her time in more comfortable surroundings.

"It made no sense to me, either," Sallie said after the slightest hesitation, "until I saw the passenger list from the steamboat that arrived this afternoon. The manifest included a Sir Harry Chamberlain. He's Barbara's brother, is he not?"

"He is."

Just in time he bit back a warning to Sallie to keep her purse close at hand. Zach's opinion of Chamberlain had not improved during the weeks he'd spent in Charleston, stretched out flat on his face while the Englishman prowled the streets in search of amusement.

Her dark eyes troubled, Sallie shared yet another bit of news. "Sir Harry hired a horse from John Stallworth's livery, Zach. He rode down the Fort Smith pike shortly before Barbara did."

In a single heartbeat Zach went from puzzled to coldly furious. Whatever the hell Chamberlain was up to, it spelled trouble of some sort. Zach was damned if he'd let the bastard drag his wife into another of his dangerous schemes.

"Thanks, Sallie. I'll make a check of our quarters. I'm sure Barbara left a note or word with a neighbor explaining matters."

A quick search of their two rooms and a survey of their neighbors revealed no note or message of any kind. What he did find was a half-finished meal and an empty peg where his hunting knife usually hung.

His stomach knotting, Zach threw aside his cane and lifted his rifle from its pegs above the mantel. He didn't know why Harry had returned to Fort Gibson or where he and Barbara were headed, but every muscle and sinew in his body was now strung as tight as a bow.

Three minutes later he was at the stables where he kept his mounts. Peter, the freed slave who'd tended to Zach's mounts during his time in the army, still served as his groom.

"Bring my saddle."

The groom's jaw sagged. "You're going to ride?"

Gritting his teeth against the pain that speared through his back, Zach threw the saddle blanket over his roan and didn't waste breath on the obvious.

"You're in no shape to climb into a saddle," the elderly groom protested.

"Jump to it, man!"

Peter complied, but muttered the whole time he tightened the cinch and adjusted the stirrups.

"Miz Louise will have my head for this. First that saucy maid acomin' in here demanding to have the gray put between the shafts of the buggy and sayin' Miz Barbara done ordered it. Now you trottin' off with a bullet jigglin' up and down in your spine. I don't like this. I'm tellin' you, I don't like this a-tall."

Zach ignored the old man's grumblings, just as he always had, but he couldn't ignore the agony that jolted up his back when he put a boot to the stirrup and a hand to the pommel. Fire raced along his nerves. His teeth clenched so tight his jawbones popped in their sockets. Dragging in a harsh breath, he swung into the saddle.

27

"Where is he, Hattie? I don't see him."

The tense, nervous passenger twisted in the buggy seat and scanned the dense woods on either side of the narrow road.

"There's a cave just off the road," Hattie said soothingly. "See, I tied that bit of cloth on a tree branch to mark the place."

Barbara spotted the limp rag. "When did you do that?"

"I...er..."

Cursing her slip, Hattie fumbled for an answer. She could hardly say she'd all but run the three miles out and back earlier this afternoon, before the *Arabella* docked.

"Months ago," she lied. "When I was picking blackberries. I stashed some in the cave and thought to come back for them but never did."

Deftly, she maneuvered the buggy off the dirt track and as far into the trees as she could. The Fort Smith road was nowhere near as busy as the National Pike. Riders or wagons rarely passed down it more than once a day. Still, there was no need to leave the buggy smack in the middle of the road.

"Here, let me help you down. You don't want to stumble and fall."

Not here, anyway. She could drag the fat cow to the cave if she had to. Years of chopping firewood and dressing carcasses had certainly given her the strength for it. But why drag a dead weight through the underbrush if she didn't have to?

"Here's the path. Watch those tree branches."

Barbara plowed ahead of her, clearing the way like the prow of a boat. Hattie followed in her wake. Her blood began to pump. Sweat slicked the palm she slipped into her pocket.

"Harry!"

With a little cry, Barbara broke through the trees and rushed into the arms of her golden-haired brother. He wrapped her in a fierce hug. Hattie's fist tightened around the knife handle. She waited, her heart hammering against her ribs, until they broke apart.

"Oh, Harry!"

The skirts of her tentlike gown swirling about her ankles, Barbara took a few agitated paces before swinging around to face her brother.

"How could you plunge into another disastrous scheme? Didn't you learn from the last one?"

"Now, Babs, this scheme is hardly disastrous. You can't imagine how much I've raked in these past months."

"No, and I don't wish to. Do you have *any* idea of the grief you've caused?"

"No, and I don't wish to," he echoed with a shrug.

They didn't so much as remember she was there, Hattie thought on a wave of hate so strong it carried her right up to the golden-haired bastard. He turned to her with a sharp look, as if questioning why someone like her would dare to interrupt her betters in the midst of a heated discussion.

In one swift move, Hattie dragged the knife from its sheath inside her pocket and plunged the blade into his belly. She yanked it upward, gutting him as swiftly and skillfully as she'd gutted any hog or deer.

28

Barbara didn't understand at first what was happening. Hattie's back was to her. Her slender figure had blocked all but the sudden movement of her arm. But when Harry tottered back a step, she saw the knife buried in his belly.

"Nooo!"

Wild with shock and disbelief, she threw herself forward. The sheer bulk of her knocked Hattie sideways.

"Harry!" Barbara spun back to her brother. "Dear God, Harry!"

As if in a daze, he looked down at the intestines bulging through the slit in his stomach. He raised his head, gave her a look of utter astonishment and sank to his knees.

Sobs ripped from Barbara's throat. She dropped

awkwardly beside him. Desperate, she tried to shove the bloody white ropes back inside his gaping wound. In her horror, it didn't occur to her that she might suffer the same fate until Harry's lips curled back in a rictus of agony.

"Babs! Look to...yourself!"

She threw a terrified glance over her shoulder, saw Hattie observing them with a smile.

A smile! She stood there with Harry's blood staining her entire dress and smiled!

"You murdering whore!" Barbara screamed, her frantic hands still squishing and plunging among Harry's guts. "Are you mad?"

"Some might say so, I suppose. But quite clever in my madness, wouldn't you say?"

"Clever!"

The piercing shriek startled a flock of birds. Wings flapping, they whirred into the sky.

"This is hardly clever, you stupid bitch. You'll hang for this."

"Oh, I think not. Who's to say what happened here?" She flicked Harry a smug glance. "Not him, certainly."

A whimper escaped Barbara as she, too, looked down at her brother. His eyes had closed. His mouth was slack. Choking back sobs, she stilled her bloody hands.

"Now, mistress, I shall attend you one last time."

With studied casualness, Hattie tested the bloody

knife tip with a finger. Nausea flooded Barbara's throat. Swallowing convulsively, she wrapped her arms around her belly.

"You can't... You must not... My babe..."

"Your bastard, you mean."

Like a snake shedding its skin, the brunette abandoned her mocking pretense. The hate Barbara had glimpsed before in her eyes now burned bright and fierce.

"You thought to tie Zach to you by spreading your legs and letting his seed take root."

"No!"

"Zach married you because of that babe. Everyone knows that."

"Hattie, listen to me..."

"It will shatter him when he learns you ran off the moment your brother came for you."

She took a step forward, the knife tight in her blood-drenched fist.

"You told your brother you couldn't continue in your farce of a marriage. I tried to stop you from leaving with him. When you insisted, I had no choice but to drive you to your arranged meeting place. I argued. I pleaded. I cried bitter tears when you went off with him, never to be seen again."

Barbara stumbled back. Her smothering fear for herself came nowhere near to the terror she now felt for her unborn child.

"Please, don't kill my babe. Please!"

All the while she choked out pleas, Barbara's terror-filled mind searched for a way to save her child.

She couldn't run. She was too big and clumsy. She wouldn't take three steps before the madwoman plunged the knife into her back. She'd have to use her bare hands to fight off the vicious blade. Or a rock! A heavy rock.

She took another step back. Threw a glance at a tumble of boulders. She'd never make them. Hattie was only a few yards away.

"Listen to me!" she pleaded. "You could cut the babe from my belly. Slice me open the way you did Harry and take the babe to Zach."

The maid's lip curled. "Do you think I didn't consider that? No, it won't answer. I can hardly show up at the fort with your brat in swaddling blankets."

"Yes, you can! You can say I went into labor and dropped the child, but didn't want to take it with me. Zach will believe you. He thinks I tried to rid myself of the child in Washington."

"Too bad we didn't succeed in that attempt."

"We! Did you…? Did you poison me?"

"I tried my best to."

Her mouth curving in that same murderous smile, Hattie stepped over Harry's body.

"The knife is faster than cowbane, thank goodness, and more—"

She stopped dead, her skirts snagged by a bloody

hand. Like a ghoul rising from the grave, Harry lifted his head and gasped out an agonized cry.

"Run…Babs!"

Shrieking in rage, Hattie twisted around. Her arm swept up. The blade slashed down.

Once. Twice. Again.

With a sob of pure terror, Barbara ran for the tumbled boulders. She scrabbled for a loose rock, tearing off her nails, bruising her knuckles. She got her hands around one. Swung her bulk around. Raised her arms. Drew her lips back in a snarl.

"You'll not kill my babe!"

Using every ounce of strength she possessed, Barbara heaved the rock at the woman rushing toward her. The missile left her hands just as the crack of gunfire split the air.

A red hole blossomed between Hattie's eyes an instant before the rock smashed into her face.

29

Her clothing and arms stained with blood, Barbara cradled her brother's head in her lap.

Zach ignored his blinding pain and went down on one knee beside them. A single glance told him it was useless, but he made the effort for Barbara's sake. Dragging off his linen shirt, he stuffed it into the gaping hole in Harry's stomach. The stab wounds to the throat and chest were still pumping blood. Zach covered the worst of them with his palm.

Chamberlain's lids fluttered up. He stared at Barbara through eyes already glazed with death.

"Babs…"

The hoarse whisper brought a bubble of blood with it. Tears streaming down her cheeks, Barbara dabbed at the froth with a corner of her skirt.

"I'm here, Harry."

His lids drifted down. Zach was sure he was gone, but the muscles under his palm moved.

"Didn't...know."

Barbara bent closer. "What, Harry? What are you trying to say?"

With agonizing slowness, his lids lifted again. This time his gaze fixed on Zach.

"White...stone. Babs...didn't...know."

Aw, Christ. Chamberlain was behind those false deeds. Zach should have guessed. Feeling a thousand years old, he nodded.

Chamberlain gave one more rattling breath and died.

Barbara clutched her brother in silent, stricken grief. Zach turned his head away to allow her a last moment with her brother and fixed his sight on the body lying in a crumpled heap a few feet away.

He'd hear the echo of Hattie's enraged shriek for the rest of his days. It had brought him plunging through the underbrush, thumbing the hammer on his rifle as he ran. Things had a way of coming back to haunt a man, Zach thought. He'd rescued Hattie by putting a bullet between the eyes of her brutish master. He'd ended her life the same way.

With a ragged sigh, Barbara lowered her brother's head to the earth.

"He told you the truth," she said with infinite weariness. "As difficult as it must be for you to believe, I never heard a word about Whitestone Title and Deed Company until the sergeant showed you that bloodstained deed."

She rested her hands on her belly. They were stained with blood and scraped raw at the knuckles.

"I guessed at once Harry was behind the company. He'd used the same name for the railway scheme that landed him in the gaol."

"Why didn't you tell me?"

"I wanted to. The night before Nate's funeral, I almost did. But you had vowed vengeance."

Her gaze lifted to his. Death had stripped away the lies and half truths. All that remained was a desolation that went bone deep.

"Harry wouldn't have let you take him. He swore he'd never go back to prison. He would have killed you…or hired someone to do it. I couldn't bear the thought of losing you."

Zach believed her. Not because he wanted to. Because he knew she wouldn't lie to him over her brother's body.

Clenching his jaw against the pain in his back, he pushed to his feet. "I'll send a detail back for the bodies. Let me take you home, Barbara."

Home. Two small rooms at a remote outpost in the heart of Indian Country. They beckoned to her like a shimmering alabaster palace.

Not until she put her hand in Zach's strong, callused palm did Barbara understand those two rooms didn't represent safety and stability. That came from Zach, and knowing he loved her despite all.

With a last glance, she said goodbye to her brother and turned her face to her husband.

Barbara delivered a son six days later.

The birth was relatively easy according to Sallie Nicks and the midwife, who washed and swaddled the babe with brisk cheerfulness. Barbara rather thought they made light of her ordeal.

Exhausted and drenched with sweat, she fell back on the birthing straw while the midwife fussed and cooed over the squalling infant. Sallie attended to Barbara, helping her into bed, cleansing her with a damp cloth, whisking away the soiled straw. Not until the new mother had donned a clean nightdress and had her hair brushed did the midwife go to fetch Zach. While she waited for her husband, Barbara cradled her son in her arms.

To Sallie's delight, the babe took to his mother's breast immediately and began to suckle. "He knows what he wants, that one."

Disconcerted by the tingling sensation, Barbara cupped a hand over his soft, downy hair. It was as black as night, like his father's.

"And his eyes are so blue," she whispered, both awed and amazed at what she'd produced.

"Most babies' eyes are blue at birth. They'll likely change within six months or a year."

"I hope so! My mother-in-law told me of a legend that has haunted her for most of her life. She's convinced a blue-eyed child brings disaster."

"Only if that child is female," Zach said from the doorway.

He limped into the room, still wracked with pain from the jarring gallop down the Fort Smith Pike. Barbara's wonder in her son dimmed when she saw the harsh lines that ride had etched in his face. His thought wasn't for his pain, though, but for hers.

"Are you all right?"

"Now I am," she said with some feeling. "I shall have to think a while before deciding whether to give your son a brother or sister."

Chuckling, he brushed a knuckle down the babe's red, mottled cheek. "My mother said the same after each of *my* brothers and sisters made their appearance. Lord, he's a lusty little devil. Have you fixed a name?"

Barbara raised her gaze to his. "I thought we might name him Nathaniel."

At the soft suggestion, Zach felt something shift inside him. He'd been sure that if she bore a son she'd want to name him after her brother. Much as he would have disliked it, Zach would have agreed. Harry had been her only family, her only anchor in her topsy-turvy world.

Instead, she wanted to honor the man who'd been as close as a brother to Zach. She couldn't have chosen a more direct means of telling him she'd put her past behind her and turned her face to the future. A future they'd build together.

"Nathaniel Morgan," he said with a slow grin. "I think that's a fine name. Let's hope he lives up to it."

Author's Note

While Barbara and Zach Morgan are figments of my admittedly active imagination, the historical events referenced in this book are very real.

In 1836, President Andrew Jackson ordered the army to enforce the provisions of the Indian Removal Act. Those Native Americans who refused to voluntarily relocate were forced from their homes at bayonet point, incarcerated in hastily erected stockades, and eventually moved West. More than four thousand Cherokee died during the infamous march that became known as the Trail of Tears.

Fort Gibson served as the terminus of that exodus. For many years, it was also the primary outpost in Indian Country, later known as Oklahoma Indian Territory. The name Oklahoma first appeared in an 1866 treaty with the Choctaw tribe. Coined by a Native American missionary, the term is a combination of two Choctaw words: *okla,* meaning people, and *humma,* meaning red.

You might also be interested to know Britain continued to use transportation and/or confinement to hulks to relieve overcrowded prison conditions as late as 1867. Overall, more than two hundred thousand convicts were transported to the Americas, Bermuda and the penal colonies of Australia. Many of the convicts who survived eventually flourished in their new lives.

Some weren't as fortunate. Like the heroine of the next book in this series, they ended their days in prison or mounted the steps of the gallows. Watch for *She Shot Him Dead,* coming from MIRA in 2005, set during the wild-and-woolly outlaw days of Oklahoma Indian Territory.

Merline Lovelace

66871 THE COLONEL'S DAUGHTER ___ $6.50 U.S. ___ $7.99 CAN.
66707 A SAVAGE BEAUTY   ___ $6.50 U.S. ___ $7.99 CAN.
66649 THE CAPTAIN'S WOMAN ___ $6.50 U.S. ___ $7.99 CAN.

(limited quantities available)

TOTAL AMOUNT $_____
POSTAGE & HANDLING $_____
($1.00 for 1 book, 50¢ for each additional)
APPLICABLE TAXES* $_____
TOTAL PAYABLE $_____
(check or money order—please do not send cash)

To order, complete this form and send it, along with a check or money order for the total above, payable to MIRA Books, to: **In the U.S.:** 3010 Walden Avenue, P.O. Box 9077, Buffalo, NY 14269-9077; **In Canada:** P.O. Box 636, Fort Erie, Ontario L2A 5X3.

Name:_____
Address:_____ City:_____
State/Prov.:_____ Zip/Postal Code:_____
Account Number (if applicable):_____
075 CSAS

*New York residents remit applicable sales taxes.
  Canadian residents remit applicable GST and provincial taxes.

MIRA®